SIGNET MYSTERY

GOING, GOING, GONE

Eliza G. C. Collins

A SIGNET BOOK

NEW AMERICAN LIBRARY

For Alfred U. and Eliza C.
with love

PUBLISHER'S NOTE

This book is a work of fiction. Names, characters, places, and incidents either are the product of the author's imagination or are used fictitiously, and any resemblance to actual persons, living or dead, events, or locales is entirely coincidental.

NAL BOOKS ARE AVAILABLE AT QUANTITY DISCOUNTS WHEN USED TO PROMOTE PRODUCTS OR SERVICES. FOR INFORMATION PLEASE WRITE TO PREMIUM MARKETING DIVISION, NEW AMERICAN LIBRARY, 1633 BROADWAY, NEW YORK, NEW YORK 10019.

This is an authorized reprint of a hardcover edition published by Charles Scribner's Sons. The hardcover edition was published simultaneously in Canada by Collier Macmillan Canada, Inc.

SIGNET TRADEMARK REG. U.S. PAT. OFF. AND FOREIGN COUNTRIES
REGISTERED TRADEMARK—MARCA REGISTRADA
HECHO EN CHICAGO, U.S.A.

SIGNET, SIGNET CLASSIC, MENTOR, ONYX, PLUME, MERIDIAN and NAL BOOKS are published by NAL PENGUIN INC., 1633 Broadway, New York, New York 10019

First Signet Printing, September, 1987

1 2 3 4 5 6 7 8 9

PRINTED IN THE UNITED STATES OF AMERICA

Acknowledgments

For real-life experiences and the murder weapon, Norman Hurst and Nadine Hurst; for many readings and hard comments, Tim Blodgett, Alan Kantrow, and Nan Stone; for keeping the fire lit and providing the space, Georgie Hansen and Onnie Hoffman; for on-line research, Carol Prisant; for all those many hours in the trenches, Derrick Te Paske, and, finally, for loving the story and helping me to bring it off, Betsy Rapoport at Scribner's.

As I sat at the top of the cellar stairs, the only light coming from the desk lamp I'd left burning, I watched the late afternoon grow grayer outside the double glass doors. I shivered slightly and pulled my coat tighter around me. Something moved outside the door and I caught my breath and held it, not wanting the beat of my heart to get in the way of any sound. Without even knowing, I was waiting to hear. But it was only a shadow of a bare tree limb and I relaxed again into the corner of the wall. And waited. There was no sound after all, but something in the quietness of the house felt deadly.

How had it come to this? How had it happened that I was here at all, that someone I'd known had been murdered almost in front of my eyes, and that I was afraid, yes, I could admit it, of someone else I knew? I thought back then—was it only four days ago?—to the last moment when things had seemed normal. It was easier to think of what happened than to think of what could happen if I should be found there, where I huddled feeling a bit foolish for being so afraid. How, then, had it come to this?

1 "Jesus, what a mother of a day this is," Al Swedner said, slashing his hat against his thigh to knock the snow off. "Christ, you'd think that Joe'd want to have the effing day off himself. Where the hell's anybody going to get this stuff to today—foot of snow already—that's what I'd like to know." Swedner jerked his shoulders forward and re-settled his large head on them. He glared at me as if it were all my fault and then at Silky Constantine, who was standing next to me.

"Hang your coat up, Al," Silky said. "We're all in the same boat."

"Yeah, Joe would hold his effing auction if we were on Noah's ark." Swedner swung his large frame away from us and walked slowly, almost as if he were in pain, across the entrance hall to the main room where the auction preview was being held.

"What's gotten into him?" Silky asked, rubbing a hand through his hair, which was still thick and black though Silky himself must have been almost fifty. Silky Constantine was a bit shorter than myself, maybe five-seven, had a stocky frame, and one of those wide faces that made you think he might really be an Eskimo. Silky was new to the business. He'd sold his appliance store only a few years back when his wife fell in love with Japanese netsuke and just had to have a collection. Silky soon discovered that it was a hell of a lot cheaper to buy the little ivory sash weights as a dealer than it was as a consumer. So now, like the rest of us, he was dealing. His main love was painting, as was mine, but

9

his main business was decorative glass. It kept his wife in netsukes. Maybe that was why he hated dealing in it. He'd spend what he had left on paintings, but it was never enough to buy something really good. I always suspected that Silky was afraid of owning a painting by a name artist, as if jumping from decorative glass to Boudin was just not imaginable for a man from Boston's North End with a face like an Eskimo.

"I've seen Al upset but never like that," Silky said, shaking his head.

"Oh, come on, Silky, you know as well as I do that Al has to sweat and groan his way through every day," I said. "Wouldn't think he was justified in living if he didn't. He's probably thanking the Lord right now for making it such gruesome weather." Just then Swedner came back through the entrance hall and headed our way.

"Seen Baron?" he asked.

"Nope," said Silky, looking at me, "you, Helen?"

"Nope," I said. "I'll be surprised if he shows at this hour. He's probably come and gone by now."

"No," said Al, "he said he'd meet me here at ten o'clock. If you see him, tell him I'm looking."

"That could explain it," said Silky, watching Swedner leave for the second time. "If he has to meet Barton, it's going to make him mad. Simple as that."

Before I could comment, the door by my right shoulder opened and another cold snow-filled flurry of air blew in.

"Coming through, coming through," two headless hunched figures shouted as they hauled an exquisite Queen Anne highboy across the entrance hall into the preview room. Silky and I dropped our styrofoam coffee cups into a trash bin and followed. As we reached the door Silky turned to me and said, "You know every time it's like the first time for me. I still get excited, still think maybe today I'll see what no one else sees."

"Do you play the numbers game?" I asked.

"No," he answered, "why?"

"Because you're more likely to make money there than here with that attitude. That's luck and this isn't.

Silky, if you don't like the damned glass business, then get out of it. The problem is credibility. Who's going to believe you really know anything about paintings when every time you stick your hand up at an auction or have a booth at a show you're buying or selling pink soap dishes? No one gets very far by playing it safe."

"Just one good buy and I'd have it," he said, his jaw muscles tightened.

"Good luck."

Silky smiled and moved away, silently agreeing to the arrangement by which we all make our living. "You don't look too closely at what I'm interested in and I won't look too closely at you, not while you're watching at any rate."

The preview was in itself much like any other. It was a Friday morning in Shelton, Massachusetts, a small town southwest of Boston, close enough to Providence to get that small but growing business. Joseph Wickham auctions were famous in the area and were steadily picking up more of the New York trade. Wickham sold only good stuff, authenticated each piece himself, moved his sales quickly, and was gaining the reputation in the business for dealing in not only good but also museum-quality items.

When he began, like most auctioneers starting out, Wickham handled mainly lesser painters, and bad examples at that. Ten years ago you'd never have run across a painting with a real provenance at Wickham's, not a painting that had once been sold at Sotheby's or hung in a museum as part of a collection. Then Joe was still in the grandmother's attic league.

Things had changed. Joe's auctions now made the *New York Times*, and auctions like the one that day drew people from everywhere. It was one of the kind Joe liked best, lots of fine furniture, mostly early American, some English imports, better than average amount of Canton pieces (rare ones), Georgian silver, about a dozen or more very good orientals—there was one Shiraz even I had my eye on—and paintings, maybe twenty or so, and all fine. Some Wyants, an Inness, some nice signed Ennekings, a Prendergast watercolor, a small

Bellows—enough to make my early American twentieth-century-loving mouth drool.

I'm Helen Greene. Luckier than Silky, I inherited my business from my father. When he died ten years ago, and I was 23, the business itself wasn't worth much. He'd bought and sold well out of his gallery on Newbury Street in Boston but he'd died younger than he'd expected and had borrowed against his inventory to buy a number of paintings plus a Ryder for me, to start me off. Then he died and underneath the rock of his death there were more unpaid accounts than I'd known he had. I'd had to sell the Ryder and others just to pay them off, and then there was not much left, but enough to keep the gallery open. Not many, but a close few, knew how near I'd come to having to shut Greene Gallery down.

What my father did leave me, however, was credibility. Greene Gallery had been on Newbury Street in the same location for seventy-five years, had handled Homer and Ryder for the artists, and had sold many of the early American realists before they were known to be "American Realists." We had established their initial value. Once a gallery is in that position, it has something only time and ancestors can buy in this game. In fact, at least two of the paintings in the auction today we had sold originally, and one I'd sold. The Ryder. My cool analytic approach to Silky masked my own excitement at seeing it again, masked my interest, as I meant to have it.

Albert Pinkham Ryder, born in New Bedford in 1847, died in 1917, leaving behind him a wealth of beauty but not of paintings. Many of Ryder's paintings had literally peeled off their canvases as Ryder had ignorantly or uncaringly painted over wet surfaces with pigments that discolored. So what there are of his works, and there are few, exist almost exclusively in museums, most exclusively in the National Gallery of Art in Washington. They simply never appear at auction anymore; those not in museums are in private collections and likely to remain so.

This one, Lot No. 140 today, was a fluke. When I sold it to a private collector after my father died, I made two stipulations; one, that the buyer wouldn't sell it privately but put it up for auction, so that at least I could have a chance at it again; two, that it would not be at an auction in New York. Although it didn't occur to me then or now that bidders wouldn't travel over 400 miles for a Ryder, I wanted the home court advantage. Ten years ago I had sold the painting for $12,000. Today who knew what it would fetch. The last one sold went for $42,000 in 1981, so I was estimating at least $50,000. For a dealer that's a good-size buy. For a private collector, well, there are few that can do it, and I expected to do it only a few times in my life. This was going to be one of them.

Different people walk into preview rooms different ways. Silky always walks straight in and over to the thing he is most interested in and stares at it briefly as if he weren't. He can't hide his feelings though; Silky is as subtle as dog droppings on snow. Al Swedner, Barton Morley's ex-partner, takes the zoo lover approach. Enough time for everything and who is to tell that you really crave the lions when you feed the elephants as well? Al prowls slowly around the walls of the room, once, twice, and three times. He is always the first to arrive at the previews because it takes him so much longer than the rest of us to see them.

Tom Ewart, who at that moment was standing across the room, isn't very subtle either.

Tom had been an acquaintance of my father's and I'd known him for years. When I was a kid he had had the most annoying habit of slinging his arm around my chest and drawing my backside to him. Then with his other hand he would stroke my eyebrows, catching the tips of the hairs in his nails. I don't think he ever knew he was odd, but he was. Everything about Tom was a little off center; the jokes he told were either not really funny or not quite right for the company he was in. They were either adolescent and smutty, or irrelevant. When he was at rest, when for all the world there was no need for alarm, his hands shook.

Tom Ewart didn't have a gallery or a shop. He would buy at an auction, and sell straight to a buyer, picking up a small commission. Or he'd place his inventory in shops around Boston where he'd have to pay the shopowner or gallery owner up to 25 percent on commission. Tom's whole business depended then on quick moves, fast turnover, and small margins. If he spent $10,000 at an auction on one day, he'd probably clear $300. Maybe that was why his hands shook.

Tom saunters into a preview room, sweeps it once or twice with his hooded eyes, then, hunching over, darts from item to item, as if by moving quickly he could hide himself as well as disguise his interest.

I generally try to walk in as if I were somewhere else. My father always said that no matter how you walk in, it won't fool anybody unless you look as if it doesn't matter to you whether you're there or not. There are few in the trade in Boston who can walk into a preview unnoticed by their peers and competitors, he said, so if you're going to be seen don't try to hide like some scumbag in the night, but act like you own the place, with purpose and confidence. My father had had the touch; when he didn't have a penny in his pocket he'd looked like he could bid on the biggest item in an auction and take it away. Half the time he simply scared people out of bidding against him; they'd figure Gaston Greene would take it to the limit, so they'd drop out early. Then he would walk out as he'd come in, as if he hadn't really noticed anything unusual going on.

I had some of the same touch; while I didn't have it all down yet, I was learning. I think Barton Morley was the only other person with a familiar face who could do it, but Barton did it because he believed it. He wasn't fooling. Barton Morley bought paintings, but he didn't sell them. Like Boston women and their hats, he owned them. He bought what he wanted because he wanted it. He'd once been a dealer maybe fifteen years ago when he and Al Swedner had been partners, but then he started spending more and more of his time restoring and repairing paintings. Now he was only forty-three, but his reputation as a restorer of museum works was established, his word on certain periods of painting was law, and his own private collection immense. As Barton's reputation and collection grew—and as his lately-acquired English accent thickened—so had his detachment from his former friends. Barton no longer dressed in sensible New England clothes; Barton got his suits tailored in London. And Barton rarely moved as a man among other men, but as if he knew they were wondering how much his fur-lined coat had cost.

I know Silky thinks I'm unfair to Barton. He thinks that Barton deserves everything he's got. Silky secretly loves Barton's fur-lined coats. But I don't. I've seen what's underneath. Once, what seems like ages ago, I was going to marry Barton. At least that's what the silent messages and longing looks he'd pass my way always meant to me. For years, Barton had lived in the loft studio behind Greene Gallery. We lived on the upper floors, and from the time I was twelve Barton had been it for me. He was straight out of art school, doing an apprenticeship with my father, learning how to restore paintings, and doing some selling in the gallery.

He had been wonderful then. At least, I thought so. He used to call me Minuke, which is a small metal doodad on a Japanese samurai sword that holds the peg that locks the blade and the hilt together in place. It's a small, delicate, but functional piece.

That described me pretty well when I was twelve, and still did as I'd never completely lost the wiry look of an adolescent. My hair is the same straight brown it was then, my mouth still too wide in an otherwise economically featured, tidy face I'd long ago accepted as New England puritan. I would call Barton Tsuba, which is the hilt on the sword. Barton, like beautiful pieces of art and antiques, moved through my young years, filling them with a beauty I thought I had a special right to.

When Barton finally moved out of the back studio to go into business for himself with Al Swedner, a move my father thought doomed from the outset, I was seventeen and there was an "understanding" between us. Of course, I wasn't to know then that one of the wonderful things about understandings is that they are merely that. Someone can always claim to have never understood at all. Which is precisely what had happened when my father died. Barton had helped me sell the Ryder and then he had simply evaporated.

Suddenly, Barton didn't understand that there'd been anything special, anything more than a sibling-like fondness between us. There's every possibility that he was right, naturally, and that my adolescent head had been filled with dreams. Certainly fantasies made up a great portion of it. At the time, I was confused and half believed him; and finally, as guilt covered over grief, I withdrew.

Over the years, though, as Barton's successes became unending and an international reputation within his reach, I came to see his grasp for what it had been. Those fond gentle hands had really been after my father's blessing, not my breasts. We'd never talked about it; we had a different understanding now.

I walked into the room and looked around me. Tom Ewart was working the north wall. Silky was standing in front of a small painting with his hands clasped behind his squat back, gently rocking on his heels as he sucked it in. About two hundred other people moved around the large room; some of them stooped over tables checking for nicks or the shapes of dovetails, some stood unconcernedly in the center checking numbers in the catalog as if they were at a horse race. In a sense they were, only here the buyer is the horse, rider, and bettor.

It was hanging against the far wall. No matter who had owned the painting, no matter for whom Ryder had painted it or what he was thinking that day, it was mine. Rarely was I struck by anything as irrational as my need for my painting. Perhaps it was a final way to seal off my father's death, a rite of passage. I don't know, but it meant a coming home to myself, a resting. Of course, it's not impossible that the painting itself evoked some of the feelings it raised in me. Typically Ryder, typically lyric, it was of a field that led to the ocean which one could glimpse between a cut in a stand of trees. The painting was a blurred wash of browns and golds, a light coming from within the frame but without the scene so that you almost wanted to peek between the two to discover its source. And that was the feeling the painting gave me, that just between the trees, on the beach I'd find, one would find—what? Something. It was called "To the Sea."

Threading my way across rugs, around tables, large wing chairs, and desks, I went to it. My eyes sought out every remembered paint stroke, every crack, every subtlety I could recall. For a long while, I was back there, ten years ago, at home.

"Fabulous, isn't it," said a voice right beside me, breaking my time warp. "Amazing how little it's aged since you had it."

Without turning I answered, "Yes, it is and yes, it's amazing."

Tom Ewart stepped up to the painting and with a small sigh stepped back again. Tom had a thin, bony face that was all nose and deep eyesockets. His narrow lip line was hard, the tips of his lank hair fell hard upon his lined forehead, and his chin came to a hard point. His tall frame was angular and sharp. There was little soft about him.

As he stepped closer, I instinctively moved away, shielding my eyebrows from his bony caress.

"What do you bet it'll go for?" he asked.

"God, who knows? A Ryder hasn't been sold at auction in years," I replied. "Doesn't look like consumer city yet, but you never can tell."

Consumers at auctions are the bane of dealers. Dealers know they have to make a certain percentage on their purchases, so in buying they allow a margin for mark-up. Each dealer figures it differently. Tom, I think, works on 10 percent, for me it depends on the item; Al Swedner works on 50 percent; Silky, whenever he buys, closer to 100 percent. When there are a lot of consumers at an auction they'll go the full market value or damn close to it. They think if they get it for 10 percent under what they would pay in a shop, they've got a deal. They do, of course, but eventually what happens is that the prices in the shops go up. Got to keep the consumer one step behind, otherwise it's all over.

"The bet is on you, you know." Tom grinned, showing his upper teeth.

"What?" I asked.

"Modesty, modesty. Everybody knows you want it back."

"Back? Who said I want it back? It's a hell of a beautiful painting but I couldn't afford to hold it. Give it to me, and I'll take it."

"Barton said you'd pop for it."

"Barton would say 'pop' and probably just to put you off. Don't you know that by now?" I was feeling slightly nauseated. There it was, what I wanted, and suddenly I felt the vultures swarming. I don't know why I had thought for a moment that Barton would have forgotten how much I loved the painting.

"Is he here?" I asked, shifting the focus away from the Ryder.

"He's in the other room looking at the silver. So, are you going to do it?" he asked, doing a fair imitation of a pit terrier.

"What do you want, Tom, blood?"

"No, a deal. I won't bid on the Ryder if you'll do me a favor." Tom reached for a cigarette, then remembering that you couldn't smoke in the preview room, stuck a match in his lips and clamped the end of it with his teeth.

"You make it sound like I wouldn't want to do it," I said.

"You won't. It's got to do with Barton."

"Oh well, you're right there, you may not know a lot about my buying capacity, but you know my central nervous system like the back of your hand. What do you want?"

"Ask Barton to get off my back. Just for awhile; he's driving me nuts."

"What for? I don't know what you're talking about."

"You won't do it," Tom said, jerking the match out of his mouth.

"Look, I'm not playing games. I don't know what in the world you're talking about."

"Everybody else knows."

"You seem to think everybody knows a lot of things."

I moved down the wall slightly so that I was no longer in front of the Ryder but the small Prendergast watercolor. I leaned forward and peered at it.

"It's not as good at it looks," Tom said, pointing to one corner with the middle finger of his right hand. "There's a stain in that corner and someone's touched up the sky." I looked closer; he was right.

"Remember the Vlaminck and the Henri?" he asked.

"Naturally," I said. Who didn't? One day about four months ago at an auction on the Cape, Tom had gone the distance for two paintings for over $65,000. It was a shock to all of us; as the bidding went up and we realized that it was Tom, Silky and I, and I think Julie Atkins, another gallery owner who was sitting nearby, stared at each other in amazement. It was as if a neighborhood kid just made it to the Olympics or as if your best friend got an invitation to sing the leading role in Bellini's *Norma*, the first having no skill as an athlete and the second known to have no voice, let alone speak Italian. But that had been months ago, and nothing. Tom hadn't broken mold since.

"Whatever happened to those, Tom? I never did find out."

"Oh, I sold them alright, but at a real loss. I'd had a buyer for both, but one ups and dies tying his frigging estate up for months and the other turns out to be a con man." Tom's voice lowered as he spoke, his hands seeming to come involuntarily out of his pockets. He started rubbing his own eyebrows.

"Jesus," I said, "How much did you lose?"

"See, I had to sell them right away, I couldn't afford to wait a minute."

"Tom, what're you doing? Do you want me to know or don't you? Either tell me what's going on or don't but don't waffle on me."

"You really don't want me to bid on that Ryder, do you?"

Now, I understood. He wanted to see me crawl, probably. I guess so he wouldn't have to crawl alone.

"You're the one who asked for the favor," I said. "What's it got to do with Barton?"

"He fronted me the money." That explained phenomenon number one.

"And?" I said.

"He bought them from me, so I could pay him back."

"But at a much lower price, right? And now he wants the rest you owe him?"

"Yeah, and it's killing me. Everything I buy he feels he owns or has a part of. Jesus, if I buy an extra cup of crappy coffee he wags his finger at me and laughs."

"Well, pay him for Christ's sake."

"I can't borrow the money elsewhere. Why do you think I borrowed from him in the first place?"

"Tom, it occurs to me that you couldn't bid on the Ryder if I begged you to," I said, moving down the wall again. A nice small piece by J. J. Enneking, who painted peopleless pastoral pastels around the turn of the century, had caught my eye. It was hung above a Sheraton bureau and barely noticeable because of the way the light fell. I moved beyond the bureau, hardly glancing at the painting as I went by.

"Will you ask him?" Tom said. "Please."

"Let me think about it," I said. "What he did sounds pure Barton, but he didn't do anything illegal, you know, and if he could do it in the first place I don't see that anything I could say would change his mind." Frankly, what Barton had done was on the face of it good business, if you didn't need the business of your buddies, and I guess he didn't. He could have waited for the money until a good auction when Tom would have had the opportunity to unload the paintings. He could have, easily; everybody else would have.

Tom looked at me with pale watery eyes that looked like martini olives. "Okay," I said. "Okay." A twitch of a smile appeared on his face, his hand shot to his forehead sweeping the greasy tips of hair out of his eyes. As if he'd never betrayed a word, he turned and walked away.

As soon as he was gone, I stepped back and took a swift second glance at the Enneking. It was sweet. $800.00 limit. I moved on again, as far away from the Ryder, the Enneking, and Tom Ewart as I could get. Besides the Ryder, there were three things I was particularly interested in seeing at the auction and I'd seen one. The Prendergast was a disappointment. I wanted to see the large Wyant, apparently one of the last paintings he'd done before his eyes went, and, of course, the one by George Inness, who had painted landscapes in a shimmering, mystery-infused light. The Inness had been sold by Greene Gallery years ago, and I just wanted to see it again for old time's sake. I was going to buy little that day, knowing I'd need all my reserves, both monetary and emotional, to stick it out for the Ryder. Maybe the Shiraz, the Enneking. I'd see.

I left the main room and went back to the entrance hall where Silky and I had run into Al Swedner. There was at least another forty-five minutes before the auction would begin. Before I looked at the other paintings I needed to sit down and breathe deeply. To myself I could admit that one of the reasons for leaving the room was to avoid Barton, the one person I knew at the preview so far capable of bidding against me on the Ryder. He was also the one person who could make me lose my cool. At that time it was imperative, or so I thought, that I didn't see him.

The snack shop was off the main hall. It too had changed as Wickham's auctions had become more famous and drew higher bidders. In the old days, Joe's wife Phyllis and his daughter Sally would stay up late the night before making tuna, egg, and chicken salad sandwiches. On occasion, they'd have brownies and doughnuts. Now there were lobster salad rolls, chicken salad plates, and the crowd pleaser, chili. I walked down the few steps to the snack bar, which was nearly empty. I got myself a cup of coffee and sat down at one of the small black-topped art deco-style tables.

Outside, the snow was still coming down. I peered out the window. Al Swedner had been right. It was foolish for us all to be here. I thought maybe I should persuade Joe to postpone the auction. Anything, I said laughing to myself, anything to get me out of here.

At the sound of clicking heels I looked up and saw Julie Atkins standing next to me. Before I could say anything she had pulled a chair around, unbuttoned her coat as if it were on fire, sat down right next to me, and taken a sip of my coffee. Her fingers fluttered like butterfly wings around the warm coffee cup.

"Oh Helen," she said, "Am I glad I found you. Do you know who's here?"

"I know some of them, not all."

"Don't be cute or I won't tell."

"Alright, who's here?" I looked at Julie. She was a small woman, with a full matronly figure, about seven years older than myself, though I thought she looked more like fifty than forty. Her blond hair was carefully coiffeured and her face solidly slathered in make-up. She wore a lavender silk blouse with a heavy droopy bow, a tight black skirt that outlined her fair-sized rump, and tiny spiked heels that had gone out of fashion years ago. Julie ran a gallery on Charles Street, and was very successful. Her idea of really making it, however, was to go to New York. The only thing that kept her in Boston was a degree of self-awareness that matched her ego.

Though a good businesswoman and a shrewd negotiator, Julie really didn't have an eye for a good painting. She bought according to the price tag, according to other people's ideas of what was good. She was shrewd enough to deal in paintings that had some provenance and she was an avid day-tripper to Sotheby's and Christie's in New York where she kept abreast of what period was selling for what. In Boston, she relied on her friends to keep her informed of what was good. If she didn't have a file on it she was dead. Away from Boston she would be cut off from her sources, and I think Julie was afraid that without us she would just be so much flesh in New York. She may have been wrong, but I think she was right.

"Promise you won't cultivate him for yourself?" she said, suddenly scrutinizing me as if seeing me for the first time.

"Not unless he's some sort of mushroom," I said.

"What's that mean? Don't bother to tell me, because I think, Helen, I really think this may be it. It's Jerome St. George I'm talking about; I've heard he's looking for a partner."

"A partner. What would he be looking for a partner

for? He does restorations, Julie, his gallery business is really small."

"Not any more it isn't. You ought to go to New York more often. He's got a big new space on Seventy-Sixth, just off Park. He isn't doing restorations any more, or just a few odd pieces."

"But why, he was so good?"

"I don't know. Barton said something about his hands being no good anymore. He's got the shakes, or something. Anyway, it doesn't matter."

"Well, I think it matters. He was one of the best." I had never met St. George, but I knew his talent. He'd done some exquisitely difficult restoration of some early Italian Renaissance frescoes as well as a Copley portrait that had hung at the Yale Art Gallery during the Bicentennial. If his hands had failed him, he probably felt like a dancer who'd lost his feet.

"May have been," Julie answered, rubbing the air with her hands as if trying to erase my words, "what I'm trying to tell you is that he's expanding his gallery and needs capital which can mean a partner and, he's here."

"Does he know you're interested?"

"No, but he will, I've asked Barton to mention the possibility of me to him first so that he'll come to me."

"Did Barton say he would?"

"Sure he did, why wouldn't he? I've done things for Barton in the past and he owes me a few. Besides we have a sort of understanding." I was sure they did and hoped for her sake that Barton knew it as well.

"Julie, I'm really excited for you if that's what you want. I couldn't take New York myself, but I'd sure love a friendly place to visit." I smiled, trying to look enthusiastic and squeezed her arm. Julie, eternally on to something, was in a bubble of excitement, and I didn't want to prick it. But she couldn't speak Italian and was too fat for the part of Norma.

"Haven't you ever seen him?" she asked.

"Who? Jerome St. George? No. With a name like that, though, you know what he's got to look like. Long, lanky, distinguished looking, graying hair, and a monocle stuck in his left eye."

"He does look a bit like that, but without the monocle. But wooo, I'm not about to start complaining."

"Julie, I hope it works, but something about today just doesn't let me get too excited about what somebody looks like."

"I know, you must be in a dither. I am amazed at you sometimes. You're just like your father, you know, cool and detached. Most couldn't do it."

"Couldn't do what?" It occurred to me that Tom Ewart was right, everyone knew what would probably happen that day. It was becoming a real coming out party, a real test. Was I able to go the distance, could I afford to take on all comers, was I really going to be someone to reckon with? When I thought no one knew, it was a contest with myself. Now that everyone had figured it out, and I began to wonder how they had, I wanted to get it over, meet my unseen competitor face to face. For one thing is sure at an auction, there is a contest. It starts out as a free-for-all, bids coming in from all over the place, but as each person reaches his or her limit it evolves into a *mano a mano*, where the game is truly joined.

Julie said, "It's hard for me to go for something that I really care about. I guess one of the reasons I'm as good a bidder as I am is I don't really care. You know, Helen, I envy you. But I'm beginning to know what it might feel like. About this New York deal, I care. You, I'll tell. If you tell, I'll punch your face off." She rubbed her beringed knuckles playfully across my jaw. She was kidding, of course, but something in the way she did it told me she was serious. Maybe it was simply that it hurt.

"Your secret's safe with me," I said, touching my jaw.

"Good, now will you come to dinner tonight? Barton and Jerome will be there and I'm thinking of asking the Wickhams and maybe one or two others."

"Barton and Jerome are beginning to sound like Tweedle Dee and Tweedle Dum. Do they go everywhere together?"

"Well, Jerome is staying at Barton's. You know they have a lot in common, both restorers and collectors."

"Julie, if it will really help, I'll be glad to come, but I

can't promise what kind of company I'll be. In any event, I may be hysterical."

Julie was about to say something when Silky Constantine bounced into the snack bar and came over to our table.

"Hey. Helen," he said eagerly, then, noticing I was not alone, he said hello to Julie before taking my arm and whispering, "Can I borrow you for a moment?" He jerked his head in the direction of the preview room, trying to hide from Julie what was on his mind.

"Sure, just a minute." I turned to Julie, and we discussed what time I should arrive for dinner. Reassuring each other we'd see each other during the day and wishing each other good luck, we mutually withdrew from our confidences, me to Silky's side, Julie to my cup of coffee.

Back in the main hall, Silky grabbed my arm again and nearly pulled me into the preview room. We passed through the main room into the second gallery off to the left where Wickham had cases for the silver and china pieces as well as some wall space for paintings.

"In the corner," he said out of the side of his mouth, "next to the Wyant. Have a look and tell me what you think, I'll be in the other room." He slipped out of the double doorway and disappeared in the crowd.

I circled the room quickly and came to rest ever so briefly in front of a small canvas in the corner of the room. The canvas was small, about nine by twelve. It was unsigned but done in the fashion of John Sloan, an American realist and leading member of The Eight, a group who painted in the 1930s dedicated to showing urban life for what it was. It was a very nice little oil of a street scene, at evening. If it was a Sloan it could be worth a nice bit of money, $15,000 anyway. But unsigned it wouldn't go anywhere near that much. How one proves it is a Sloan when it is unsigned is by getting two or more authorities to agree that it is. If it turns out not to be the real thing, you still have the painting and won't lose money, you just won't have the bonanza you might have thought. I'm not an expert on Sloan, but I thought it was one. It had the right feel. If Sloan hadn't painted it, he had stood awfully close to that canvas at one time; it smelled like him.

I took all this in in about half a minute and moved slowly away from the Sloan to the Wyant landscape, about as different a painting from the Sloan as you could find. (Wyant was a nineteenth-century National Academy regular who would have hated sharing wall space with a painter of ashcans.) The Wyant was one of the paintings I had wanted to see, and so had a perfect excuse for staring at it, every once in awhile glancing at Silky's Sloan. I wouldn't bid against him on it, he could have it. I figured that's why he'd asked me, as well as the fact that I did know something about American art at the turn of the century. I gazed admiringly at the Wyant for a few minutes, taking my time, and then slowly walked back into the main room across which Silky was unconcernedly pacing and shooting worried glances in my direction, like a bad spy out of a bad World War II movie. We met halfway, in the middle of the room.

"Well?" he said.

"Could be," I said, "could very well be. If I were you, I'd take the risk."

"How much would you go?" Silky asked. "What if I can't?"

"Silky, either you want to go for it or not. I can't tell you what to do if you can't. Assuming it's a Sloan and you want to verify it, how long can you afford to hold it, say if you have to lay out two thousand to twenty-five hundred for it now? Maybe even more, because even though it's unsigned it's a very nice piece and someone else might take the same gamble."

"I can go to two thousand tops. If you think it's a Sloan, I can do that," Silky said, rubbing his small hands together in a gesture foreign to him, as if people who spent $2,000 expressed glee that way.

"Silky, don't do it on my say-so. Please. Not if you're counting on it being a Sloan."

"I know, I know you're not responsible. It's okay. I just feel this one is right. One favor though—no, two."

"Anything as long as you don't do it because I said so."

"If I need the cash, would you put it in your gallery, if I have to sell it?"

"Sure I would, it's very nice. That's no problem, but I would take the usual commission."

"Sure, sure, I gotta be prepared to lose something, right? Second, don't tell. Just let it find its sweet way to my hands, no one else knowing what I got. Okay?"

"I won't tell, Silky, but get yourself something else you like too. It helps."

"Got it, and thanks." He smiled and walked off, glancing obviously into the next room. I hoped he got it but if every person in the room didn't know Silky had some interest in something in the next room, I didn't know these people very well. Still, no one took him seriously yet, so maybe he'd get away with it.

There were still about twenty minutes until the auction, and I didn't want to spend them hanging around on preview myself. Here, ladies and gents, is what a very nervous bidder looks like. I knew I probably looked cool, Julie had said so, but I felt awful.

I was standing in the middle of the room wondering where to hide, when Joe's second-in-command, Kevin, a nice young man, though overanxious, caught my eye and came across the room to where I was. Kevin had all the makings of a good auctioneer. He moved things along well and despite his somewhat hustling qualities, seemed to get almost as good prices for things as Joe did. From an auctioneer's point of view, the amount the item goes for is the most important thing, so the speed will always cater to what an auctioneer thinks an item should fetch. How he manages the audience deeply determines how much it will bid. So an auctioneer who can move things at a speed and still get a price is doing okay.

From my point of view, Kevin's great failure was his need to make a person laugh at whatever he said, as if humor guaranteed acceptance.

"What item number are you?" he said, looking around me as if to find a sticker with a number on it.

"Whatever it is it's a bad lot," I said, flattening my voice.

"I give the estimates around here and I'd have to say

you'll fetch a good price. You may be going out of style in a year or so but right now you're top of the market."

"I'm not in the mood, Kevin," I said, moving away.

"No cats here, so who's got your tongue?" he asked, following me.

"Please lay off it. I don't feel up to your jokes this morning."

"Oh I wouldn't worry, I'll come down to yours."

"Kevin, shut up," I said, finally turning on him. I knew I'd lose my temper sometime that morning but I didn't want it to be at someone who might not feel he could fight back. I picked up an ugly wooden African chieftain's sceptre, the top of which was carved into hideous grinning baboon faces with jagged bits of ivory for teeth, and pounded the bulbous head of it into my hand.

"I'm sorry," I said, "really sorry. I'm just all prickles this morning. I guess it's hard for me to see a joke."

"What's wrong?" he said, his vocabulary remarkably limited.

"It's snowing," I answered, borrowing a page from Al Swedner.

"That's not it," he said. "It's the Ryder isn't it?"

"Gee, now there's an idea," I said and immediately, "Sorry for that too, the sarcasm, I mean. I don't seem to have much control over my tongue." I put the sceptre down and started to walk away.

"Have you seen it yet?" he asked, following me.

"Almost first thing."

"What did you think?"

"It's still in great condition. Amazing really. I don't want to look at it again, though."

"Why not?"

"I guess you don't know Barton very well, do you?" Of course, he couldn't. Barton doesn't readily associate with people who remind him of where he came from.

"Not really, no."

"Well hang around and learn a lesson," I said. "In the meantime I need a breather. See you later." I left him standing there looking a little awed as if it just occurred to him that personality might have something to do with this business and that he didn't really know much about that. He was smart and he'd learn, but not from me any more that morning.

A door at the side of the preview room across from its main entrance led to a narrow passageway about sixty feet long at the end of which was another door that led to the auction hall itself. The door off the passageway dropped you in the back of the hall facing a stage with a back wall, the other side of which formed the back wall in the preview room. During the auction, the items would be lifted onto the platform from the preview room, then the wall would revolve and the object would appear facing the auction hall. The auctioneer, Joe himself or Kevin, would stand at a small podium to the left of the revolving wall.

The auction hall was fair size, with seats for maybe 300 to 400 people. Joe had, along with his lobster rolls and chicken salad plates, recently acquired some new chairs and had carpeted the hall so that the room was damped and quiet, as if silence would add to the price an item would fetch. In a way, I believe it probably does.

I walked across the preview room through the door and down the passageway to the back of the auction hall. Just as people have different ways of viewing at previews, most who regularly attend auctions have a special place they like to sit. None of us sit together. Unlike some of the furniture buyers who pool their resources and split what they've bought at the end of the auction, most art or antiquities dealers buy for their own galleries or on commission and don't want to pool with anyone. Understandably, we sit as far away from each other as we can get, although we all know where each other is.

If a bid comes from the back of the hall, center, it's always from Al Swedner. He doesn't sit, he stands, slouched against the wall, indicating a bid by flapping his hand into the air in front of him. He doesn't smile or move a muscle, he's just bearing up under the load of doing his job. Whenever he gets what he's after he grimaces as if disposing of the piece were a task someone had just foisted upon him.

Julie sits in the front row directly in front of the

auctioneer. Tom sits to the far left of the hall about three-quarters of the way back. I generally try to sit on the center aisle, also about three-quarters back, so that like my father, I can easily move around. Sometimes I leave my seat five or six items before a lot I'm interested in so I can actually bid from another spot in the room. The walking soaks up some of the adrenalin and a bid coming from an unknown spot simply throws uncertainty into the bidding, giving me an imperceptible edge over someone else. It's the edges that very often count. Sometimes, however, it's important that the other buyer knows that I am bidding against him or her; at those times I don't move, I take on the persona of Gaston Greene's daughter, and act as if the bidding were merely a formality. If only they knew.

I had been in the hall earlier, to leave my briefcase on the chair I wanted, and it had been empty then. Now there were people scattered around the room, some in groups talking quietly, some sitting pouring over the catalog as if they had not seen it before. Almost every seat that didn't hold a person held something belonging to someone, a coat, a hat, gloves, books. It looked more like a room that people had just evacuated rather than one that would shortly fill up.

Across the room from the chair I had selected, Tom was settling himself into his seat. He looked over at me and raised his eyebrows in inquiry. I shook my head slightly wondering whether I ever actually would ask Barton to lay off Tom. I might that night at dinner if the right moment presented itself and if I were in any shape. But something about Tom made it hard to help him. Although Barton could be unmerciful in his teasing, Tom would make Barton want to do it even more. I looked over at him as he gazed at the catalog and saw what it was; he was smug. No matter how much he owed you, Tom would act as if you owed him something. If they ever dragged him off to debtor's prison, he'd spend the trip picking at the car seat to indicate that it wasn't clean enough for him to ride in.

Sitting in my seat wasn't much help. I wanted this to be over and if it was to be done, "twere well it were done quickly." I glanced again at Tom who was either picking his nose or just playing at it. Somehow that made sitting there worse. Suddenly, I felt as I hadn't for years, as if I were at a dance waiting to be asked while I sat by the wall. This won't do, I said to myself. Up. This should be an exciting day, a day I'd remember for a long time and there I was spending the first part of it as if unredeemable gloom were all it had in store for me. Then, I knew what was wrong. It was Barton. He lurked out there like a leopard waiting to pounce. Better to meet him head on than sit and wait for him to see me first. Another one of those incalculable edges that might pay off.

Putting my briefcase on my chair, I went back through the door and up the passageway, now lit. I noticed it was lined with pieces of furniture and odd items, lamps, andirons and such that would be auctioned off. I determined to find the Inness—at least that would be a pleasure—and then I'd find Barton.

Back in the main preview room I asked Kevin where the Inness was hiding and was directed to a small room behind the one where the silver and Silky's Sloan had been. The door to the room had been obscured by a large Japanese screen which I had just seen in the corridor between the auction and the preview rooms. The small room was very nearly empty; apparently others had not found it either. Joe is slipping, I thought. People rarely buy what they don't get a chance to examine beforehand.

The Inness was one of the better ones I'd seen; he's not a great favorite of mine as I think so much of his stuff is murky and dark. But this was a good one. It came after the Ryder in the auction and taking my own advice to Silky I decided that if by chance the Ryder disappeared down Barton's or anyone else's throat, before I cut my own, I'd take the Inness. It wasn't much but it helped. When I entered the room a tall, no, *huge* fellow was inspecting the canvas with a pocket flash enlarger. I decided to wait to look at it after he moved, not wanting to sneak around his considerable bulk. I sat down on a large carved walnut chest to wait him out.

He took forever. I glanced at my watch impatiently

as if I could transmit to him that there were other people waiting. Still he didn't move, and to me then time seemed like an enemy. He must be half blind or not have seen a painting before in his life, I thought, to be so absorbed. Either that or he doesn't think much of others. That obviously was the explanation. As I was involved in hurling my tension at his back I noticed that his shoes were run down at the heels and that his left sock had a hole at the ankle where it had rubbed against his shoe's edge. Clearly, he was not someone to reckon with. Unaware of Joe's rules, he was smoking a pipe, which sent streams of smoke to the ceiling over his head. Bending over to inspect the bottom edge of the painting he knocked his pipe on his shoe. A lit ash fell onto a small Hamadan prayer rug, singeing it.

"Hey, watch it, you're burning up the place," I said, not as testily as I was feeling, but almost. I jumped off the chest and stamped out the ash with my foot.

"You're not supposed to smoke in here, you know," I added, shaking the corner of the rug.

He turned and looked at me, smiled slightly, and went back to inspecting the painting. I suppose if he'd even acknowledged that I'd put out his fire with a mere thank you, I would have just gone back and sat on the chest until he left. But his complete absorption in what was quickly becoming "my painting" and which by all appearances he was considering "his painting" forced the worst in me out.

"You know, Superman would have a problem seeing that painting through you," I commented.

At that he did turn and stare at me again, but this time he wasn't smiling. He *was* big. He was wearing a herringbone tweed suit that must have hung in his closet for ages, the lapels being an early sixties width and the trousers having no crease except where they had lain over a hanger. The fronts of his pants had small burn holes at the knees. Obviously, he was in the habit of burning things and not noticing. His face was wide, his features rounded like a huskier John Voigt; his blue eyes didn't shift their gaze from my face.

"All you had to do was ask instead of whining like some spoiled kid," he said sucking on his pipe, wrapping his lips around a well-chewed stub. Of course, he was right, there wasn't really any question about that. I knew it and he knew it. But his size invited chest pounding; because of his size, he was pretty unlikely to pound back.

"I'm not the only one lacking in verbal expression, as I recall. You might have said thank you," I said, feeling very clever.

"I might have if you hadn't spoken to me as if I were six. Why do you think nagging someone is going to get you a 'thank you,' unless of course you picked up your ideas of reciprocity from the Mad Hatter?"

"I suppose your ash did not fall on the rug, and you were going to stamp it out if I hadn't?"

"Probably. Listen, if you really need to hack away at someone, don't do it on me. I can't see how I've hurt you, and frankly, I don't like this one bit." He stepped away from the picture and opened his hand toward it, "The painting, madame, is yours; the rug, I see by the scorched nap, is mine." He stooped to pick up the rug, which looked like a handkerchief in his hand, and with a big dragging suck on his pipe stepped away from me and left the room.

If someone had tried to talk to me, he or she would have found me speechless. The big slob, and I had thought that Tom Ewart was smug. This fellow was smug with a capital S. I may have acted terribly, but the least he could have done, I caught myself thinking, was to be nice about it. I wasn't always that way. But he wasn't to know that. There was no reason on Earth for him to be nice about my being terrible. Wasn't there anything wrong about what he did? The only thing I could think of was that he hadn't given me a chance to apologize but had strode off mid-battle. It wasn't much of a consolation, but it would have to do. Fortunately, I thought, I wouldn't see him again, so I wouldn't have to apologize, as I didn't think I could.

What had happened though was that I felt terrific. I could take on Barton and all the tigers in India if I had to. When there isn't much dignity left to lose, one can go all the way. I sat on the chest rubbing the rounded edges of the carving on the top. It was a hunting scene, men on horseback, leaping dogs, stags at bay. It was intricately carved and must have been used as a household object somewhere for years: The wood was smooth with the passage of many hands over it. I always get calmed in the presence of beautiful things. If the Inness and the chest had made it through all those years, so could I. They'd be around after I would, and my ownership of any of them, let alone the Ryder, would make very little difference one way or the other. All I could offer them was good guardianship, but that might be as good a reason as any to pursue what one wants.

I heard someone come into the room behind me and automatically sniffed for the smell of pipe tobacco. It wasn't him. The person who sat down next to me on the chest was Al Swedner. And an unhappy, grumbling Al Swedner doesn't sit down on a chest lightly.

"How's it going, Al?" I asked, knowing that the answer would contain a mixture of blaspheme and woe-is-me's.

"God-damned shitty," he said, artfully combining the two.

"What's the problem?" I asked, wondering only for a second if he needed to pound on someone smaller than himself, which might explain why Silky and I always got it.

"Snow's up to my hubs already. We'll never get out of here."

"Joe's got good equpiment, Al. We'll make it," I said, gazing at the Inness and wondering whether Al might not have a point.

"Well, just you try to convince Joe to start plowing now. He must think it's a joke. He doesn't have to drive miles to get home. He sits in his office drinking tea with Barton and that homo dandy with the Alzheimer hands he brought with him from New York. Can't get a word in to either of them."

"Thought Barton said he'd meet you here. Didn't you get a chance to talk yet?"

"Oh sure, two minutes of excuses and explanations. You'd think I was a leper or something. Barton treats me as such, when he was glad enough once to learn everything I knew."

"I can sympathize with that one. What do you want from him?"

"Only my fair share of some of his inventory. He owes me. If it was ever to go to court, you know, it would stand up."

"Why don't you sue then, Al?"

" 'Cause fancy pants Morley keeps comin' up with excuses and 'we'll settle this together old buddy' kind of statements. Besides, it's expensive, and I don't have the resources he does. Jesus, he's a pain. Catch me waving at him with my pinky finger someday when he wants something and I just feel like having another spot of tea." Al said the last sentence in a very bad imitation of Robert Morley.

Sitting next to Al was like sitting near a sewer that might explode. It if did, the shit got all over you and even if it didn't, it didn't smell too good. Al simply was a bore. But his complaints were so frequent and un-endingly inventive that it was almost a game to see what he could come up with next. The only problem was once you got him going he never shut up. As a result, conversations with Al tend to go on much longer than with anyone else. I'd heard that he once told someone that he had tons of friends but they were always hanging around trying to suck off him. Funny, I thought, how some people can't see themselves for their furies.

"Hey, Al," I said standing up, "hope it works out. Excuse me, but I've got an appointment myself."

"If it's with Barton, don't bother."

"Just so happens it is."

"Some people never learn," he said.

"That's right, Al, you ought to know. See you later." I left him staring at me dumbly as if he'd recognized I'd said something. For a fleeting minute I had sympathy with Barton. The fact that he could stand Al for five years was a testament to his ambition. I wondered, as I left to go face Barton, whether the day would be a testament to mine.

2 Joe Wickham's office was off the passageway between the auction hall and the preview rooms but closer to the latter, so that his door almost faced the door to the gallery itself. I went back into the main preview room and crossed the passageway. Joe's door was shut, but as I raised my fist to knock on it, it opened from within. Barton came striding through, so fast that I fell backward in the direction of a Japanese screen that was leaning against the back wall. Instinctively trying to protect the screen from my hand, I scrabbled for a bit of wall to hold on to and, not finding it, slipped off my feet on to the floor.

"Pride goeth before the fall, as usual," Barton said, reaching a hand down to me. "Hope it isn't irreparably stung, if so I'll do my best to puff it up." Great windbag, I thought as I allowed myself to be indecorously jerked off the floor.

"The pride isn't stinging quite as much as something else," I said, wiping at the back of my skirt as if my hand's proximity to it could console my sore rear end.

"I'd be glad to attend to that as well, if you'd allow," he said, smiling his most charming and insinuating grin at me. Damn him if he didn't take a swipe at my rear, patting my rump familiarly. Few people can reduce me to sheer infantilism as quickly as Barton. Really sophisticated epithets such as "asshole" and "dumbbell" flew through my head as I gently removed his hand from my behind, grinned (I hoped as insinuatingly as he had at me), and stuck my tongue out.

Naturally, he loved it and laughed in his "so I can still do it to you" way. I have to give it to him. Barton is smooth. If I didn't find his laugh so annoying I would be charmed by it. He has a flair for making everything seem a bit like a party, nothing to be taken too seriously. But if you do have something important or serious to say, you end up, or at least I do, feeling like a spoiler. It seemed, for instance, that it would be out of place for me to even question why he had to rush through doors not looking where he was going, knocking people, me especially, down in his path.

"Well," he said, "after all is said and done, are you all right?"

"Of course I am."

"Thank the lord for that. We wouldn't want anything to ruin . . . how shall I say it . . . the great day," he said, the latter phrase as if he were Ed McMahon introducing Johnny Carson.

"I guess I have you to thank for all the advance publicity, the billboards, the public notices," I said.

"You know me, Minuke, never was one for allowing any silent victories."

"Or silent suffering, I suppose. Really, Barton, you amaze me. What was the point of telling everyone?"

"Why not. You don't own the procedure, the moment, and the whole shebang. This is a public business we're in, as your dear Da used to say, so don't let sentiment cloud the works."

"There isn't one part of your life that sentiment has touched, is there?"

"Not exactly true, but for the moment, I'll accept that as almost accurate. I haven't yet heard of anyone, except maybe Lillian Gish, making it on sentiment."

I heard myself telling Silky just awhile ago that you couldn't treat an auction like the lottery, and here I was trying to treat it like my own private confirmation. I knew I was hysterical, but I'd have to get over it another day. Today I wanted the Ryder, and I did not want Barton to have it.

"Well, are you?" I asked.

"Am I what?" he responded, fondling a Satsuma urn that was standing on a low Korean chest.

"You know perfectly well what, Barton . . . the Ryder. You don't even like Ryder," I said, aware of the pleading tone my voice had acquired.

"Now that would be telling, wouldn't it?" He smiled his charming grin again, leaned forward, and kissed my cheek. The epithets started their scheduled flight around my head once more as I grimaced. When, when, I thought, will there be an opportunity to get my own back without my seeming the idiot and Barton the innocent victim. Though I knew the answer, I didn't want to admit it.

"Regardless," I said, trying to reverse the tide, "let's pledge to have a lovely dinner at Julie's."

"Oh, yes, of course, Julie. Well, we'll have as good a time as we can, I guess."

"Are you going to speak to Jerome St. George for her?"

"Of course not, whatever gave you that idea?"

"Julie. She said she'd spoken to you and you'd promised."

"What Julie interprets as a promise and what is one may be two entirely different things. I said I'd ponder it, and I have, for maybe a second, and decided not to. No, that's too big a word for what I did, I intuited 'no.' "

"But she's counting on it. Can't you just say something nice about her to him?"

"About her cooking? Yes, she makes a lovely coquille. About her abilities as a judge of paintings? No. Absolutely not. I'd be betting my reputation on Julie's abilities, and I can't imagine a more guaranteed way to lose it."

"That's a bit grandiose, Barton."

"Maybe, but fortunately for you it's not your affair, correct?"

He was right, it wasn't. And I thank my lucky stars, I said to myself, wondering how I could ever have thought that the world began and ended with Barton Morley.

"True enough, but can't you do something simply human and kind? For instance, I can understand why you demanded the money back from Tom Ewart, but why hound him? Can't you give him a little slack?"

"My dear, what is this, the inquisition? Have all your

little pals hired you to plead their causes? Aside from the fact that I refuse to discuss my business with anyone, Helen, leave it alone. You used to be more interesting than this."

The cruellest blow of all landed deep in my center, somewhere between my hip bones. A sick smile flickered around my mouth, but before I got a chance to say anything another figure appeared at the door of Joe Wickham's office. I assumed it would have to be the mythical and wonderful Jerome St. George. A moment proved me correct.

He stepped into the light. He was as I had imagined him: tall and lanky, with hair smoothed over a well-shaped head, a good suit of European cut, and an air of quiet refinement that spread over a face of normal, regular, and totally acceptable features. He looked like a model. Julie and Jerome St. George were an unlikely match on physical appearances alone. Not a very sound basis for judgment I'm aware, but when you make visual judgments daily and often very rapidly, it's hard to stop at art.

"I should have known," St. George said in a George Plimpton voice, "you'd be waylaid by a lovely lady."

"Jerry," Barton said reaching his arm behind me and pulling me toward him slightly, "this is Helen Greene, Gaston's daughter, your dinner partner at Julie's, and my unyielding gadfly." We shook hands. His grasp was not strong, and I tried not to stare at his hand that he quickly put in his jacket pocket.

"I'm very glad to meet you," he said. "I met your father once and got from him my first exposure to how good a gallery could be. I think it was during my sophomore year at Harvard, my mother dragged me behind her on one of those Saturday trips you Boston women do down Newbury Street and suddenly there I was having tea with the most wonderful lion of a man in a room like a pasha's palace. Never forgot it—straight out of Proust."

I said, "I always thought it was a little chaotic."

"But you haven't been to a pasha's palace, and Jerry has, so he knows what he's talking about," Barton said.

"Apparently, I lived in one," I said to Barton, wondering if he'd ever get over thinking he owned me.

"As you two have so much in common then, if you'll both excuse me, I have a little more viewing to do." Barton placed a comradely hand on Jerome St. George's shoulder and looking at me said, "Remember the Alamo" and then was gone, moving swiftly and gracefully through the crowded preview room.

"I suppose that meant something," Jerome St. George said. "I'm too polite to ask."

"You mean you don't know?" I said, wondering if Barton had missed a chance to expose my weak flank.

"Aside from the obvious reference to a rather disastrous battle, I haven't a clue."

"What a refreshing thing to hear. Sorry if I'm being cryptic, but I intend to stay that way for a bit. You'll find out all about it at dinner. Meantime, though, I do want to compliment you on your work on the Copley. It's a terrific job. I don't know anyone but my father who could have done it and that's saying a lot."

Jerome St. George's mannequin features seemed to crumple as if he had been made of papier-mâché all along. "An undeserved comparison, I wish I could accept it. But I didn't do the Copley."

"You didn't restore the Copley? I've heard you're not as active now," I said, "but I thought you'd done the job before you . . ." I couldn't finish, not knowing what to say.

"I started it," he said, sounding beaten, "and I appreciate your delicacy. The rumors are true. I can't even hold a brush steady anymore."

"It was beautifully done," I said, resisting the urge to lower my voice as if in mourning. Jerome St. George was losing whatever fleeting polish he had had.

"Barton finished it," he said. He turned his head away and looked in the direction Barton had gone. "I suppose I should be grateful, but I'm not. I'm angry." Anger can make a person's hands tremble, I thought, but if he couldn't see that I wasn't going to be the one to point it out.

"I can sympathize but I'd think he'd at least understand," I said, finally.

"Quite frankly, all I think Barton understands is that my misfortune is his gain."

"But I thought you were such buddies," I said, forgetting who we were talking about for a minute.

"Oh we are. There's no one I can talk to about my work or paintings like Barton, you ought to know that yourself. His fund of knowledge is encyclopedic, his instincts impeccable. And I trust him to do exactly what is in his best interest all the time. One really does know where one stands with Barton, there's no mistaking how he feels. I'd be missing too much if I didn't see Barton regularly."

I thought of what I missed and realized the only thing I regretted losing was the opportunity to see Barton's new paintings, which he always put on an easel in his study so he could have it at the same eye level the artist probably had when painting it. The first thing one saw entering Barton's house, in fact, down the hall in the study was the easel with his newest acquisition on it. With so many new and beautiful things in his life what need did Barton have of people?

"You seem rather cool about what seems distasteful to you," I said finally.

"Maybe I learned a lesson from your father, at a distance at any rate. I don't like Barton at all, I really rather despise him. I wish people like him couldn't succeed, that there was some moral court that forbade them entrance. But then I'm an old reactionary; I think people who don't own land shouldn't be able to vote."

"That's reactionary enough for me," I said seeing how innocent I was in thinking that *I* shouldn't judge people. Here was Jerome. St. George condemning Barton to some sort of parvenu purgatory when all I'd done was to surmise that Julie and St. George were an unlikely match. The more I knew him though, the more I knew Julie and he would get along. She'd love his finickiness and he her smothering. I thought briefly of mentioning Julie to St. George myself but like Barton decided against it. If I were honest with myself I had to agree that by recommending Julie one was making a statement about one's own abilities. No more than Barton was I ready to make that statement.

I looked quickly at my watch and saw that the auction was scheduled to begin in ten minutes. In the time that remained I wanted to check the Shiraz rug quickly and then give my gallery assistant, Liam Cabot, a call to see if there was any business and to tell him to go home when the snow reached the letter slot. (It had been a Greene Gallery tradition for years and was, on Newbury Street anyway, a signal to others that it was time to shut up shop. I suspect the other merchants on the street had gone along with it simply because, my grandfather being a stern-hearted Yankee, the letter slot was reasonably high.)

"I'm boring you," Jerome St. George said.

"Not at all," I replied, "but I have a few things left to see myself and I need to make a phone call. I look forward to dinner." If nothing else it should not be boring, I thought to myself. I wondered if Barton was aware of the emotional shoals he was steering his ship around. He probably was, and it probably didn't bother him a bit.

"Until dinner then, and don't forget the Alamo." He smiled. Jerome St. George was a very nice person if a shade too much like a fading hothouse plant. I smiled in return and backed away into the main gallery once more.

The Shiraz rug was in the middle of the floor, and I had barely stooped to lift the edge of it when Julie swooped down upon me like an eagle spotting her prey.

"What did you talk about all that time? You were cultivating him for yourself, I just knew I should have kept my big mouth shut."

I stood up and looked at Julie who had changed from eagle to poppinjay in a second. "Calm down, Julie. I am not interested in being Jerome St. George's partner in office, in bed, or anywhere. And if it really is your chance no one else can swipe it. Good lord." What I said was true, but I didn't think she'd understand it. I was right.

"Do you mean that?" she asked.

"Of course I do."

"Had Barton mentioned anything, could you tell?"

"No, I don't think he had, and Julie, I wouldn't count on it."

"What do you mean, of course he'll do it. Helen, I don't believe this of you. You're being spiteful."

"No, I'm not. Julie, if Barton thought you were the best partner in the world for St. George he'd not recommend you, because he doesn't want St. George to succeed any more than he wants me to, really. If you were the worst he wouldn't recommend you because his judgment would be on the line. And as you're neither he won't recommend you because he doesn't deal with the middle."

"Are you saying I'm mediocre?" she asked plastering her hands to her hips.

"No, I just know Barton."

"God damn him," she said. "He promised."

"You may have thought he did."

"No, he did, and I believed him. The bastard, the unholy, unforgivable bastard."

"Hey Julie, calm down. Barton probably promised in the way men and women have been promising things to each other for years, in the heat of the moment."

"Nobody promises something to me in the heat of my moment and doesn't come through. Nobody." She glared at me and stormed off, nearly tripping as one of her spiked heels caught a rip in a rug.

It was shaping up to be one hell of a dinner. I contemplated calling a documentary film producer friend of mine at the public TV station in Boston, alerting him to get over there with his action camera. This evening promised to outdo *I Claudius*.

I liked the rug. It would go well in my entrance way. If it went for under a thousand I'd have it, anything over was off limits. Only with the things you need can you not set limits. It's like saying you'll give up smoking or stop loving someone. Thank God, I thought, there aren't many Ryders in my life. I'd be out of business in a week.

The pay phone was in the entrance hall, right outside the snack shop. After waiting for two other callers, who took ages trying to describe various pieces they'd seen to potential customers and closet authorities, I finally got through to Liam, who took forever to answer the phone. Maybe the snow was already up to the slot, in which case, I thought, Al Swedner's gloom may be on target after all, my cheery assuredness about Joe's equipment notwithstanding.

"Anything happening?" I asked when the breathless voice came over the line.

"Sold the Luks," Liam responded, the triumph sounding in his voice. We had argued over it at an auction about six months ago, me saying, people just don't buy sofa-sized nudes these days, not in Boston anyway, and that we'd have to live with it. Liam, convinced that anything by George Benjamin Luks, another member of The Eight who was better known as a painter of low-class city life, would sell and wanted to take a flyer. I let him.

"Congratulations," I said, "well done. Who bought it?"

"A Mr. Stanford De Ruyter."

"Never heard of him. Local?"

"Yup, Charles Square. Not only local, but rich local, right?"

"You're learning. That's terrific, Liam. Why not close up and head home? I'll give you a call later."

"Okay. Think I will. I'll never get my car out if I don't. Good luck."

"I'll need it. Barton's going for it too," I said, no need to say what *it* was.

"Oh, God," Liam said.

"I'll do my best, but he's got the resources, damn it."

"Hang tough," he said.

"You'll be the first to know. Thanks." I hung up and thought for the millionth time what a treasure Liam, a 24-year-old ne'er-do-well son of a distant Irish cousin of the Cabots, was. I'd taken him on about three years ago when he'd arrived in this country as part-time help in the summer. He came to work because his aunt had said she'd kick him out of the house if he didn't get some sort of job, and working in an art gallery seemed a pretty painless way to qualify. But he'd not bargained on loving it. I hadn't bargained on getting a worker with a flair for buying, a genius for selling, and potential talent for restoring. It worked out beautifully for both of us.

The clock on the wall said 10:58, and I needed another cup of coffee. Standing in line at the now-crowded counter, I was joined by Silky who, not wanting to miss a moment of the auction, stocked up enough goodies to last him for three days, not the five hours these auctions usually take. Tom Ewart sidled into the line between us and turned his head in my direction and raised his eyebrows.

"Well, do I bid on it or not?" He did his best at smiling.

"That's up to you. As for the other matter, it's thumbs down. Sorry." His eyes glazed over and he left the line without a word.

"What's with him?" Silky asked, piling his cardboard box full of doughnuts and brownies.

"I don't know," I said. "Some of us just aren't having a great day."

"Yeah, well I am," Silky said grinning.

Maybe, I thought, just maybe, I would too. Though from how I felt and what I knew was coming, if it turned out to be a great day I was going to have earned it. "Well, one more time, good luck," Silky said as he paid the cashier.

"You too, Silky, I'll have my fingers crossed for you," I said to his departing back.

In the next moment the auction began. It was 11:00 exactly.

3 Most auctions begin slowly. The first piece is inevitably a sacrifice that, by ending the bidding prematurely, the auctioneer makes to the audience. Once a buyer thinks bargains are to be had, then he or she will be convinced that whatever goes is a bargain and will bid more. There's a funny mentality that grabs hold of people at auctions; they forget that it is not a game, that in fact they don't win anything. For the neophyte, the game or competition aspect is always the most tantalizing. When someone else bids he is saying figuratively that he doesn't want you to have what you say you want, he says he wants it. Its gimme gimme time.

When I went to my first auctions with my father, as long as I promised to sell it he let me bid on anything that he was fairly sure would go for under $50. No matter what it was, if I said I liked it, he let me bid on it. We'd come home from those auctions, when I was twelve and thirteen, with the car trunk filled with old brass pots and lampstands, the most hideous Beyreuth lobster-ware that I developed a taste for (and still have), daguerreotypes, waterstained prints, sets of tumblers, chipped, and worst of all, a stuffed sloth that sat in the living room for years, a witness to my lessons in not winning.

Eventually, what my father had planned on happened. I got tired of "winning" things I couldn't sell. He'd set me up in an antique show, one of the larger junkier sort that was often held at the Commonwealth Pier in those days, and I'd man the booth and sell my wares. It was at those shows that I learned it really helped a lot to like what you were selling and even more important to know everything there is to know about it. Finally, it became far more fun to buy the things I knew were good and right.

Once I'd passed that stage my father really started considering me his partner. It's a hard thing to do what he did, and I shudder when I think of the doubts he must have had about my ever learning what I was doing as he sat there watching me buy lobster cream pots. Not only was my taste questionable but also I was costing him. We figured later that his education of me had cost about $3,000. He'd said that was pretty cheap for a trade school.

At that auction, Joe started with a speech. He came out on the platform and stood with his hands in his pockets smiling at his audience.

"Friends," he said, "I know you're all worried about the snow, but rest assured we've got some local boys here plowing our roads already and the state highway says that the main roads to Boston and Providence are being worked on. You people in from New York, well, you'll just have to rest here awhile. It might be in your best interest to take a second look at the lovely early American spool beds we have today." An appreciative titter went up from the crowd. More adrenalin than humor, I thought.

Joe was a medium-sized man in his mid-fifties who in the last few years had slimmed his shape down so that it now fit the more elegant three-piece suits he wore. He was balding slightly, his graying brown hair was pulled thinly over the top of his head. His face was the only part of him that still looked the same as it always had; the paunch in his jowls and the bags under his eyes wouldn't give way to elegance. Also he had a slightly flushed, pink-cheeked pertness, that gave him the look of someone always a little embarrassed, always a little on the edge of being found wanting.

"Item number 1 is a miniature Tiffany creamer, irridescent gold, signed L.C.T. Favrile. What will you offer for it, please? May I hear fifty dollars to start?" Joe said, ushering in the creamer that was barely visible on the black velvet stand on the revolving platform. And so we were off, rider, horses, and bettors alike.

I looked around the room trying to spot Barton and St. George. They were sitting perhaps ten rows behind Julie and maybe six over from Tom who I noticed had slipped down in his chair with his arms folded tightly across his chest. Silky was in my half of the room, perhaps six or seven rows ahead of me and to my right. Also to my right and only two seats away was the pipe-smoking horror from the little room with the Inness. One of his legs was resting on the other while an ashtray nestled into the crook of his bent knee. He tapped his pipe onto the edge of it. It was the sound that drew my attention.

I looked at him while he reamed the burnt tobacco out of his pipe and thought that never in my life had I seen anyone so immensely self-satisfied. I knew for sure that he knew I was there and yet he refused even to acknowledge me. And then I realized I was staring. As soon as I turned my head away I could tell that he turned to look at me. God, I thought, this is all I need. A silent battle with this creep while I need all my resources for Barton. I decided to concentrate on every object that came onto the stand and price it fast before it sold. It was a game I often played with myself to while away the time and to test my awareness of the market. If I wasn't buying, at least I was learning.

"Lot number 2 is a pair of thirteen-inch eighteenth-century balltop andirons," Joe announced from the platform. Five hundred, I said to myself and wrote that amount in the left-hand margin of the catalog. The bidding was quick, only three people seemed interested, and the andirons quickly sold for $500. Not bad, I said to myself, not bad, writing $500 into the right-hand margin of the catalog.

The betting game served its purpose until Joe closed in on item number 70, the alleged Sloan, and a small ball of tension settled into my stomach. Looking for Silky, I peeked over the heads of the crowd. My eyes met his staring back at me through rows of heads. For a moment I thought he looked crazy, his stare was so intense and unflinching. I tried to make my eyes smile or at least look encouraging by raising my eyebrows and nodding my head slightly. Finally, his forehead creased as well, and he turned around. For a brief second, I had felt very like one monkey talking to another.

"Lot number 69 is a large six-foot hutch table. Can I have a start, please?" The bidding went quickly and the hutch table sold for $1,600. (I had bet $1,575.)

"Lot number 70, an oil on canvas early twentieth-century American street scene in the style of Sloan, maybe a Sloan, who knows? What am I bid for this really very nice little painting?"

Unprofessional, Joe, I thought, but terrific for Silky. No one in his right mind is going to get lured by a description like that. Mentioning that a painting is painted in the style of someone else is a classic auctioneer's technique to slip in the name of a famous painter while describing a painting by an unknown artist. Class by association. However, no dealer worth his or her salt buys according to what an auctioneer says and will be put off by blatant pushing. If you haven't seen it yourself and know what it is, don't buy it.

"Who'll give me five hundred to start the oil painting?"

A voice from behind me to the left said, "Two-fifty."

"I've got two-fifty. Do I see three hundred?"

Three hundreds came from all over the room. Joe had a lot of people interested in the little canvas. Silky had tipped his hat and was among them. The same voice came from the back of the room. "Four-fifty." That's the way to shake them out. I turned to see who it was but couldn't tell. It was someone standing near Al, but I couldn't make out who.

"I've got four-fifty from the back of the room, an interesting little bid for such a nice painting. Who'll give me five hundred?" Joe searched the hall for a bidder.

Silky would. His bid was quickly followed and the price got up to $1,000 in only three bids. It hovered between $1,000 and $1,500 for a moment, then like a spiking fever leapt to $1,750. The audience, at first phlegmatic and uninterested in the item, quieted some

and became a little respectful. We were nearing the
$2,000 mark where things get serious.

"Eighteen hundred," said Silky, into the low mur-
mur. There was not a response from the audience. I
held my breath. Maybe just maybe he'd pull it off. I
bowed my head as if by not seeing it, the worst wouldn't
happen.

"I have eighteen, do I hear nineteen?" Joe said. There
was no sound from the room. A voice yelled "sell it!"
and the crowd hooted approval. Things seemed to be
going Silky's way.

"Eighteen hundred once, eighteen hundred twice . . ."

"Eighteen-fifty," said the voice from the back. Oh
Christ, I thought, a dog fight. Poor Silky, I don't think
he's got the heart for this kind of thing.

"Nineteen," Silky responded very quickly. Good, no
hesitation, sure sign of going all the way. No indication
that he was approaching his limit. Determination will
often scare someone out faster than the actual price.

"Nineteen hundred once, nineteen hundred twice . . ."

"Twenty-five," said a voice to my left in a tired impatient sort of way as if asking the auctioneer simply to
get it over with. I didn't even have to turn my head. It
was a typical Barton move. He smelled the $2,000 limit
as easily as if it had been Sunday lunch. He knew who
Silky was, and he may have known the voice at the back
of the room as well. He knew they were in a dog fight,
and while they weren't looking he grabbed the bone
with one swipe. Very few can leap over a $2,500 bid
when they've been haggling under $2,000.

"Twenty-five hundred once, twenty-five hundred
twice, sold to number fifty-seven." Barton held up his
little card with his number on it as a gesture to the
auctioneer. Everyone in the room knew who Barton
was, including Silky who at that moment must have
been feeling he'd just lost his woman to another man. I
looked over to where he was sitting and saw him stand
up and walk quickly to the back of the room. His eyes
wouldn't meet mine. His face was a deep red. I felt that
we'd witnessed the blooding of Silky.

As if nothing had happened Joe moved the auction
along and we were back in the race with item number

71, the mammoth six-foot Satsuma urn that Barton had fingered so lovingly in the hall. It went for an unsurprising $3,300.

Through item 75, when Joe left the podium and was replaced by Kevin, I hadn't done too badly. I had bid over by an accumulated amount of only $775, which meant, considering a markup of only 30 percent, that I would have made money had I bought and sold. Not exactly as much as each individual buyer but for the whole works not bad.

I snuck a glance at the person to my right who I noticed had a number of items circled on one page of his catalog. Straining to see without appearing to look, I recognized the page from the type layout as the one with the Inness listed. It was item number 152. So, I thought, he is going for it. If I was going to bid against him I didn't want to be sitting two seats away. It was then I knew that I probably would, Ryder or no. And that seemed odd to me, as I knew I didn't really want the Inness. Curiously, it just seemed like a good idea. A warning voice inside my head that sounded familiar, as if it was my father's, said, "watch it." Another voice, which sounded like mine at age thirteen with a little of the Liam Cabot accent said, "Go ahead, the worst that can happen is you have to sell it." With a George Inness a lot of worse things can happen.

I needed another cup of coffee and I wanted to find Silky. The snack shop had about fifteen people in it but Silky wasn't one of them. I got a cup of coffee, and climbed the few steps into the entrance hall. It was empty except for some of the objects that had been sold already which were being crated up to be shipped elsewhere. No sign of Silky. Outside the snow was still falling. It appeared heavier to me, though it seemed as if one could still get out. I searched the parking lot, found Silky's car, but not Silky.

As I went back in through the main door, however, I saw him standing in the preview gallery in front of the Sloan, which had been put back on the wall. Something about the way he was standing, so unapproachable, so rock-like, made me back away rather than go forward. I knew he shouldn't even be in the preview room while the auction was in progress, but I wasn't about to blow the whistle on him. If Joe couldn't keep people out, that was his problem.

I got back to my seat in time to see the Wyant sell for $4,750. A nice buy for someone. It was number 92. The next item of interest was the little Enneking, number 105. As my nerves were "getting up" like a wind-whipped wave, especially after Silky's catastrophe, I thought I'd better go for it. I had to do something. I snuck a peek at the person to the right whom I was quickly dubbing "the hulk." He had a pad of paper on which long and involved looking formulas stretched across the page resting on his thigh. Each time he lifted his pencil he'd suck on his pipe so deeply that I could hear the beads of moisture rumble through the stem. I became so attuned to the sound that I found myself unconsciously holding my breath, waiting for him to exhale. He had enormous lungs.

As if he knew I was thinking about him, he shifted slightly in his seat, got up, and sidled past the seats in the other direction from me. As soon as he was gone I leaned over and looked at the pad that he'd left on his seat. It was covered with the formulas I'd seen but that was not all. In the lower right-hand corner was an extremely deft sketch of me which had a mustache and witch's hat attached to it. My face got very hot. Not only had he drawn me but also, I knew as solidly as if it were fact, he'd meant me to see it and had left his seat just so that I would. The worst thing though was not that he'd drawn me as a witch with a mustache but that I couldn't get back at him without revealing that I'd peeked at his pad. Also damning was the fact that he could draw well.

I squirmed in my seat and considered moving, but quickly saw that would merely prove that I had seen what he'd drawn and that it had bothered me. But what was to keep me from saying something pleasant for a change? That would surprise him. It would take some doing but it wouldn't hurt to think about it.

"Number 101, a George II small silver coffee pot, Gabriel Sleath, London, dated 1739. What am I offered for it please?" Kevin's voice finally pierced my consciousness. I quickly checked the catalog photograph of the Enneking, No. 105. The coffee pot went for $5,000. As I was writing the figure in the margin I felt a slight tap on my left shoulder. I turned my head and saw Tom squatting next to me, his mouth close to my ear.

"If you get the Enneking, I'll take it off your hands immediately at 10 percent," he said in a scratchy whisper. He then cleared his throat in my ear.

"Buy it yourself then, Tom," I said, aware that he'd probably noticed my looking at it and that I hadn't been as clever as I thought.

"Can't. Hands are tied. It'll cost me, but I've got to buy something to keep alive."

"What do you mean you can't?"

"If I bid, Barton'll merely ask for it at cost 'til his bill is paid off. I can't eat that way, for Christ's sake; he's killing me."

"Everything you bid for? Barton doesn't have room enough."

"Well, he just took that old print of "Washington Crossing the Delaware" off me; I got it for $400 and he bodily removed it and stuffed it in his car."

"What the hell did you buy that for, ugliest damn thing I ever saw."

"Some of us can't afford to buy only what we like, Helen," he said, pulling his lips tight across his face, making him look more skeletal than ever. "Will you?" he asked again.

"If I get it, and decide to sell it right away, you can have it at 10 percent," I said, not liking it. "But don't count on it, I may decide to keep it."

"I've had it. I've reached my limit."

"Barton's pretty good about sniffing out limits, Tom," I said, thinking of Silky out there somewhere nursing his wounds.

"Yeah, well maybe not good enough," he said quickly then was gone.

Lot numbers 102 and 103 had gone while we talked and Lot number 104 was just nearing the finish. I sensed a movement next to me and recognized that the hulk was back. The tap-tapping of his pipe started up again. For a moment I thought I just might scream.

"Lot number 105," Kevin announced, "a small eight-by-ten oil on canvas, signed J.J. Enneking, some small damage in upper right would need repair, but does not diminish the value or beauty of this lovely little painting. What am I given for the Enneking, please, who'll start it at $100?"

"One-fifty," said a voice from the back of the room.

"Two-fifty," I said. Out of the corner of my eye I could see the hulk turn to look at me.

"Three-fifty," quickly followed from another corner of the room.

"Four hundred," from the back of the room.

"Five hundred," said Julie from the front of the room. Kevin, having taken my first bid, shot an enquiring glance at me. I nodded my head, indicating I'd go to $500.

"I have five hundred. Do I hear five-fifty?"

"Six hundred," said Julie with confidence. Damn, I thought, she's testing. If I like it enough to go to $650 she'll go $700 figuring $50 is a cheap price to pay for being sure. There was no way, knowing Julie, I could win. I forced myself to hold to my original sum. I could take it up, but I wouldn't under normal circumstances so I wouldn't for Tom. That was the quickest way to make me really angry at him.

"Eight hundred," I said, and knew my voice said it all. That was it.

"Eight-fifty," Julie answered back. Kevin looked my way again and without a trace of hesitation I shook my head. It was a nice Enneking, but not nicer than $800. I knew that; and Julie didn't care.

In a second, Tom was back at my shoulder. "Why did you stop?" he asked through clenched teeth, twisting his tie around his fingers.

"Tom, you didn't ask me to buy it for you, you asked if you could buy it from me when and if I got it. If you wanted it so much you should have given me a price or even better got someone else to do it for you. I'm on the job myself, you know."

"Barton got to you, didn't he?" he said, looking at me as if I were small and smelled bad.

"No, Barton didn't get to me, but you are. You're the one that's in debt, not me."

"A lot of good talking to you is." He was nearly spitting in my face.

"Tom, I'm not trying to hurt you, but no one can get you out of this but you." I'd had it with Tom and his selfish jabs.

"And you better believe I will, with no help from you."

"Tom, it's not me, it's Barton you're mad at, remember?" I said, mocking his voice.

"That's something I'll never forget either," he said, jamming his hands into his pockets and then just as quickly flinging them into his hair to wipe it back from his forehead. He stood there motionless, holding his hair back tight from his face as if he were about ready to put on a bathing cap. He looked transfixed by something beyond me. For a moment, I thought he'd gone into a state of shock, and was on the verge of touching him to see if he'd respond when he turned abruptly, like a soldier on parade, and marched off.

I was stunned. It occurred to me to ask Barton again to lay off for awhile. But almost as soon as I considered it, I decided not to. Enough had happened to me that day to set me off course and I didn't want to give Barton a chance to sink the ship altogether. After the Ryder maybe, but not before.

I bought Lot number 127, the Shiraz rug, for $800, and thought I had a steal. The hulk obviously thought so too. As the bidding ceased, I chanced a look in his direction and saw a hint of a lift at the corners of his mouth. He inclined his head slightly my way and soundlessly patted his hands together in applause. I nodded my head in recognition of his recognition, and not wanting to seem pleased at the mere show of a smile, turned quickly to face the center of the room again.

I leaned forward slightly in my seat to check whether Barton was still his ten or so rows over across the aisle. He was. His Bally shoe and his neatly turned ankle were visible in the triangle formed by Jerome St. George's legs. Then Barton himself leaned forward and waved at me, wiggling his fingers. He had taken his hat off and I could see the deep satiny cushion of black hair that had once seemed to belong to me.

Like a beloved stuffed animal can always provide comfort, so could Barton's hair. I can remember, too vividly, times when the three of us would be sitting in my father's office, Dad behind the desk, Barton in one of the big leather armchairs that had been at Williams with my mother's father, while I'd sit on the arm lying along the back of it twiddling with Barton's hair. Before my mother died, I don't think my father would have let me, but she died when I was ten, at a time everyone told him I needed as much affection and loving as I could get. When I think back now on those afternoons and other times equally as intimate, such as Barton and myself stretched in front of the fireplace both reading the same book to keep each other company, I knew it was less than innocent, and that my father must have known it too.

And now I didn't miss much of it except my father, the quiet hurt of which Barton's hair could both calm and stir in me. About Barton himself I didn't have any illusions. He'd given me a wonderful adolescence, but he'd also taken it away.

I wiggled my fingers back and winked wickedly, trying to be flirtatious. Where he used insinuation to unbalance me, I'd use acceptance to unhinge him. I saw his confidence in how well he knew me fade ever so slightly as if a flag blown stiffly by a breeze had gone limp for a second. I smiled even more engagingly and withdrew before he had time to respond.

4 As the lot numbers rose and we neared number 140, the Ryder, so rose my desire to flee. The moment I'd waited years for was almost there, and I was afraid that at the instant of engagement, all the years of training would desert me and I'd see my painting disappear forever. I tried breathing deeply, shutting my eyes, and pressing my back to my chair. Anyone looking at me would have thought that I was either practicing transcendental meditation or was simply bored with the procedure. I was neither, being acutely aware of everything going on. The item on the platform, number 138, was a very rare pair of Staffordshire figures of doves that went quickly to a woman in the front row for $3,500. Lot number 139 was two Chinese export bowls that came and went too quickly for my liking.

As soon as the bowls were whisked off the platform, Kevin, who had been there since lot 75, also disappeared, and Joe stepped out from behind the curtain and took his place behind the podium. He stood there silently for a moment smoothing the hair on his head with one hand while he looked over the audience. For its part the audience grew quiet and looked back at Joe. How quickly the long-awaited moment had come and how the time almost seemed to stretch to accommodate it.

I don't think that everyone in the room knew what was happening, but a large enough number did. My seasoned heart began flipping over. Not before the bidding, I thought, calm down. I listened for the slow inhalations of my friend next door and heard them deep and regular. I think if he'd got up at that minute to leave I'd have killed him.

"Lot number 140, ladies and gentlemen, needs almost no introduction. I'm sure it's what brought half of you here, to see if not to buy. 'To the Sea,' by Albert Pinkham Ryder, oil on canvas, measuring twenty-eight by thirty-five inches; the condition, excellent. What am I offered for the Ryder?"

Understandably, no one wanted to open the bidding. No matter how much of a veteran you are, if you feel a little silly offering $10 on an object worth ten times that amount, just think how you'd feel offering $1,000 for something worth fifty times that. What often happens then is that the serious buyers don't open the bidding, they wait until it rises to their level. So on a piece that starts low, the first bidders are the young dealers and naive consumers who all want to go home and say they bid on a Homer, a Bellows, a Ryder. When they're exhausted the next tier begins, until wave after wave of bidders tumble in on each other, the last and strongest reaching the furthest up the shore.

The silence that followed Joe's introduction was the longest I'd heard at auction. On the platform Joe cleared his throat.

"Come now, ladies and gentlemen. This is an unreserved sale. One of you will drive home, albeit slowly, with this magnificent painting. Let us not be too shy before a masterpiece. Who will give me five thousand to start?" There was no response still.

"One thousand?" Joe asked.

From somewhere below me and to my right the first wave rolled up the beach, "One thousand." There was now a collective sighing in the room and a perceptible shift in the atmosphere. What had been detachment was giving away to commitment; only toward the end would that give way to unbearable tension.

The first bidders took the price to $15,000 rather quickly. They leapfrogged over each other's backs to get the highest bid in they could afford before they had to stop lest by a horrible miracle they had to buy what they'd just bid on. The second wave was in good form that day. Bidders skirmished sassily with each other. For awhile I wondered dumbly why there was all the frolicsome play with the bidding. Slowly the realization came to me that everyone knew that until I'd spoken the bidding was a formality only. These people were like dolphins preceding a ship. Until someone like Barton, St. George, Sev Lahti from the Worcester Art Museum, or myself spoke up, the price could rise beyond where even we would expect to take it. And there was the rub. Barton must have known that too. The question was, who would stop the dolphins? Even though neither of us had yet said a word, the battle had silently begun.

Here's how it stands, I thought. Barton knows for sure that I want the painting, and he knows that I know he intends to have it. The question for me is does he want it only *because* I do, or simply for what it is. He never really liked Ryder's work, always teased me about my romantic streak. So it must be the former, I thought. In which case, I knew he'd wait for me until eternity. So if I bid first I'd never know what his emotional investment was. If I showed my hand, the only question remaining was how much Barton was willing to pay to have his little game with me.

The bid was at $35,000, and what had been fairly rapid fire raises suddenly stopped. Joe looked around the room for another bid, and there was none.

"This is ridiculous," he said, "but I'll say it; thirty-five thousand once, thirty-five thousand twice . . ." The sound of Joe's voice filled the room, the unasked question hanging there, looming larger than anything else.

The obvious thing happened, of course. I should have guessed that it would, and as my heart nearly stopped beating in the silence and then began again, I thanked Barton silently for making it easy on the both of us. The bid for $35,000, of course, came from St. George. A graceful move on Barton's part. He could hide behind St. George for as long as he wanted, while I exposed myself all over town like a hussy. Barton could stay in the race and I'd never know how much of his heart was really in it. Lunacy, it was all lunacy, and what I did next was assuredly the most lunatic of all, especially to the man on my right who may have been just getting over the notion that I was a crazy woman.

St. George's voice still echoed in the room when I turned my head and hissed at the hulk, who was sucking on his pipe and doodling with infuriating concentration on his pad. From where I sat he seemed to be drawing snakes slithering over lily pads, but I didn't want to think about the Rorschach implications of my assumption.

"Psst, psst, hey yoohoo, I'll explain and apologize profusely later; I'll even not bid on the Inness if you'll just bid $37,000 for me, right now. Please."

He turned and gave me a long hard stare, and something in my eyes must have convinced him that I wasn't crazy, because at least he didn't run away. Well, almost convinced him anyway.

"What?" he said, his mouth gaping open. He took a pair of glasses out of his jacket pocket and put them on as if he could hear me better if he saw me more clearly. Joe, too, was looking straight at me obviously waiting for me to do something.

"Look, my credibility is good, I can cover any amount, I just need a front."

"Who are you?" he said, sounding like the caterpillar in *Alice in Wonderland,* which is where he must have felt he had landed.

"Helen Greene. Greene Gallery. Newbury Street," I said, not sure that would mean anything to him at all.

"Thirty-seven," he said loudly and confidently, putting his pad away and settling into the chair as if he assumed disguises and took over $37,000 bids every day of his life.

Joe looked stunned for a moment, but he recognized immediately what the situation was. He smiled slightly, shook his head, and looked around the room apparently searching for the tell-tale signs of a bidder brewing a bid. I turned my head to the left just enough to catch a glimpse of Barton's toe. He was still there, and I wondered what he must have been thinking. He would be curious about who the hulk was and how I'd sneaked him past his ever-watchful eyes. Of course, the whole maneuver was simply that, a maneuver. Eventually, if it seemed as if another shake-up was in order we'd come out from behind our disguises to throw the other off balance. Or it might end up that either St. George or the hulk bought the Ryder, and Barton and I remained silent bidders all the way through.

The man on my right was waiting, and rightly so, for me to say something. "That was very important and you were gallant. After how I treated you, I had no right to expect you to be willing to help. Thank you."

"My pleasure, I enjoy bidding on paintings I don't have to buy. Even on those I do buy."

"Would you go all the way with it if need be?"

"Sure, seems like a very interesting way of getting through an auction. Besides I'm impressed by your resourcefulness under pressure. How could I refuse? My price?—who and why."

"Understandable. I'm curious about why you're doing this despite the pleasure. For all you know I could stick you with a $60,000 painting, and you'd own it."

"You're good for it. I know for a fact that you've got at least fifteen thousand in cash assets and about half a million in inventory, so what's the big worry?"

It was my turn to gape at him. But before I could make verbal my astonishment, the rejoinder was made from the other side of the room.

"Forty thousand," St. George said calmly.

I thought of leaping very quickly and playing out the endgame in $2,000 not $1,000 bids, but decided against it. That might make me look too ready to have it over with, too nervous. Better lay back and let Barton take the leap. I whispered to my front, "Forty-one."

St. George replied with an immediate $42,000. I had succeeded in setting the pace. That might seem insignificant but it matters. Every bit of control over the number, rate, and amount of bids gives you an advantage. We went up by the thousands to St. George's bid at $50,000. Then I decided I could leap. Now it wouldn't look like nerves, merely that I was tired of this dallying around and wanted to get down to serious business. Of course, the small acid trickle in the pit of my stomach told me the truth. If Barton really wanted the Ryder, no matter how many cunning tactics I employed, he could outbid me. I simply couldn't afford to blow my resources on the one painting. I hadn't before and I wouldn't this time.

But Barton could. He could keep the Ryder for a month, and by his ownership increase its value then sell it to a museum, and make money. Keeping it didn't matter to him. As far as he was concerned, all he and I were doing was setting the value of the painting at which he could later sell it, plus.

"Fifty-five," I whispered to the hulk. "Good going," he whispered back, before proclaiming that amount to the room as if it were a call for dinner.

There was a slight perceptible pause before St. George came back with $56,000. He said it as if he were saying "in my own sweet time," to the invitation to dine. Damn Barton, I thought. If I leap ahead too fast I'm going to look ridiculous. I can't answer every bid with a $5,000 leap, but if we go on this way I don't think my nerves can stand it.

I remembered suddenly a picture in *Life* magazine taken many years ago. It shows one moment in a lion's chase of a baboon. Clearly, the second before the camera clicked on the scene, the lion was in full control chasing the baboon to an inevitable end. Just as clearly, both the lion and the baboon must have known it. Then the baboon turned and showed the lion one last defiant snarling visage, almost daring the lion to want to go after such a hideous thing. The lion pulled back in shocked surprise. For one second, but only one, the baboon had the tables turned, and if by some miracle at exactly that second the lion had got diverted by an easier prey, the baboon might have escaped. But implicit in the photograph is that he didn't. This was a momentary reprieve brought about by his own fierceness. In the next moment, as a series of photographs showed, the lion recovered his aplomb and battered the baboon's life out of its body.

And, suddenly, with all the animal wisdom I possessed, I knew that was going to happen to me. No matter how long I prolonged this chase, no matter how many clever miracles I caused to happen, no matter how many snarls I offered in Barton's direction, they would be only momentary diversions, sudden surprises, doing nothing in effect but making the hunt more interesting for him. How would I have wanted the baboon to respond? Any differently? Not really, given it didn't have any alternative. But I did. I could do a number of things. Stop bidding altogether, which would leave Barton with a Ryder but not one valued at an absurd price unless of course someone else joined the bidding. Or I could keep pushing him so that it was going to be a very expensive chase for him, or even better, I could divert him to an easier prey.

Leaning over toward my friend the front, I asked him to keep the bidding going at the $1,000 level and take his time, let the painting almost go each time before coming back with a bid. He nodded his head in complete understanding and gave me the thumbs up sign as I slipped out of my seat and almost crawled up the aisle. I didn't care who saw me as long as Barton and St. George didn't, and as they were well into the other section of seats I didn't think they could.

Once at the back of the room I stood up and walked past a surprised and glowering Al Swedner, nodded to him as I passed, thinking that he'd never understand the diversion I was going to create. I reached the far aisle and hunching over, scuttled down it until I reached Tom's shoulder. He had his head down, seemingly paying no attention to what was going on. His posture didn't fool me, however. His fingers drumming away on the bottom of the chair gave him away. I tapped his shoulder lightly and his head snapped around, his tongue seeming to lag slightly behind.

"Tom, take over the bid on the Ryder. I can't do it. Barton will take it the limit, and I don't want him setting his own prices. If you bid against him he'll have to let you have it cheap because he'd be bidding against himself. Please!" All I really wanted was to keep the price low and for Barton to eat crow in public. I hated him thoroughly, knowing he'd have tweaked me along letting my heart and lungs cry desperately for relief, exhausting me, until he merely gobbled me up. It was clever bidding, and I was learning a lesson I'd never forget, but right then it was happening to me.

"Why should I help you?" He seemed to push the words out of clamped lips.

"It's not helping me, you dolt, it's getting Barton," I said, recognizing a little late that calling Tom a dolt was not likely to get him to help me.

"I'm sorry, I didn't mean that. I'm the dolt."

"Explain it again," he said, sticking a match in the corner of his mouth.

"If you bid on the Ryder and I drop out, Barton will have to let you have it, cheap, otherwise he'd be raising prices against himself, assuming of course he's still taking everything you buy off you."

"He was half an hour ago, don't see why the leopard should change his spots."

"Okay, so he'll drop out of the bidding, leaving it in your hands. So you turn it over to me. You pay him off, getting him off your back."

"Sounds great all except for one thing."

"What?" I said, noting that my friend had just taken the bid to $57,000, and St. George answered with $58,000.

"Where in hell do I get the bread to float upon the waters?"

"Me. I loan you the amount of Barton's loan, and buy the painting off you at cost."

"So I'd owe you?" Tom said. I could tell he was thinking how to turn this whole situation to his advantage, hanging onto the notion that somehow out of it he ought to be able to make it so that I owed him. Give him long enough and he would. "Deal," he said.

"OK, so bid now. Right now, go to fifty-nine right now." And he did, shrieking it out in a cry not unlike what the baboon must have uttered.

Joe's head snapped around so quickly you'd have thought that he had sensed a wild animal in the room. The silence that had accompanied St. George's and the hulk's contest became even deeper. Tom and I discussed quickly how the deal would work, then I scurried back up the aisle. I tried to catch a glimpse of Barton. His head was bent toward St. George and he was whispering something in his ear. Joe looked straight at Barton as if waiting for instructions, then took a glance at my empty seat. The hulk shook his head. He clearly wasn't going to bid until I got back; bless him for being an intuitive hulk. I dashed along the back wall and down the aisle again until I was in my seat and panting hard.

"It's over," I whispered to the hulk, suddenly feeling the swell of victory.

"I have fifty-nine thousand once, fifty-nine thousand twice ... do I hear sixty? Sold to number 92, for fifty-nine thousand dollars." Numbers of people in the audience who didn't know what had happened, and that was probably 99 percent, clapped appreciatively at what must have looked like a brilliant bid on Tom's part. How had he known, they must wonder, the exact moment when the dogs would quit and he could scoop up the bone? Brilliant. The applause went on for a few minutes and I heard it swelling around my head. I interpreted it as applause for my tactic, and it sounded wonderful, even if I knew that while I'd won the painting I'd lost something else.

I looked toward where Barton was sitting and saw him rise and go toward Tom who had also risen and was walking away from Barton as fast as he could toward the cashier's desk. I watched as he wrote out a check to the cashier. Barton stood right behind Tom almost, his head was stuck forward as if at a moment's twitch by Tom, Barton would lunge for his throat. That pleased me. Barton's poise had been dallied with. Score one for the baboon.

Barton took Tom's arm and tried to lead him out the back door toward the passageway between the auction room and the gallery where he thought he would pick up "Tom's" Ryder. The plan was that when Barton demanded the Ryder, Tom would present him with a check for the amount he owed him. I would, of course, first thing in the morning cover the check to Barton from Tom as well as Tom's check to the cashier. I watched as they stood a few feet from the cashier's desk, Barton pulling at Tom and Tom resisting. I could imagine what they were both feeling and thinking, and it gave me a great deal of pleasure to watch them, though I hoped Barton was getting the worst of it. It was the first time in my life that I had felt my own power at such a distance.

The tableau continued. Tom had written out a check and was handing it to Barton; Barton was refusing to take it and was talking intently to Tom, looking not at him directly but at something to Tom's left, as if anything were more important. I also knew he meant what he was saying, however. Barton couldn't look you in the eye when he was serious. I didn't like the time this was taking. Why the hell doesn't Tom just go get the Ryder, I thought, and get the hell out of here. The longer they stood there arguing, the more anxious I got.

Obviously, I wasn't the only one. On the platform Joe, who had continued to the next item, paused and looked over to where Tom and Barton were now arguing closer to the top of Tom's voice range. As Barton argued, I knew from experience, his voice got softer and more menacing. Joe called a helper from the wings and slipped off the side of the platform to join Tom and Barton at the back of the room. I craned my neck to see what was happening. As long as Tom kept his head we were home free, but Tom's head had been increasingly missing as of late.

"Ahem, ahem, excuse me. I certainly don't mind sitting here saying numbers into the air, but it would make the day a whole lot more satisfying for me if I knew what the hell just happened . . . and what is happening. Curiosity has always been a failing of mine." The man on my right smiled and shrugged his large shoulders, holding his large hands palm up to the air.

"Just a minute, just a minute," I said quickly, not even looking at him. My attention was totally focused on that scene fifty feet away. Joe had now joined them and was standing between Barton and Tom, turning his head from one way and then to the other. Tom was still waving his check in Barton's face, Barton still refusing it. In a second Joe left them and went to the cashier's desk. I could see her ruffle around in front of her and produce what I knew to be Tom's check for the Ryder. He took the check over to where Barton and Tom were standing and I knew that it was indeed over. The momentary ploy had turned out to be only that, and the lion had not been diverted.

Tom grabbed the check out of Joe's hands and ripped it up and fled the room. Barton and Joe stood together, Barton seeming to console Joe by throwing his arm around his shoulder and walking with him back up the side aisle. Barton slid into his chair and Joe continued to the platform. He waited until the item being auctioned was sold, and then with amazing spring for his size and age, vaulted onto the stage.

"Ladies and gentlemen," he said, holding his hands up, "I'm afraid we've had a small unpleasantry, something that we all deplore happening, but which unfortunately in this business sometimes does. Someone has bought something which he has decided he can't pay for. I'm afraid we will have to auction the piece again. For you all, a second chance at 'To the Sea' by Albert Pinkham Ryder."

Feeling embarrassed and naked like a child exposed after being caught trying to steal, I slumped down in my seat. I don't know what Barton had said to Tom and Joe but I could guess. I had known it would be a tension-filled day, but I hadn't been prepared for this complete sense of loss. It was very quickly over. I took the bid to $50,000 but had no heart for the fight so dropped out at fifty-one. I knew whatever I bid, Barton would top it. So Barton walked away with the Ryder at $51,000. For him it couldn't have worked better, I had done him a great favor and saved him at least $8,000.

I felt a touch on my arm. "I'm sorry it didn't work," my erstwhile front said, trying to smile in the face of what must have looked like someone just seeing the end of the world.

"Oh well, easy come, easy go," I said, trying to return his smile but knowing I was failing miserably.

"Would a cup of coffee help?"

"No, but something stronger might."

"I have a small flask I always carry for ladies in distress," he said, reaching into his briefcase.

"I was actually thinking of arsenic, but thanks." He handed me the flask and I took a quick swig of what I perceived was Remy Martin. I nodded at him in appreciation.

"Want to tell me now?" he asked, packing up the flack again.

"In a minute, I'll be right back. I have to see some-one first." I knew I owed this guy an explanation of everything that had gone on, but first I wanted to find out what Barton had said to Tom. I was sure Tom wouldn't have gone very far.

I left the row and the room and soon found Tom sitting in the coffee shop taking some of the same medicine, only he was pouring his out of a bag into a cup of coffee. I slipped into the chair next to him and waited. He looked miserable. He took a look to see who it was and just as quickly looked away.

"Well," I finally said, leaning forward and trying to get myself into his field of vision.

"You and your bright ideas. Leave me alone, will you?" He took another drink from his coffee cup and gasped a little at its strength.

"It was a good idea, and it might have worked. You know that otherwise you wouldn't have agreed to do it. What happened?"

"Barton happened, as usual."

"Right, but what did he say?"

"Threatened to ruin me, that's all. Said if I insisted on buying the Ryder he'd smear me all over town so that I'd never be able to buy another piece at auction, ever."

I knew Barton would be angry at my touchdown but I hadn't expected he'd kick Tom out of the game. "That was a bit of overkill, wasn't it? Honestly, Tom, it never occurred to me that Barton would be so invested in the Ryder. I don't understand why he is. Anyway, I don't think for a minute he'd really do what he threatened."

"I do. He said he doesn't like dirty tricks. He said it was a dirty trick."

"Did you tell him I'd cover your debt?"

"Yeah, that didn't matter to him, what he didn't like was being had."

I should have known it. It was a dirty trick, but no

dirtier than Barton had been playing. But Barton doesn't like surprises. I remembered once, before I'd known him very well when he was still a fantasy and me a kid, a friend of mine and I had short-sheeted his bed on April Fool's Day, and then watched from the studio loft stairs while he tried to get into bed. At first he had been merely annoyed trying to fight through the sheets but when he discovered we were watching he went wild. I should have known that being made a fool of in public would bother him more than anything.

"I'm sorry, Tom, I set you up for it." I *was* sorry too.

"You can afford to be," he said.

He took another drink from his cup and then seeing it was empty poured more from his whisky bottle. I stood up. I did feel sorry for Tom but he was not making condolences easy.

"See you," I said. "It'll be over soon."

"You still want to lend me the money to pay him back?"

"Not really."

"Shove off then," he said.

I started to leave the coffee shop when Tom himself stood and pushing me aside ran through the entrance hall. I followed to see what Tom had escaped from and saw Barton standing there, the Ryder tucked casually under his arm, talking to St. George. As much as I had loved him once I hated him then. There was no reason to hate him, of course; there is never a "reason" for hating anyone. Barton had all along simply used the tools of the trade to get what he wanted. Often the tools were fear and love, but apparently that didn't make any difference to him.

He stood there talking to St. George, his posture easy and loose. I looked critically at his handsome profile, the slightly hooked nose, the deep-set brown eyes, the thick black hair, the high chiseled cheek bones, everything that ought to make him lovable, and saw nothing there for me, ever again. My silent gaze must have touched him for he turned slightly and merely returned it. He clearly had no intention of talking to me either, and in seeing that, I wondered how his vision of me had changed through the years. Whether he just saw me as a nuisance now, and a rather predictable one at that. Or was he seeing that I wasn't so predictable after all? My maneuver with Tom had not been one I'd learned from Barton or from my father, it was an original.

Finally, St. George, sensing the truth of the silence, and being too much of a gentleman to ignore me and cater to it, came over to where I stood, gently nudging Barton along with him. Barton let himself be prodded; to be sure, he would never have moved otherwise.

"I had no idea you were the Alamo," St. George said. "I'm sorry our first encounter had to be such a warlike one."

"Bloody but unbowed," I said, smiling to reassure him I held no malice toward him. And I didn't, any more than Barton could hold a grudge against the person who had fronted for me. It flashed through my head that I didn't even know his name yet.

"Congratulations, Barton," I said, finally turning toward him, "I hope you appreciate the real price you've paid for your painting."

"Of course, I never buy without knowing the price. But, my dear Minuke, remember, what you think of as costly and must in your heart of hearts regard as too great a price to pay, I regard as necessity. I don't have to like it, but it is necessary."

"Threatening Tom was necessary?"

"Do you know the nature of our contract, Tom's and mine? Were you there when we made our agreement, and being there, fully cognizant of the implications of what he did? But no matter. You think you know what is right, and that's enough for you. You think you have some moral right to this painting, that Tom has some moral right to get his way when he wants it. I disagree. This painting like everything else is up for grabs."

Barton motioned with the Ryder and did what he could to shake it in my direction as if trying to knock some sense into my head, as if I simply couldn't perceive his meaning and would never understand. I confess I couldn't. He stood there rock-like, hard, and unapproachable. He was the one seeming so right, appearing somehow to have developed a point of view that justified whatever he did. I couldn't fathom what it was. All I could tell then was that I found myself in an absurd way wanting to believe him, at the same time feeling guilty that I should even contemplate it.

"Oh, come now, Barton, really, that's rubbing the salt in a bit hard isn't it?" St. George cooed, his words soft like the call of a peacemaking dove.

"No, it's not. If I wanted Helen to have the painting, I would have given it to her outright if I could afford it, or I would not have bid on it. But I don't owe it to her, nor does she owe me anything, which for one brilliant flashy moment I thought you understood," he said looking at me. "When you tried to get Tom to front for you, you weren't thinking you owed me anything, were you?" He smiled knowing he had me, and as I remembered my sense of power, my influence from a distance, I knew he was right.

"See you at dinner, you later at home I trust, Jerry. I'm off." Barton gave us a slight wave of his hand and was gone, leaving as always a larger than human-size hole where he'd been.

"He's unforgivable," said Jerry, shaking his head. "He shouldn't speak to you like that. It's insensitive, thoughtless, and cruel." St. George clenched his trembling fist, "And what I find most unsupportable is that he didn't have the decency to tell me who he was bidding against. I wouldn't have done it if I'd known." His hand landed lightly on my shoulder; its tickle was unpleasant.

"Why not," I said. "What do you owe me?"

"You nothing, myself everything. I couldn't contribute to doing what Barton did to you and find myself very good company. I'm finding it very hard as it is."

"You're talking as if there were some blot upon your escutcheon." I never thought I'd ever use that phrase appropriately but St. George made it possible.

"I'm beginning to feel there is. I feel dirtied." His pale blue eyes gazed over my head and he seemed to drift away. He shuddered slightly, removed his hand and placed it across his forehead as if taking his own temperature. Amazing, I thought, how quickly the condolences passed to St. George. His comfort of me had quickly been converted into a hymn to his own shame. No wonder his hands shook if he could be made distraught so easily.

"I ought to get back," I said softly, "I owe someone an explanation. See you at dinner."

"You'll still go? After what's happened?"

"Have to eat," I said, "and Julie makes a mean coquille." I heard Barton's mocking tone echo in my voice and marvelled that it sounded so like me. I touched the bewildered St. George lightly on the elbow and left the entrance hall.

5 Back in the the auction room when I slid into my seat I noticed my friend was engrossed in his catalog. As soon as I checked mine, I saw why. The Inness was lot number 152 and the item then being auctioned was number 150. Fully aware that I'd promised myself I'd go after the Inness when I thought the lout was a lout, I had to question myself carefully whether things were any different now. Did knowing that this person had graciously helped me just a little while ago, make a whit's bit of difference about how I should bid on the Inness? Did I owe him something? The question quickly became translated into an issue of whether in ten years I'd become a hand-shaking wreck like St. George or—and it seemed at the time the only other option available—become selfish and friendless like Barton. There didn't seem to be any way to win. For a fleeting instant, it occurred to me that a sense of futility was behind Barton's insistence that anything is up for grabs. Of course, it's lucky for Barton that everyone else didn't feel that way as well.

Lot number 151 was a Chinese Foo dog, a bronze incense burner, that sold quickly and unremarkably for $800. I tried to sum up years of wisdom as if one could grow up all in one minute and make the "right" decision. The question was whether I wanted the Inness or not, and at what price? Before I could answer my own question, the moment itself wiped my mind clean of anymore fruitless and all-too-familiar self-questioning.

"Lot number 152, 'Before the Rain,' by George Inness, what am I bid for it please?"

As usual there was silence. I shifted slightly in my seat and the movement must have caught my front's eye.

"After you madam," he said, bowing his head and making a sweeping gesture with his hand. Some of the ash fell out of his pipe and landed on his pant leg. I watched while a small hole appeared.

"You're burning," I said.

"Asbestos knees," he said, not even bothering to wipe the ash off.

"Do you always burn things up and not notice?"

"Do you always sound like someone's mother?"

Facing the podium, I caught Joe's eye. "Five thousand," I said loudly, announcing my bid as if it were a challenge. The silence was painful. I felt as if I'd just burped at a tea party. Bids like that for openers are rare and either brilliant or stupid. It took a few moments for the crowd to decide which. I looked around me and saw a few admiring glances shot my way and decided that, if nothing else, today was going to shake up people's image of me. "Six thousand," someone from the back row said. The same voice I now recognized as being of Sev Lahti from the Worcester Art Museum who had bid against Barton on the Ryder.

"Seven thousand," the lout said. Immediately, I got up from my chair and walked up the aisle to the back of the room. I stood behind the lout against the back wall. If he was going to watch me he'd have to turn his head completely around. From where I was I could see him as well as the man on my left. At the moment there weren't any other bidders.

I raised my hand and caught Joe's eye. "I have eight thousand from the back of the room," he said. "Do I hear ten? We know, ladies and gentlemen, that this is a fine Inness and that it's so low right now that we all ought to be embarrassed."

"Ten thousand," said Sev Lahti from the Worcester Art Museum.

"Eleven thousand," said the hulk. His voice had a rasping dull sound to it that I hadn't noticed before. I was beginning to think he was probably a bit stupid.

The fact that his pad had been covered with incomprehensible formulas didn't impress me one bit.

I nodded my head again, and Joe announced my bid of $12,000. It went on like that up to $20,000. I was getting prepared to take another leap forward when another bid came from the lower right quarter of the room. As soon as I heard it I knew it was over for me. It was Silky; out of the depths of his fury he was about ready to propel himself into the heights of debt. He should not be taken seriously, nor should he do this to himself. I didn't know how well Joe knew Silky, how easily he could perceive that Silky at that moment wasn't to be believed.

I slipped away from where I had been standing along the back wall to the aisle on the right. The door to the passageway was almost exactly opposite where Silky was sitting in the third row from the front. The seat next to him was empty and, as I sat down in it, I put my hand on his arm and tried to get his attention.

"Silky," I said, "you can't be serious?"

"Of course, I'm not serious, what do you think I am, crazy? I'm just practicing." He shifted the angle of his head as if to hear better the $25,000 bid just made.

"Well, I have to admit it—I did think you were crazy. I thought you'd gone straight round the bend and were heading off into directions unknown."

"Whatever gave you that idea?" Silky said. He still hadn't turned to look at me, so I wasn't convinced yet.

"You seemed upset last time I saw you and, frankly, you still do."

"What would upset me?" he asked. His broad face lacked any expression as it turned my way. I had the eerie feeling that he could have been talking to anyone. Of all the people I regularly ran into at auctions I was most fond of Silky. He was the most approachable, the easiest to touch. But at that moment he was walking alone in acres of pain that were closed to trespassers. I was left standing outside, not wanting in, but wanting him out. On the stage the bid went up to $36,000.

"The Sloan, Silky, the Sloan," I said.

Finally, his features crinkled. He put his hand to his face, so I couldn't see it. "Oh God, I feel ashamed," he said. I didn't understand what made him so ashamed. My seeing him distraught or what? I'd lost paintings at auctions, hadn't I just lost one myself, but shame? I told him I didn't understand.

"I should never have let him see me that way, wanting something so badly and he saw it. I must appear weak and disgusting to him."

"Who's him?" I asked, grateful that Silky was at least talking.

"Him, of course, Barton. He's the only one around here worth anything, he's got the dough, he's got the success, and I've been shamed in front of him."

A bid of $40,000 broke into my consciousness but I no longer cared. "What about me, don't I count? Hell, you weren't shamed by Barton any more than I was. It's hardly as if he'd gone around putting yellow dots on our noses to let others know we'd been outdone."

"I'm sorry, Helen, of course you're worth something, you're my best friend in this business. I'm just so frustrated and angry." He beat his arms with his hands and for a moment looked like a little kid in a too-tight snow suit. He then put his head down and I could see that he was gritting his teeth, against either tears as it would have been in my case, or the world. I heard him mutter something and leaned forward, but couldn't catch it.

"God-damned fur coats," I said, again suddenly shaken out of my concern for Silky by the recognition that the bidding on the Inness was over. Joe was just wrapping it up, with a $53,000 bid from Sev Lahti. I wasn't even aware of how far the hulk had taken the bid, but I was aware of being sorry that he hadn't got it and glad that I hadn't forced it to a point where he couldn't take it. I knew too that I hadn't really wanted it, it had been merely my way of being angry. Silky and I weren't that different after all.

I sat with him through the next few items then touched him on the shoulder and started to leave. He raised his hand slightly to acknowledge my leaving, and got up abruptly himself and walked past me and through the door into the passageway. I figured he'd be okay, I was just very glad that he wasn't still wandering around inside his head.

As I walked back to my seat, I thought that this was going to be the longest auction of my life. Most of the items I had been interested in were gone, and there was little reason for me to stay. At some auctions, however, especially ones where some of the bigger items go first, some surprising bargains fall out at the end. Many people come to see the big ones sold and after they realize the enormous prices these things go at, get depressed and go home. Unless they want a specific item the consumers don't hang around, and the dealers, who most often have a certain market they're looking to fill, also won't go for just anything. Under those conditions, some things fall through the cracks. Only a chasm would fit the Bierstadt canvas that was understandably going cheaply at that very moment.

Late in one auction I had picked up a small Culverhouse oil for $300 that I later sold for $2,500. Of course, that is the kind of deal that Silky dreams about and expects to happen. It is in fact the kind of deal that happens only when you sit out auction after auction pulling the muscles in your fanny to keep them from going to sleep, drinking cup after cup of gritty coffee, and watching lot after lot of cut epergnes and bon bon dishes pass before your tired glassy eyes.

Eventually, as one becomes successful like the Voses of Vose Galleries of Newbury Street, the less one has to hang around for the deal. And, in fact, I was in that category myself, not depending on a "good" buy to pay the rent, taking a nice summer vacation on Nantucket, and flying to London when I wanted to do some buying there. I stayed mainly because I liked it. As much as I hated it, I liked it. And I think no matter how big we get, all of us in this game at heart really like turning a dollar. As much as we love a good painting or a finely carved chest—and most of us really are wedded to our fields—we love buying and selling. If we didn't we'd all be museum custodians.

As I walked back up the aisle I wondered what the hulk was; a consumer, a dealer like myself, or maybe he was a museum custodian. The formulas made me think he was the creature we like the least, the speculator. Those people don't care a whit for the art itself, but have so much impact on the marketplace that they change the art vogue and thereby what other people like. They, the rich ones anyway, can drive up the prices of a certain school of painting, lead everyone else to think it's the hot thing to have, then dump it all at the top of the market they've created. They start buying, say, American impressionist while everyone else is buying Italian renaissance. But, because by their action the impressionist market booms, everyone will switch to it. The real speculators, then, start buying the Italian schools before the market has crested on the impressionists. In any event, they play a tune to which we all must in some fashion dance, jump, or stand still to.

I looked around to see who was still there. I could make out the top of Julie's head in the front row. I hadn't been paying careful attention, so I didn't know if she'd bought anything since the Enneking. I thought of what the night's dinner would be like and what on earth anyone would find to talk about. I imagined St. George being impossibly correct and solicitous to me, whom I was sure he'd always see as some sort of seduced and abandoned maiden. To Julie, he'd be coolly proper, and to Barton? How would he treat Barton? The same with Julie. I thought of quickly darting over there and telling her what I'd found out about St. George. It might not make her feel any better about losing her chance to go to New York but it might console her some to learn that St. George wasn't the pillar of strength that she thought and that he would have depended on her for survival rather than the other way around. Also there was something about him that convinced me he wasn't a great candidate to be a lover either; passion would threaten his dignity. That was probably why he found himself so ambivalent about Barton.

At that moment, I saw Julie get up and walk up the side aisle to the back of the room. The top of her blonde hairdo (one couldn't really call it her head; to assume it was attached was to do her an injustice) appeared between other heads along the row like a bouncing ball. I watched her leave the room. I'd tell her tonight, I thought.

As I swung that way I searched the line of figures at the back of the hall for Al. He wasn't there. He'd shown a side of him that day that I hadn't seen before. Always I'd thought he was rather a stiff and dumb bully, not getting ahead merely because he wasn't bright enough to figure out how to do it. But today I'd seen him in bondage. Unable to do anything for himself, unable even to make very many friends, Al dragged his limitations around like a ball and chain which he loved because they were the only things that stayed by his side. He couldn't and wouldn't give them up.

Before I turned back, I saw Al come in, his hat covered with snow. He'd probably been watching the snow bury his truck, wondering "why me" and cursing Joe for having his auction.

I looked at my watch. It was 2:05. Lot number 175 was being sold, which meant things were moving at a rate of less than seventy-five an hour. Joe would have to speed things up if he was going to get through 354 items before dark. I'd wait until three o'clock then make a decision depending on the number of lots and people left. Today might just be a bonanza if a lot of people decided to leave early because of the snow. When I got back to my seat the hulk was gone. That settles that, I thought; he's not a dealer or if he is, he's not a very good one. Or maybe he's a very well-stocked one, that's a possibility. Of course, it never occurred to me that he might have moved his seat, or in fact just might have gone to make a telephone call, taking his briefcase with him.

Something like the latter looked to be the case as no sooner had I got my briefcase open and spread the lunch I'd brought with me across my lap ready to eat, than he returned. He stood in the aisle right next to me, waiting for me to move my knees so he could get by. I shifted them slightly and he squeezed past, but not without upsetting the briefcase that I had carefully balanced on my knees. The weight of the lid plus his touch pulled the case over and it fell off my lap.

"Oh, I was looking forward to eating my food, not standing in it," I cried, feebly trying to catch my lunch as it slid to the floor.

He bent down to help shaking his head. "I have managed somehow to get around for all of my thirty-five years without upsetting every person I meet. Some people even like me, though you may find that hard to believe. And I think I'd better move rather than send the whole of this room into fits of laughter at your being forced to throw this squashed deviled egg into my face." He said all this while picking up my papers and stuffing them back into the briefcase.

He handed me the egg, the gooey stuffing of which was dribbling out the edges. It was a bit mushed but clearly edible: a bomb in my hands. I couldn't do it, as much as I'd like to, I couldn't. Besides, I was really hungry and loved deviled eggs and wouldn't waste one on anyone. I slowly unwrapped the egg from its wax paper and while he watched, took a deliberately big bite of it. I chewed very carefully and slowly. He watched just as intently.

"You've got egg on your face," he said.

"Cute," I said, knowing I'd set myself up for it. He placed the now closed briefcase on the chair next to me and continued past to his seat. He sat down and using his briefcase for a desk, started making calculations on a pad. I turned away and wiped the egg from my face so he couldn't see me.

"Look," I said, "it's been a bad day and just when I think it's over it gets worse. But that gives me no right to take it out on you, though you have to admit you sort of ask for it with that clumsy routine." He turned and poked his head forward at me.

"It's not a routine, it's a characteristic, and I can't help it any more than you can help being bitchy when the day falls apart. The only difference is that I know I can't help it, and you don't," he said in a loud whisper.

"How do you know I don't know I can't help it?" I asked, nearing my limit again.

"Because of statements like that."

"And your comments are perfect?"

"Nobody's perfect," he said.

"No, but some of us are pretty damn smug," I said under my breath while rearranging the stuff he'd crammed into my briefcase. I didn't even want to look at him because I sensed he was looking at me, and because I suddenly felt very exposed.

"I'm sorry you are having a rough day," he said finally, "but it wasn't my intention to make it rougher. In fact as I recall, I did try to make it easier."

"Yes, you did," I said, still staring at my jumble of papers, "and I am grateful, and I apologize."

"A truce?" he asked.

"Definitely," I responded.

He nodded and smiled and immediately opened a book and started reading. I don't know what I'd expected him to do but it wasn't that. Just as well; despite the truce I was still feeling raw and couldn't have bet for a moment that I wouldn't break it. I finished my lunch self-consciously trying to make as little sound as possible with the wax paper, and then decided the hell with it. Wax paper is wax paper and who's afraid of the big bad wolf.

As I suspected, the audience had begun to thin after the major items had been sold and I decided it was probably worth it to hang around. By then it was two twenty-five. Kevin had come back with lot number 215. They might make it after all.

I spent the next half hour or so bidding against the winners, playing my hand once more at beating the market. I didn't do very well; somehow my acquisitive sense had been put into neutral. Besides, I had this eerie feeling that every time I made a mental bid, the guy next door was laughing.

I checked the right side of the room and saw Tom slip in the door from the passageway. He searched the room with his eyes then slid along the wall to the back of the room. I tried to get his attention as I was beginning to feel I'd treated him poorly, but he refused to look my way. So be it, I thought, if I lose more people than paintings today.

At three o'clock, Joe, back at the podium again, was at item number 263. The speed was really picking up. But it occurred to me that I didn't want to hang around that day any more at all. I'd had it. No bargain I could get would make it worthwhile sitting there gazing at my buddies and friends as if they were so many wounded bodies lying bloodied and dying on a battlefield. Because that was how they all appeared; it was probably a pretty good indication of how I felt myself. And it was. I was monstrously tired, unbearably saddened over the loss of the Ryder. I knew I hadn't even begun to recognize how much I was hurting over it and what it represented.

It seemed there was nothing to keep me there. I packed up my briefcase and started slipping into my coat when I saw that there was. I did owe the man who was still sitting on my right an explanation, an apology, probably a drink, or all three. It would be easier to write him a note but somehow that seemed too intimate. But it also seemed more than I could stand, or thought I could, to explain the whole day to him the way it ought to be explained. Intimate or not, a note would have to do it.

I scribbled on a piece of paper "if you'll be my guest at lunch I'll explain the who and the what. How about Tuesday or Thursday next week? Just give me a day's notice." I was folding the note and preparing to pass it to him when the next item came up on the platform. The center revolving wall turned slowly and upon the platform was the beautiful walnut chest with the carved hunting scene that I'd sat on in the small room with the Inness. It was large, about six by three, but looking at it from a distance I could see its proportions were perfect; the light on the stage glinted off its shiny round surfaces. Joe described it as walnut, seventeenth-century English. It had a coat of arms of the Duke of Richmond on a panel on the front. Joe opened the bidding.

It seemed as if everyone in the audience was feeling the same lassitude that I had just the moment previously. There was a joke bid of $500. From the back of the room one of the pool of furniture dealers bid $1,000 in an impatient tone as if he were being interrupted from something more important. I bid a quick $1,200 and felt the comforting familiar rise of adrenalin in my stomach. I wasn't dead yet.

A serious bid of $2,000 came from the left-hand corner of the room, and then one of $2,500 from the right wall behind me. I bid $3,000 fast on his heels. We three played that way until they dropped out at $3,500, and I had it for $4,000. Actually with that and the Shiraz, I hadn't had that bad a day after all, though business had been lousy. Joe looked my way from the platform and I held up the plastic ping pong paddle with my bidder's number on it.

"Item number 280 to number sixty-two—four-thousand dollars. A very nice buy; I was thinking of taking this one myself. Did everyone get a chance to see the top of the lid?" Joe was being a bit of the showman trying to interest the few remaining customers in what they'd lost, juicing their glands for the next item. Also, revealing some "discovered" item on stage sometimes leads the uninitiated into thinking that there are diamonds to be found in the drawers of old bureaus and secret caches of money in old desks.

Joe called Kevin and one of his helpers from off-stage. He motioned them in with a wave of his arm and asked them to tilt the chest so the audience could see the fine old carving on the lid. The two young men walked on stage and with one at each end lifted the chest slowly off its feet and tilted it forward. Given the glare of the lights, however, we couldn't see much at that angle. Joe squinted up at the ceiling and signaled more with his hands.

"Can't you get it over farther?" he said, trying not to be exasperated with Kevin but sounding it nonetheless.

"It's really heavy," Kevin said, as they tipped it. And clearly it was, because of its own weight it began to tip even further than they obviously intended. The lid, which had been shut, opened slightly. Helped by the weight of something that pressed against it, it opened even more, and what had been inside rolled out on to the floor. The moment froze.

I can still see Joe standing there, his hands pulled away from his cuffs as if he were performing a magic act, Kevin and his mate, backs humped, heads bowed low, feet spread in identical positions like two life-sized bookends, the chest—my chest—tilted open so that its lid swung on its rusty hinges like a gaping mouth, and on the floor, Barton's hair, his coat, with some of the fur lining exposed, his shoes, his suit, his face even, but not him, because the form was totally lifeless. The silence of the moment continued; to begin the next was to respond and the reaction went too deep.

I must have jumped up and grabbed the hulk on my right because I found myself standing and clutching his arm when the silence was broken and the body was recognized. Kevin put down his end of the chest and announced to the air, "It's Mr. Morley. He's dead."

6 No one moved. Then Joe lowered his hands and clasped them in front of him as if he could pray Barton to his feet. Everyone on the platform was still. It reminded me, absurdly, of a children's Chrismas play.

The scene stirred when a small lady in her mid-fifties pushed her way across a row about five ahead of me and walked to the front of the room. "I'm a doctor," she said. In a moment she was on the stage bending over Barton. Everyone knew he was gone. There was something about the way his body had hit the floor, all parts landing at once, solid and heavy, like a large jelly fish. One imagined that if he'd been living, something would have bounced, had some resilience to it. It wasn't demonstrable, but we were a room full of animals who had a collective sense that one of their kind was dead.

As the tableau was clearly visible, there was no need to crane necks or jump for a good view, and some had stood only to sit down again. Like everything else in his life, Barton's death had been performed center stage. But I had to see and touch. I let go of the arm of the hulk and walked up the aisle to the steps at the side and onto the stage. The doctor was just pulling the lids down over Barton's eyes. I got one glimpse of them, filled with no recognition and distant, then they were winked, and were gone. I moved over to his head and looked down at his face, which though totally still didn't look any different. Atavistically thinking there was something there, a small molecule of life remaining that might want comfort, and as if nothing had happened in all the years, I reached down to stroke Barton's hair. When I pulled my hand away it was greasy and streaked with blood.

"Please don't touch it," said the doctor. I stood up, nodding my head, suddenly recognizing that I had no official right to be there. I stepped back and sat on my chest which had been replaced on its feet. Kevin disappeared behind the revolving stage, then returned with a piece of tarpaulin which he placed over Barton. The doctor stood up and went over to talk to Joe. I peered out into the audience, only half seeing.

I must have been a little in shock at the time because I couldn't keep my mind concentrated on what was in front of me. I'd look at the gray-green mound and know it was Barton but not know. I sat there and all I could think of was a mountain climbing party I'd been on years ago when in college. A group of us had gone to the Alps for the summer to try some novice climbs. On one of them, by not following directions and going off on my own, I'd got lost from the others. I found myself climbing a path that got steeper as it went up and more difficult to climb. The higher I went the more difficult the return became as well. Neither up nor down seemed likely to get me back to where my friends were, neither offered any comfort, and yet I had to choose one of them. Each second I didn't move and each one I did were equally important. There was no sitting it out, no going back to Tara to find another way. There wasn't one, except jumping. At the time the knowledge that I had to make a choice immobilized me and I sat there for a long time on that path, watching the afternoon fade away knowing that as I sat there it only got worse.

And yet there was something wonderful about feeling the sharp edge of indecision so cleanly, in the face of it I felt truly helpless and because of that, free of responsibility. It occurred to me that I'd die and that seemed okay too. Anything seemed better than making a choice. Somehow while knowing that and feeling it to be true, content to die, maybe even to jump, I stood up and started walking back down the path. I never made a decision that I knew of, somewhere in some dark cave of my subconscious a battle was raging and I had had to sit by, a prisoner, until it was over. Then like someone who's received a governor's pardon before the death sentence is executed I was let go, dazed, feet walking mechanically away from the prison walls, stumbling a bit, not used to activity on my own behalf, alive, but still on a battlefield.

Sitting on the stage overlooking the audience, I couldn't move either. Because I'd been through it before I knew the combat was raging and that I'd have to wait until it was over. What I hadn't counted on, of course, was that the battle was not between some subconscious motivating forces but simply between the stuffed eggs and my nervous system. The former won and propelled me off the chest, across the stage and behind its back wall to the preview room where I gave up my deviled egg to a Meissen tureen that was sitting on a stand waiting to be displayed next. I swayed a bit and grabbed the stand tightly.

"Wickham's sure giving away some surprises with his stuff today," said my erstwhile neighbor from the next seat, putting the top of the tureen neatly on the pot, covering what I had just deposited there. He handed me a handkerchief with which I removed the last of the egg, for the second time.

"Thanks," I said, "I'll have it cleaned." I stuck it in my pocket.

He then withdrew the precious flask from his pocket, opened it, and handed it to me. I took a large swig, a larger gulp of air, and another drink. The brandy raced to the pit of my stomach where the egg had been, took a quick survey of the cavernous interior and decided it liked it there, and settled. I handed the flask back.

"Friend of yours?" he asked, twisting the top back on.

"No, not friend, family," I said.

"Close?"

"Very like a brother."

"I'm, sorry."

"Me too," I said. "I'm very sorry ... what's your name?"

"De Ruyter, Stanford de Ruyter." The name was familiar, but why? Then I remembered, from this morning, the telephone call to Liam in the gallery, the monster sofa-size nude.

"Thank you very much, Mr. de Ruyter, for being such a nice person while I've been such an irredeemable bitch," I said finally. "I also hope you enjoy the Luks. You should have told me who you were. That wasn't fair."

"And spoil the fun? How often do I get the chance to sit next to someone knowing who she is and something about her while being the mysterious stranger myself? Not often, and I'm not about to give up the chance. When you're my size you don't have many opportunities to hide."

"It's still sneaky."

"Agreed, but then as I said, nobody's perfect. You probably ought to sit down, you look green."

"What do people call you when they know who you are?" I asked, taking his assessment seriously and lowering myself onto a Queen Anne country chair.

"I don't know, it's a constant surprise to me. I hate Stan and there's not much else. Those who hang around long enough to try to tackle the problem with ingenuity and intelligence usually end up with 'Ritter.' "

"I think I'll start there if you don't mind."

"Be my guest," he said, smiling down at me, and then moving away slightly to look out on the stage where the tableau hadn't shifted. From where I sat I could see the gray-green mound, and Joe still standing at its head talking to the doctor. While I watched, a third figure appeared on the stage. What had been a shock and a horror among people made intimate by its occurrence was suddenly to become a matter of official concern. We would soon hear the word that had lain dormant, no one uttering it, no one wanting to think, but like a tumor, it pressed its way to the surface. The doctor said it first. As the policeman pulled back the canvas to look at Barton's face, I heard it from the wings:

"It looks like murder," she said.

7 Officially, there wasn't any question about it. Barton had been killed by someone wielding that hideous African chieftain's sceptre that I'd held while talking to Kevin. The sceptre was still in the chest, with strands of Barton's hair caught in the monkey teeth that studded its tumulose top. From the wings where I still sat, I watched as swarms of policemen, photographers, detectives, and whatever officials converge at a death, hovered around the body. I saw them find the sceptre, examine it, then put it carefully into a case that one of the people had with him. I saw a plainsclothes officer talking with the doctor, who had first looked at Barton, then at Joe. Eventually, as I figured they would, the police requested everyone to return to their seats and remain there.

Without a word, Ritter and I started across the preview room to get back to the gallery through the passageway. But then I remembered the tureen. As Ritter went on ahead, I signaled to Joe from the side of the stage. I got his attention and he came over to the side.

"I hate to add to the confusion but I have already. It's the tureen, Joe, I vomited in it."

"You what?" Joe looked a little stunned and I couldn't blame him.

"Look, I'll buy it at 10% just for the pleasure of cleaning it up, I can't leave it there and let anyone else do it. Somehow after you've done what I did, you sort of own it."

"Do what you want, Helen, I can't think beyond what's out there."

"How much is it?"

"I don't know. Whatever the estimate is will be fine. How could this have happened? It's beyond me, absolutely beyond me." Joe shook his head and some of his thinly combed hair fell off the top of his head and hung down over his back like a chinese pigtail.

"I don't know," I said. Joe looked at me closely as if suddenly realizing that I might be even more affected by Barton's death than he.

"How callous of me, I'm sorry, Helen," Joe said putting his hand on my shoulder.

I nodded, but couldn't speak. I hugged the tureen as if it were a pillow, then remembering what was in it backed away from Joe a bit and started to leave.

He asked, "You okay?"

"Sure, sure, just wanted to get this cleaned up and back to my seat." I gestured to the policemen and with a weak wave of a hand moved away. I'm sure I sounded fine to Joe but I wasn't really. I was shivering. In the shock of Barton's death, his dramatic appearance on the stage, touching him, being sick, then sitting there watching for half an hour or so while policemen and examiners of all sorts poked at Barton's body, I hadn't had time to think of anything more than the what. As Joe had said, one's mind was full of what was out there. But suddenly my mind focused on the murder itself.

Someone had picked up the African sceptre studded with baboon teeth and whacked it into Barton's head until the teeth were stained and bloody and Barton a lifeless lump. Trying to shake the image from my mind, I went to the ladies room and sat down on a bench. While hot water ran in and out of the tureen, the sounds comforted but could not rid my mind of the sight of Barton. It gripped me and wouldn't let me go. I rose to turn off the water. I needed to get back to the auction room and people as soon as possible.

It turned out that not everyone was sitting obediently in his or her seat. Just as I was about to open the door to the ladies' room it pushed in toward me and Julie came rushing through, her arms filled with grocery bags. Snow lay sprinkled over the bushy tops of celery, the fox fur collar of her coat, and her hair. She brushed past me and dropped her bundles on the floor in front of the sink. I watched her as she peered into the mirror catching a trickle of mascara before it became a stream. I saw her face in the mirror, her eyes resolute and unyielding. Why, I thought, is she still so angry, what difference does it make now? What difference does any of it make? Then it occurred to me that if she had been out shopping, she might not know.

"You go out?" I asked quietly.

"No, I always walk around in my coat carrying god-damned heavy bags." She stuck her head forward at the mirror, and flapped hard at the underside of her chin with her hand.

"You're really pissed aren't you?"

"Damned right I am, not so much at you, Helen, I'm sorry for that, I'm just so frustrated at everything. I know I'm no damn good at this game. Oh sure, I've got a good shop and a good reputation and all that, but I'm not interested in earning money anymore, I've got enough of that. But I don't know anything. I really wanted to learn something so I'll understand and care what the hell goes in and out of my hands." She suddenly looked old. "I don't want to hustle anymore," she said, sounding like a tired whore. "It scares me sometimes, but even more it scares me how angry at Barton I am," she said, as if Barton were the pimp who wouldn't let her stop.

"I wouldn't say that to too many people, Julie," I said.

"Why the hell not?"

"Because Barton's dead."

Her mouth dropped open and she turned to look at me. Her knees seemed to buckle slightly and she slid onto the edge of the sink and caught herself with one hand while the other fled to her face to cover her eyes as if by not seeing she couldn't hear. A moment passed while I watched her breathe deeply and slowly peel her hand from her face.

"But I just saw him," her voice sounded reedy and thin.

"We all did."

"No, no I mean it. Just before I went out I saw him. What happened? I didn't know there was anything

wrong with him, that he had a bad heart or anything."
She shook her head in disbelief.

"He didn't, he was killed. His body tumbled out of a
chest onto the stage, about forty-five minutes ago," I
said looking at my watch. It was then four-fifteen.

"Oh my God." Julie collapsed back onto the sink. Just
as I was about to go over to her and hand her a wet
towel there was a knock on the door.

"Hello in there. Everyone is supposed to be in the
main gallery. The police want everyone, in their seats."

"Coming," I called and heard the footsteps move
away. We'd be there for hours. There must have been
at least fifty people left.

"We'd better go," I said.

"You go, I'll be there in a minute. How was he
killed?"

"The monkey sceptre."

"It would be something collectible."

"I know, see you later." I left the ladies' room, the
tureen cradled in my arm, and walked past the coffee
shop back to the main gallery. A line of people were
moving up the aisle to the stage as if they were about to
receive communion. The mound was gone, the stage
was filled with people milling around. My chest had
been moved off center stage and in its place was a table
behind which a non-uniformed officer sat.

"What are they doing?" I asked Ritter, who was reading his book and smoking his pipe for all the world as if
he were home in front of a fire.

"They've asked everyone who knew Morley to stay,
the rest of us are supposed to go up and give our
names and numbers in case they want to get hold of us
later. Then they'll talk to each of you independently.
How are you feeling? I see you're not taking any
chances," he said, pointing to the tureen.

"Can't be sure of anything anymore," I said, wondering how often two people who don't know each other
very well are exposed to each other as much as we had
been.

"I'll always think of you that way," he said. "Such
sweet memories." He smiled and I did as well. I looked

at him then and wondered how he could have ever seemed like such a lout.

"Did you go up yet?" I asked.

"No, I was waiting until you got back. I want to know what happened because I just realized that the dead man is the very one whom I was bidding against for you, right?"

"Correct."

"So, it occurred to me that I am involved if only tangentially, and I'd really like to know more about the Ryder, and what happened. Who was he?"

"There's nothing to tell, really. Barton was an old friend of the family, a protégé of my father's, sort of, and I'd known him all my life. And he knew me. He also knew that I'd want that painting very badly as I had once owned it and had had to sell it. Well, so did he, though why I am not sure of, and there was no way out but for us to butt heads. It made it easier I guess on both of us to have other people do the actual bidding. What happened was that the other guy that I got to bid owed Barton money so I thought Barton wouldn't bid against him thinking he'd get the painting anyway and, well, it gets complicated."

"I think I understand. Barton ended up with the painting and you with nothing."

"Well, not exactly nothing, I've got a rug, the chest, and of course, the tureen."

"Why do you think he was killed?"

"I haven't the foggiest idea, and less idea who could have done it. Anyone might have wanted to. Barton was not a favorite person."

At that moment the police asked for anyone who had not yet given his or her name and address to go to the stage and do so. The rest of us were to wait. Ritter and another man both rose and walked to the stage. I looked around and counted Tom, Silky, Al, Julie, St. George, Joe, myself, and three others. One was Sev Lahti from the Worcester Art museum who obviously had known Barton, and two others, Claire Lucas, a dealer from New Hampshire, and Phil Woodruff, another auctioneer. None of those three had left the room during the auction so wouldn't have much to offer, or to hide.

I watched Ritter walk up to the stage and found myself wondering how heavy he was. I smiled despite myself that here, only yards away from where Barton's body had lain, his blood probably still fluid in his veins, I should be looking at the back of another man and literally and figuratively trying it out for size. The blood in my veins felt warm for a change.

Ritter walked with a long stride up the aisle. His shoulders were slightly stooped, his head preceding the rest of him by a fraction of a second, his pipe preceding that. I watched him walk up the stage stairs then lean on the table with his back to the audience, his stretched arms taking his weight as he leaned forward to talk to the officer.

They seemed to be having a friendly chat as if they had just met at an afternoon's tennis match. The officer stood up and came out from behind the table and they talked for awhile together, both with their arms folded across their chests. Every once in awhile Ritter would take his pipe out of his mouth and dot the air with it as if he were stabbing flies. Then suddenly he turned and pointed to the bunch of us in the room, me in particular. I slid down in my seat slightly as I was aware of everyone else looking at me. Ritter then waved in my direction and, with a final handshake with the policeman, was gone. The detective, for that is what I assume he was, came to the front of the stage and looked us over. I think we all shrank into our seats. It had been a long time since I had felt so ready to be scolded.

"Ahem," he began inauspiciously and I sat up a little higher in my seat, "ahem, thank you all for waiting. As you all knew the deceased personally, you may know something about him that will help us. That's all. This is no grilling or anything like that." There was an audible sigh in the room as if air held in ten sets of lungs had been released at once.

"What we'd like to do," the detective continued from the stage, "is to talk to you now only if you know something specific about where Mr. Morley was this afternoon. As it is continuing to snow we don't want to keep you here. We can contact you in the next few days at home."

No one moved. The detective stood there for a moment turning his head slowly from one side to the other. I didn't think I had to stand up because Julie had seen Barton after me, but why wasn't she standing up? Had she talked to someone who had seen Barton after her? Why wasn't St. George standing up? The moment seemed to get longer and longer. Finally Al, of all people, stood up and walked to the stage. Then Julie stood and followed Al. St. George and I searched each other out, nodded imperceptibly, and stood simultaneously. We met at the head of the room where we formed a line waiting to go up the stairs.

"Why don't you sit down," St. George said, "I'll take care of this."

"Why should I sit down? I'm okay. How are you?"

"Shattered, simply shattered. I always knew there was something violent about Barton, but to think I have stayed with him and in a sense been his friend when all along he was this violent person."

"He didn't exactly murder himself you know, Jerry," I said using his nickname, as it seemed absurd to be formal under the circumstances.

"No, but it was a passionate death, wasn't it?" Now that he mentioned it, it did seem to be just that. Skipping over St. George's interesting identification of passion with violence, I wondered, had Barton been having an affair with anyone that I hadn't known about? It hit me first as a shock that he could have an affair without my knowing, and second as a shock that it was a shock. In Barton's and my open estrangement, one of the unspoken agreements had been that at least each would know who the other was having an affair with. We had been bound together far more than I had realized. I knew then that although I couldn't like him, I could never deny his importance. I felt my throat close and my eyes sting.

The line moved slightly as Al shifted his weight across the stage, swinging his shoulders slowly from side to side as if shuffling a burden from one aching part of his back to another. Jerry and I moved up the stairs and stood at the corner of the stage while Julie walked forward and talked to the officer behind the table. I looked out at the hall and saw Silky and Tom talking together at the back of the room. Both of them shot glances up at us. Claire Lucas and Phil Woodruff were sitting at opposite ends of the room, and Sev Lahti from the Worcester Art Museum was talking to Joe who had slipped into a seat beside him.

Julie told her story very quickly and moved on. Then Jerry, straightening his tie and pulling back his shoulders slightly, walked across the stage. He looked terrific. In a moment or two he was done and it was my turn. I gave the detective my name and address, and explained what I had been doing on the stage when they arrived, my relationship to Barton, and when I had last seen him.

"I suspect that confirms Mr. St. George's story," I said finally.

"Yes, it does."

"Would there have been a lot of pain?" I asked suddenly, not wanting to leave.

"I'm not an expert on these things," he said, "but I wouldn't think so. A crack on the head like that one knocks you out pretty fast before you feel anything."

"Oh, I'm so glad."

"You cared a lot for Mr. Morley?" he asked, drawing his pencil slowly from his pocket where he had just put it.

"Yes I did, once. But now we were barely acquainted. Is that all?"

"Of course, we'll contact you if we need to ask further questions. Thank you." I saw him scribble a few notes on his pad while I walked slowly across the stage to where Julie and St. George were waiting for me. We went around the side of the stage into the preview room where some of Joe's helpers under Kevin's watchful eyes were listlessly stacking things and shuffling pieces of furniture around. My chest had been impounded and I wouldn't be able to pick it up until the investigation was over. But my rug, I wanted.

"Wait a minute more for me," I said to Julie and

Jerry, and walked away to where Kevin was checking items off on a ledger pad.

"Kevin, excuse me, but do you know where my rug is? Lot number 127."

"Oh sure, that's the Shiraz, isn't it? Over there by the phone dialing a number. See it?" When I didn't smile, he added, "I'm awfully sorry about Mr. Morley. I know he and you were close once. I just wanted you to know I'm sorry. It's too bad," he continued, "you two had to have that fight. I mean in a way it's too mean, isn't it really, that the last contact you had with him had to be that kind. Sort of wrecks your good memories doesn't it?"

"It hadn't until you mentioned it, Kevin. What Barton and I did was strictly business, you ought to know that."

"Oh sure, I just meant you couldn't have felt too kindly toward him, especially after he did a double on Tom. That was pretty serious stuff. At least it was on our side of the house. That was no joke. Pretty slick try though I must say. Sure had Joe leaping through hoops."

"Kevin, what are you trying to say?"

"I'm not trying to say anything, I guess I just wanted to know if you and Morley had a chance to make up. It made me feel bad that you would feel so bad." He walked across the room and picked up the Shiraz and brought it back and handed it to me as if I were a war widow and it a flag.

"Thank you," I said, "but no, we didn't make up."

Julie and Jerry drifted over to where we were standing. Julie, sensing a hint of drama, had to hold her own. "Helen, I've been absolutely unspeakably unforgiveable to you today," she said. "This is a time when we should all be extra kind and I've been awful. I've just asked Jerry if he would still come to dinner and I hope you will too. No reason for us all to sit separately and mope, and besides I think Barton would like it."

"Barton wouldn't give a damn what we did," I said. "All he'd care about would be his painting." As soon as I said it, as soon as the words spilt forth, so did the vision of the Ryder form before my eyes and the question that was so obvious, I wondered why no one had asked it.

Where was it? Had anyone seen it? Had anyone looked in Barton's car? Did the police even know about it?

"Where do you suppose it is?" I asked. "If anything has happened to it, I think I really will have a nervous breakdown, right on the spot. Kevin, do you know?"

"What are you talking about, Helen?" Julie asked.

"The Ryder, of course, in all this has anyone thought of the painting?"

"Mr. Morley had it when he left, that's all I know," said Kevin.

"It always comes down to the painting with us, doesn't it?" St. George said to no one in particular, "as Ruskin said, any kitchen maid and scullery boy can make a person, but it takes a genius to make a Raphael."

"When did Ruskin say that?" asked Julie moving an inch closer to St. George and looking up at him.

"Watching Rome burn or something like that," I answered testily. "Kevin, do you know where the Ryder is?"

"Mr. Morley had it when he left, that's all I know," he answered.

"Come on Jerry, I can't believe your disinterest. Where's Barton's car?"

"I don't know. If it's in the same spot it was when we arrived, it's in the back near the loading dock. We came up the back stairs. But as he left and came back, lord knows where the car is."

"Well, it's little matter. The lot's got to be pretty empty by now anyway. Look, I can't stand it. Jerry, do you have a set of keys?"

"No, I don't."

The detective was still sitting at the desk talking to people. I asked Julie and Jerry to wait a moment and went back onto the stage. Explaining the situation about the Ryder, I asked if anyone had checked Barton's car. He said they knew about Barton's purchases and had examined the car closely but had found nothing in it but a fur rug, a leather box containing two bottles of brandy, and some broken glass. The car was now part of the estate and would be held by them until Barton's executors decided what to do with it. I thanked the policeman for the information and went back to St. George and Julie who were now talking to Tom while sitting on a Hitchcock bench like a spooning but tentative couple from the 1890s. As I approached, Tom moved away and started wandering listlessly around the room as if he were looking for something he didn't expect to find. It was odd, he was acting as if he were waiting for me to leave.

"Jerry," I said, "I'll give you a lift if you want. I'm going to Barton's to make sure the Ryder is all right. If you don't want to stay there, I'd be glad to put you up."

"He's already got a place to stay if he needs, Helen," Julie said, injecting deep meaning into her words by saying them slowly and in a lower tone of voice.

"Fine, I just want to go with him to Barton's."

"Julie," Jerry said, "why don't you go ahead. Helen and I will go to Barton's, and then arrive at your place giving you time to do whatever you have to do."

"Well, all right," she consented, standing up. I was beginning to think this might be a match made in heaven until she added, "but drive carefully, Helen." I hoped Jerry needed as much mothering as Julie appeared to have in reserve.

Jerry and I made our way across the preview room. I raised my hand to Kevin as we passed into the hall. We stood quietly for a moment by the door; I was somehow reluctant to go out. It wasn't just the snow and cold, I knew that.

"Come on," he said, "he's not here anymore, there's no reason for us to be."

"You're right," I said, "Thanks. This is harder than I thought." He held open the door and the two of us pushed ourselves into the swirling snow. My car, a battered old green Mercedes station wagon, was parked at the edge of the lot. We made our way to it, the last moments being a frantic wrestling with rugs, tureen, doors, and keys. Once inside we sat quietly again, catching breath and wiping eyes.

I looked at Jerry while he adjusted his fur hat on his head. Maybe he wasn't such a stick after all. The light sandy colored twirls of hair snaked out under the edge of the hat and over the edges of his ears. From where I sat all I could see was a small portion of his face; his fur collar was up around his neck, making him look like a fuzzy Daruma.

"You know," he said, looking straight ahead, "I think the thing that appalls me the most, and this might be appalling in itself, is that I don't feel sad about Barton at all. When he was alive I depended on him because he seemed so vital and cavernous in complexity. I had to explore . . ." He turned to look at me. "Do you know what I'm talking about? There was something about Barton, wasn't there, that one needed more of even if you didn't know where it would take you. This must sound hopelessly sophomoric." He shook his head.

"No," I said, starting the car and backing slowly out of the space, "I know what you're talking about. The confusing thing is to realize that you can love a person's strengths but hate them for their weaknesses. Barton wasn't really very nice to any of us, you know, and yet we all fell around him like trees before a wind."

I turned out of Joe's driveway onto the road back to Boston. The roads were bad but the plows had been working hard and were still at it. Normally, the trip takes about twenty minutes. The traffic was very light, however, as Jerry and I drove silently along. Every once in awhile Jerry would take his tremulous hands out of his pockets and place them softly against his own cheeks then rock his head gently between them. He looked as if he were nursing himself.

Once into Boston's narrow cowpath streets, the driving was much more difficult, but the streets were well plowed and miraculously I found a parking place only a block from Barton's house on Beacon Street.

We got out of the car and picked our way through snow drifts to reach Barton's house at 114½ Beacon. I don't think either of us looked forward to going in there. The house itself was an old brownstone with stairs coming down to the street level, from the main floor. At street level, three steps went down to what used to be a trades or servant entrance. The steps going to the main level were made out of a dark cinnamon sandstone. It was four stories high and a little narrower than most of the houses on this section of Beacon Street where some of Boston's finest lived still. Barton had bought the house ten years ago and, though his participation in the city life of Boston was limited to a few dinners a month at St. Botolph's, he had become an accepted member of the "Beacon Street Club."

The steps led to a large dark wood double door. Jerry and I stood at the top of the steps while he searched his pockets for the keys. It was cold and I shivered. The house in front of us was totally dark except for a trace of light.

"I can't find them," he said.

"It's okay," I said, swiveling the name plate beside the door. Behind it was a depression in the wall just deep enough to hold a key.

I inserted the key and opened the door. This led us into a small foyer where we stamped our feet and left our boots. The foyer was separated from the main body of the house by another door, this a single massive one the top half of which was glass. From the foyer we could see a light on in Barton's study which was at the back of the house down the hall on the main floor.

Once past the inside door, we stood in the doorway looking across the black and white marbled floor to Barton's study. As I walked down the hall and into the room I could see that the light came from the small brass student lamp with a green glass shade that sat on Barton's desk. The room was unchanged. Book shelves lined the lower part of all the walls. Above them, hanging against the deep cream-colored wallpaper, was some of Barton's collection. Simply furnished, the room had a law partner's desk to the left and behind the door as one came in, and a tall mirror that reflected the hallway stood between the two windows on the back wall behind Barton's easel; to the right of the door, two leather couches faced each other on either side of a marble fireplace. On the floor was an exquisite Bokharra; the heavy velvet curtains that reached the floor were a deep chocolate brown. A small English bar table holding four decanters stood against the wall behind the couch closest to the door.

I sighed deeply when I saw it. The Ryder, propped up on the easel. I couldn't bear to look at it. I sat down on one of the leather couches and rested my head on its fat rim. Jerry stood in front of the fireplace. There was nothing to say.

"Would you like a drink?" he asked finally. Jerry left the fireplace and went behind me to the bar table. I could hear the clink of crystal top against crystal lip as he closed a decanter.

"What'll you have?" he asked.

"Scotch'll be fine."

He handed it to me from behind the counter. I took a sip but still I shivered. It was as if I couldn't get warm.

"I think I'll make a fire," I said.

"It's already been laid."

I looked in the fireplace, and he was right. Of course, Walter, Barton's houseman, would have a fire laid for him; neat birch logs in the grate with enough kindling easily exposed so one could light it. I slipped the damper switch, struck a long match on the side of the fireplace, and set the twigs alight. Then I stood up and took a deep sip of my drink.

"Well," Jerry said, "I'll leave you to your own devices. I want to change out of these soaked and freezing shoes. Won't be long." He put his glass on the mantle and with four long strides left the room. This bone-chilling feeling was not to my liking. Maybe, I thought, it's merely because this is Barton's room and he's gone. True, that could be part of it, but I had felt something more chilling than a memory could arouse. Something seemed wrong.

To take my mind off it, I looked around the room, looking for something else to concentrate on. Some of the paintings on the walls were familiar, but my eyes kept returning to the most familiar of them all—the Ryder. I looked at it from a distance. I felt I ought to salute it.

It had survived my father and now Barton, and apparently me, because it was unlikely now that I'd ever have a chance at it. I wondered where Barton would leave his collection. Probably part to the Museum of

Fine Arts, part to Worcester, and the rest I hadn't an idea. I didn't even know if there would be any personal legacies. It was a long time since Barton and I had had a talk about anything other than art. And whenever we started he had always broken them off as if what I were saying were simply a disappointment to him. My perusal of the room had lessened my chill but in its place came an uneasiness of another sort. What was it? A door opened somewhere in the house and gently closed again. I felt a draught of cold air hit my ankles. Where was Jerry? I thought. Why would he be opening an outside door? I put down my drink and crossed the room, but before I could put my hand on the door knob the door opened. It was Walter.

I'd completely forgotten about Walter. Walter who had worked for Barton ever since he'd moved to Beacon Street. Walter who'd managed Barton's life with the gentleness and devotedness of a St. Bernard. If I felt wounded by Barton's death, Walter would feel abandoned. He was a small round-shouldered man, like a penguin. He stood in the door then, his hat in his hand, his small pink face drawn and sad. His overcoat seemed to pull at his shoulders making him seem smaller than usual.

"Oh, Walter," I said, "I'm so sorry." I moved to him and took his arm. "Won't you sit down?"

"Miss Greene, you're here. I can't believe it. Mr. Morley was so alive."

"It was awful, Walter, it *is* awful." I tried to make him sit down but he stood there by the door. I suppose to sit in Barton's study would be for Walter an admission that Barton was dead.

"How'd you find out?" I asked, not knowing what else to say.

"Mr. Morley's lawyer, Mr. Dodge, called me. I'd gone this morning to my sister's for the day. When he called I knew something awful had happened but I never, never thought." He seemed not to be able to finish. He looked around the room several times, and backed away toward the door.

"What are your plans?" I asked. "I'm sure it would be fine for you to stay here."

"I told Mr. Dodge that I'd stay as long as he needed me to, until the estate is settled that is—then I don't know. I never thought. . . . Would you like tea?" he asked, finally.

"No thanks, Walter, but perhaps you'd better make yourself some. I think then Mr. St. George will be staying for a few more days at least. You might see if he needs anything." Walter needed to be needed. I'd have to remember to tell Jerry. We had lost Barton. Walter was in the position of losing his home.

His face shifted into life and he backed out the door. I could hear him moving down the hall turning on lights making extra noise as if to drown out Barton's silence. Poor Walter, poor all of us.

Jerry came into the room and stopped and stood next to me by the easel.

"I can see why you two locked horns over this, it is magnificent. Though, of course, you're lucky it has lasted as long as it has."

"The people who owned it had it in a humidity-controlled room, and we had it in the gallery, which is also. But you can't protect a Ryder completely, as you know."

"If there were more people like that I would have gone out of business." He sighed, looking at his hands, then said, "We should probably be going. I found my keys."

I went downstairs and told Walter we were leaving. When we finally left the house it had stopped snowing completely, and we drove easily to Julie's.

Julie lived in Brookline in a modern condominium building where everything worked. Compared to my ancient and creaking pasha's palace, Julie's apartment was single-minded and functional. Her bathroom tiles fit and crucial chunks of mortar didn't fall from between them everytime she took a shower. Her front door opened into a large living/diningroom with one enormous glass wall that gave a view of a massive cluster of hospitals. But at night, lights look just like lights, and I supposed she could imagine herself in some other terminus.

She had set a table with candles and crystal in front of the glass wall. While she busied herself in her kitchen, Jerry strolled around the room peering at the paintings on the walls. I wondered what he'd think. Julie's collection couldn't be faulted, each piece in its own right was good, and she had a small Prendergast that was magnificent. It was simply that the room lacked a coherence, as if it were a way station for treasures. There was no guiding hand here.

Julie called from the kitchen, "Fix yourself more drinks if you need."

"We're fine, Julie," I called back, thinking to myself how handy polite phrases are. I felt anything but fine and wished mightily that I hadn't come. I'd spent most of the day wishing I were someplace else and it looked as if my sense of displacement hadn't run its course.

"The Wickhams aren't coming after all," Julie chirped from the kitchen, "Joe is all adither," Julie said, sweeping into the living room bearing a tray of steaming bowls of cream of celery soup which she placed on the table. She guided Jerry to his seat as if he were an invalid. I thought for a moment that she was going to tie his napkin around his neck.

"Well," she said as she plopped down at the table and swept her napkin into her lap, "here we are! Isn't this cozy."

Before I could get my soup spoon to my mouth she said "So, I suppose you'll inherit everything, Helen." She turned to Jerry. "Barton and Helen were very very close once, you know."

"I couldn't have told that from today's proceedings," Jerry said, wiping his mouth with his napkin.

"You'll be rich," she said to me, "but you probably already are. You can always tell rich New Englanders, Jerry, by the fact that they look like poor cousins in from the country."

What could I say? Nothing. So Julie went on. "Me? I love the big city. New York is my idea of heaven. Helen couldn't leave Boston in a million years, but me—I'd be in New York like a flash if the right reason came up." She leaned forward to peer at Jerry's face to see if her meaning was clear. "Barton always said I was meant for bigger things." She smiled and leaned back in her chair. It was clear to me now that Barton was dead Julie was going to use him as she needed, as probably we all would in our ways. Things he'd never meant or said would be attributed to him, and that sickened me.

I put my soup spoon down on the saucer. "Julie, please, Barton's body is barely cold and here you are acting as if nothing happened. If we have to chatter, let's at least talk about what's on our minds."

"But, Helen, why talk about it? It'll just ruin the evening."

"Seems to me the evening's pretty much ruined anyway. Not very thoughtful of Barton, I'll agree, but there it is."

"Well, if you must talk about it, talk," Julie sniffed. "I don't have anything to say because I don't think any of us knows who did it, why it was done, or anything. Barton was just in over his head in something that none of us knows about, and that's all there is to it." She reached for the wine bottle and almost toppled her glass in her rush to get it.

Jerry, who had been staring out the windows at pitch blackness, shuddered visibly. Turning off Julie's suggestion that he might be cold, he faced me.

"What I can't get out of my mind is that the murder seemed so angry, so violent, so explosive. Did anyone hate Barton that much?"

"Or love him that much?" Julie added, looking at me.

I wanted to kick Julie hard under the table but instead stared at my soup and concentrated on the celery bits floating in it.

"I think someone wanted to stop Barton." Jerry added in a voice I had to strain the tension in the air to hear.

"Stop him from doing what?" I asked, grateful for the diversion from my soup.

"I don't know, just stop him. He was too much for any of us, like a fever that had spiked too high. He was too alive, and had to be stopped."

"Stopped dead?" Julie asked. "That's a lot of stopping."

"Nature has a way of taking care of its excesses," Jerry responded quietly. I looked at him sitting there, such an unlikely avenger, but he was a man whose hands shook with his own fury. I was stunned and could say nothing in response. Even Julie's twittering was strangled and we were left with nothing but our chilling soup and a gloom that settled over the table like a cold impenetrable fog.

"What we need is coffee," Julie said, finally, and leapt from the table and disappeared to the kitchen only to return a second later with a pot of coffee.

Before she could sit down again the doorbell rang. Back in form, Julie uttered "shit" under her breath. It was Joe and Phyllis Wickham.

"Oh, you've come after all," Julie said unhappily. She must have figured I'd be easy to get rid of, but Joe and Phyllis were notorious late-nighters.

"Not to stay, not to stay, Julie, my dear, frankly we're just about done in and on our way home. Wanted to deliver the Enneking, that's all. One of the boys had time to glue the frame so it's A-1 now." Joe reached into his commodious briefcase and pulled out the little painting that Tom had so desperately wanted and which I'd given up on. Jerry and I had both risen from our chairs when the Wickhams walked in so we were all standing in the center of the room when Joe handed the Enneking to Julie.

"Oh, that," she said, "I'd almost forgotten about it." She looked at the mended spot on the frame and then handed it off to Jerry as if they were in a relay race, and he couldn't refuse to take it.

We all saw it at once. The hand that accepted the painting did not shake. He looked at the Enneking quickly and handed it on to me saying, "Very nice, I missed it at the preview." He walked away from us to the table but didn't take his hands out of his pockets. He just stood there, I supposed wondering how to drink without risking our seeing again that his hands were no longer tremulous but steady and strong. No one else had spoken.

Joe and Phyllis quickly left, saying they'd see us all later, on a day that would have to be better than this one. I supposed it was good for me, so I stayed until about nine o'clock. But then I was overcome with the day, the fine Meurseult, and the thought of sleep, and shortly thereafter I left as well. Jerry had pulled off what Julie on her own couldn't have handled. Conversation would have been too difficult in the face of what we'd seen. As I drove home through the snow-silenced streets I wondered about Jerry's hands and just when they'd stopped shaking. Was he really the dove he'd appeared to be? Would a dove mate with a game hen?

8 I drove home probably faster than I should have. But home really was home, and I needed to be there. I still lived above the gallery on Newbury Street. I had lived for awhile before my father died in Cambridge with some friends of mine from college, but in the evenings when nothing was doing I'd find myself drifting across the river, slipping down Newbury Street, and through the back door of the gallery. Dad would be in his study or in the workroom stretching some painting or cleaning a piece of statuary. He was never surprised to see me appear, taking my love for art as right and natural, though he'd give a perfunctory nod in the direction of normalcy by expressing dismay that I wasn't out with some Harvard gentleman.

He had been right, and eventually Harvard gentlemen did compete and naturally. But that night after Barton's death I simply wanted to be able to slip into the back door of the gallery, see my father, pour us both a good slug of Drambuie or Benedictine and settle down in the study in front of the fire and talk it out. But knowing I couldn't and feeling the double loss, by the time I did get back to Newbury Street, I was peevish. I was also fairly annoyed at the glee Barton would be experiencing at the amount of times his death caused me to have a head-on collision with my own sentimentality.

I turned my car into the alley that ran behind my gallery. My parking space was in the last remains of an old garage across the alley from the back door to the gallery.

The gallery's back door led into a combination mud-room, receiving area, storing room, and cleaning room. This was the heart of the business, Liam's favorite place where he could work for hours matching colors for paintings he was going to restore, the room where I used to find my father up at nights working on paint-ings, and where to this day some of his and Barton's work still stood in the storage cabinets that formed the walls of the room.

Off to the right was my office; it too had been my father's. The door to it from the workroom was always open except when the gallery itself was. To the left was a stairway, wooden and a bit rickety, that went to the loft studio upstairs. It was there that Barton had lived for nearly six years, during which time heaven had been the spot between Barton's studio and my father's office. I stood there then and looked around. I was struck by the place's timelessness. Thank God for the bright touches Liam had added to it to make it clearly what it was. Simply my workroom, Liam's workroom, a place where I had grown up, a place that would be forever empty of the others who had been there. I sighed, shut the door behind me, and hung up my coat on the rack by the door.

The ceiling light was on. Liam always left it burning when I was at an auction in the winter as I invariably got home after dark when he would have shut up for the day. The room was quiet and still. Across from Liam's work table a painting stood on an easel. Seeing it, I remembered that feeling that something was amiss, no, that was too strong, just not right in Barton's study. What had it been that had seemed so strange? In Bar-ton's perfectly controlled life (his rooms were so finely temperature-controlled that the thermostats adjusted to within a quarter of a degree), something had been out of whack. I didn't even know if it was important or connected to his death in any way. I even half-suspected myself of wanting to discover some messy bit of hu-manity in Barton even after he was gone, such as finding out at least that he squeezed his toothpaste tubes in the middle or didn't fill his ice cube trays.

I turned out the light and went into my office, flicked on the desk lamp switch, and dropped into the old leather chair by the fireplace. What was it? I went over Barton's study in my mind ticking off all the things that had always been there and were still there. Everything was in place; Jerry and Walter, who had both seen it far more recently than I, had said nothing.

I got out of the chair and threw some kindling and a new log on the charred logs in the fireplace and opened the damper. With one touch of a match the kindling curled into a warm blaze. An old walnut cupboard that my mother had found in Ireland stood on the other side of the fireplace behind another leather chair. I pulled a bottle of Drambuie from the top shelf and settled myself into the chair again and stared into the fire as if it were Barton's study and I could see what I was looking for.

I was getting up to turn the log on the fire when I heard the backdoor quietly open and shut. In a moment there was a tentative knock on the office door.

"Come on in, Liam," I said from my chair without moving or turning my eyes from the fire. I knew my voice sounded done in, but I couldn't help it.

Liam's face, then his whole body, appeared around the door. Liam was tall and gangly, as if he hadn't fully filled out yet, with a thin neck and long arms that ended in large hands. Because of his height his head looked a little small, but it wasn't the size of it, it was the features that gave him a slightly bottom-heavy look. They were small and almost girlish. He had the Celtic look, dark hair, almost black, and shocking light blue eyes. His skin was pale, but his cheeks always had a light rosy glow. If he had been a woman he would have been beautiful. As a man, he was as well, but he was saved by his swagger. He was more pirate than princess.

"How'd you know it was me?" Liam said, opening the door and stepping into the room.

"Now who else but yerself was it going to be, the pixies?" I said, trying to capture his own Irish way of putting things.

"Good try but the yerself is in the wrong place. And how's yerself?" he said after a pause.

"Fair to awful."

"I heard about it at a party at the museum school. I almost got drunk trying not to believe it."

"You want to know something really hard to believe? I don't know honestly which bothers me the most. Losing the Ryder in that stupid display of bravado or losing Barton. I find it awfully embarrassing to admit I don't. I'm so damned confused by the whole hysterical day."

"The way it was described to me it didn't sound stupid. It sounded bloody brilliant. If it hadn't been Morley you were up against it would have worked. And wouldn't it have been grand if it had? Worth it, absolutely worth the gamble."

"Who told you about it?"

"One of the lads from the restoration department, name of something sounds like cabbage."

It was obvious that Liam didn't know about Barton. And I'd thought it was over for the day.

"Help yourself to a drink," I said. "Did your friend cabbage stay for the rest of the auction?"

Liam poured himself a drink and plopped down in the other chair across from mine. The firelight touched his hair making it shine. Half of his face was in shadow, the other half a warm flickery red. He smiled at me and raised the glass to drink. Something in the way he did it seemed so familiar, so comforting and homelike that for a moment I was not sure who was sitting in the chair. Was it Liam or Barton? They didn't look anything alike really, but in the half light, it was hard to see. One saw what one wanted I supposed. Was I missing Barton that much? I sat forward and looked closer. As if it were a game, Liam too sat forward and peered at my face.

"Hello there," he said.

"That's not all that happened today," I said.

"Before that, tell me honestly, how you feel? It was so important. Will it really make a difference?"

"Oh sure, it will always make a difference and I'll always love the Ryder, regardless. But I'm not going to end up selling pencils on the corner to put myself in hock to get it back. There are other paintings, always will be."

"I'm relieved. I was afraid to come back here you know, thinking I'd find you in black stalking around the studio muttering strange incantations over Morley's palettes."

"Liam, stop. I have to tell you. Barton's dead."

"What?" he exclaimed. He sat forward abruptly then slammed his body back into the chair, his head banging back against the rim. The liquid in his glass sloshed over the edge and trickled unnoticed down the back of his hand. "I can't bloody believe it. You're having me on," he said, sitting slowly forward.

"I'm not kidding, Liam. Barton's dead. Not just dead. Killed, murdered."

Liam leapt out of his chair and wiping the Drambuie off on his pant leg started pacing around the room. "What the hell happened? This is crazy. What do you mean?"

"Sit down, I'm trying to be calm and you're making me nervous."

"Oh lord, you must feel wretched. I had no idea the awful was so awful."

He came over to my chair and put his face down close to mine and peered into it as if he could read some emotion that I hadn't even felt yet. The scrutiny, the concern undid me, and I started to cry in a little high-pitched whimpering that I hadn't heard come from myself since I was very young. Slowly it seemed to increase in volume and size until my full adult self was clutched in sobs. Poor Liam, he was so stunned but offered first his hand and then his shoulder literally to cry on. I must have held onto him for at least ten minutes until I could feel the tension release me. Beneath my weight Liam groaned slightly and I realized that he'd been stooping while supporting me.

"I'm sorry, your knees must be jelly by now. I don't know what overcame me. I'm just absolutely done in more than I know, I guess."

"Hey, it's all right. I can't even begin to know what

you must be feeling. Lord. Do you want to talk about it? Maybe it would help. I'd like to know."

So I told him everything about Barton's death, about touching Barton's hair, and seeing him taken away. It felt so eerily like talking to my father after a bad day at college—Liam pouring the Drambuie and handing me Kleenex while I talked and tossed soggy tissues into the fire.

"Jesus, Mary, and Joseph," he said. "You have been through it. Even sitting through a dinner with Julie, now that's going for martyrdom."

"Oh, come on, she's not all that bad," I sniffed.

"She's not all that great either. Your trouble is. that you like anyone who's nice to you, and who wouldn't be nice to you." He came over and put his hand on my hair and held it there until I could feel my head go warm.

"Tell you one thing," he said, "you're not going to stay here alone tonight. I'll sleep in the loft."

"Oh, would you? I hadn't even thought of asking you but that would make me feel so much better."

"Are you scared and not saying so?"

"No, I'm not scared. Why should I be scared?"

"I don't know. But it gives me goose flesh I'll tell you."

I didn't tell Liam, but I was a little scared, but not by Barton's death so much as by the fact that it left me quite on my own. Even though I'd been on my own for years, I'd always known Barton was there to fall back on if I really needed his knowledge, his judgment, and most of all, his eye. Now I only had my own. And maybe Liam's, I thought. That was a comfort. Feeling better than I had since the Ryder was auctioned, I went off to bed, leaving Liam to shut up the workroom and sit out the fire.

9 What do you do the day after you lose your favorite painting and an old part of your life gets murdered? For one thing you get up and pretend it is a normal day. The snow plows had been there the night before and I woke to the sounds of shoveling outside my window. I looked down to see Liam's back bent to the job. It was eight-thirty, which gave us an hour and a half before the gallery opened. I was tempted to get back into bed but decided I'd better not. Being in shock was a luxury I couldn't afford. In fact, I wasn't anymore; it had worn off and the new day brought a different kind of shock.

I shuffled along to the kitchen and put on a pot of coffee. Who had killed Barton? Somebody had. Most likely someone I knew and knew reasonably well. As soon as I had framed that possibility to myself I realized I didn't want to know. The police would find out, the person named, and probably a motive would be made clear, but I didn't want to know anymore about it. All those people had reasons for killing Barton and in some way I was involved with everyone of them.

The workroom door shut and I could hear Liam's feet climb the backstairs to my apartment. The kitchen door opened and he stood there, red-cheeked and puffing.

"Morning," he said. "How'd you sleep?"

"Well, and you?"

"Like a statue."

"Have some coffee?"

Liam slipped into a chair at the table and tipped back

115

in it while pouring milk into the mug I set down before him. I watched him dip his croissant end into the coffee.

"I don't see how you can stand it that way," I said.

"It makes the croissant wonderful soggy and warm."

"Not the croissant, bozo, the coffee. Now it's full of crumbs."

"Such is life," he said. 'What's on the docket for today?"

"Business, as usual," I said beginning to clear the table.

"You're not going to talk about it, are you," he said reaching for the Dundee marmalade jar. He stuck his croissant into it.

"I don't really want to."

"Why?"

"Because I realized a little while ago that I must know the person who killed Barton, and probably had something to do with it."

"That's crazy talk."

"When I told you what happened yesterday, I told you about Barton's death and the Ryder but I didn't tell you about what went on before and how every person there was mad at Barton in some way or another. And every person there—and I don't know how this happened—had in some way involved me in their fight, or thought I had a special ear with Barton or something."

"Like what involvement with whom?"

"Well, Tom is in debt to Barton, or was, and I wouldn't help; then I set him up in that bedlam bidding situation. Julie wants St. George's partnership and Barton wasn't going to recommend her and she thought I was partly after St. George myself. Al Swedner thinks Barton owes him money and I fanned those flames. St. George thinks he's on a white horse and out to slay the dragon and I'm the lady in distress, and worst of all Silky. I encouraged him beyond his means and Barton beat him to the draw. Regardless, I feel guilty."

"From what you've told me about Barton, and from the times I've met him, I'd imagine anyone who knew him would have some grudge toward him. Remember last year at the Christmas party at his house and he wouldn't stop ragging Sev Lahti from the Worcester

Art Museum because he'd bought a Della Francesca and it turned out to be a fake?"

"I remember," I said.

"Well, he could have done it, couldn't he? I mean he was mad enough to. How can you be so sure one of the people you talked to did it? There were a lot of other people there who must have known Barton, you know."

"I know you're right, it just seems so odd that there was all that confusion and then Barton is dead. I would love to believe it was some escaped loony, but I just feel it wasn't. If you'd seen all that fury you'd know what I mean." I went to get the coffee pot and poured another cup.

"I'm going to get dressed and do some paperwork before opening up. But I want to thank you properly for last night and still do for your being here. It really helps."

"Hey, listen, what use is it being a man if you can't play one once in awhile," Liam said, giving me a broad grin.

"Okay, man, for that I'll wash the dishes," I answered.

When I'd done the dishes and Liam had gone back downstairs, I didn't know what to do next. I got dressed and prowled around upstairs until 10:00 and then went down to the gallery. The day after a snow storm is usually brilliant and clear and this day was no exception. The light bounced off the snow in eye-blinding shafts. I stood at the gallery windows for a while looking at the few shoppers on the street and then went into the office and cleared up the glasses and put away the bottle.

The bell over the Newbury Street door tinkled and I could hear Liam walk across the gallery to open it. He talked for a moment to someone who'd come into the shop, and then walked toward the office door. When he opened it his face was uncommonly pale.

"It's the police," he whispered.

My first thought when I saw the two men standing in the gallery behind Liam was "cheez it, the cops."

"Miss Greene?" asked the one in front who I recognized as the man Ritter was talking to Friday at Joe's. He was a small undistinguished-looking man with metal-rimmed glasses that sat on a nose surprisingly pudgy for such a slim face. After talking to Ritter he had stood close by, I supposed, listening carefully for slips.

"Yes, good morning," I said. "What can I do for you?"

"We'd like to ask you a few questions about Mr. Morley if we might," he said. "I'm Captain Sheehy and this is Sargeant Rizzo."

A dread about the police crept through me. Why me? So early? Am I first on their list? I don't know a thing, I insisted to myself, fully aware of the list of things I'd rattled off to Liam and then had tried to forget.

The two detectives were standing in the middle of the gallery. That they weren't even bothering to inspect my paintings before they inspected me made me hostile to start with, which I knew wasn't a very good way to begin the proceedings. Before I opened my mouth I reminded myself that art wasn't their business, it was mine.

"Come on through to my office. We can sit there more comfortably." The detectives followed and stood in the middle of the room looking around until I sat down behind my desk at the far end of the room. Captain Sheehy also sat but Sargeant Rizzo kept standing, obviously, I thought, to keep me from making a break for it. By the end of the conversation that assumption didn't seem so funny.

"We're very sorry to have come so early, Miss Greene, but as you know we've numbers of people to talk to and thought we'd begin with you as it seems you probably knew Mr. Morley better than anyone else."

"Over the long haul I suppose that's true."

"In your opinion then is there anything that stood out about Mr. Morley that would make him an object of murder?" I couldn't believe Sheehy really talked that way, but he did. I stifled a smile.

"I don't think anyone liked Barton," I said, "but I can't think of a thing Barton had done that would make someone want to kill him. Most of what he did was just the sneaky side of clever. Once you examine it, it wasn't all that sneaky."

"You were quite fond of him yourself at one time I gather?"

"I thought I was the first person you've talked to. Who's been gathering for you?"

"We did talk to some people yesterday at the auction gallery, and you mentioned it yourself."

"We were quite close at one time. Yes. Barton lived here with my father and me for some years, so we were close in that way. Almost brother and sister."

"I understand it was a more intimate relationship than brother and sister might have had."

"I was twelve when he came."

"And how old when he left?"

"Eighteen."

"I know this must be painful, but we need to get as much information as we can. Is it true that you and Mr. Morley were going to be married at one time?"

"No. That's not true, and what has this got to do with Barton's murder?"

"In an investigation like this we have to find out everything we can. It may seem irrelevant to you, but the whole may seem very relevant to us. Why do you think people would think you and Mr. Morley were going to be married if it wasn't true?"

"Because just like me at the time they assumed it. I was young, my father had just died, and Barton had always been a protégé of my father. It had seemed natural."

"What happened?"

"It wasn't natural, that's all."

"You must have been very bitter?"

'That's a leading question, Captain."

"Right. Well, let's go on to the auction itself. You and Mr. Morley had quite an interesting confrontation from what I understand."

"You sure understand and gather a lot," I said, suddenly realizing that this conversation was not what I thought it would be. Where I had been afraid of what I knew about others, it had never occurred to me what others might know about me.

"I wasn't the only person who had a confrontation

with Barton Friday. Everyone did," I said, feeling like a worm.

"That may be true, and I assure you we'll find out about them all. Right now we're interested in your relationship with Mr. Morley. About the Ryder, Miss Greene."

"What about it?"

"You wanted it very much?"

"Of course."

"Why was that painting so important to you?"

"Because I'd had to sell it when my father died and being able to buy it back meant something to me."

"I can understand that. So in a sense you saw Mr. Morley as barring your way."

"I didn't say that, you did," I replied, at the same time recognizing that he was correct.

"Does it sound like a description of how you felt?"

"No," I lied.

"How did you feel?"

"Grand for having really tried."

"How about after you lost the painting, how did you feel then?"

"Defeated but not depressed. Upset, but I assure you, Captain, not so upset that I'd kill Barton," I answered, doing just what I knew guilty people did. So do angry people, I thought.

"When was the last time you saw Mr. Morley at the auction?"

"Didn't I tell the Sargeant that?"

"Yes, but I'd like to hear you describe it."

"Well, it was after the Ryder was sold. I'd gone out to find Tom Ewart who had done the last bit of bidding for me because I thought he'd be upset."

"Why would he be upset?"

"Tom doesn't like being made a fool of, and everyone had seen what had happened. Anyway, I found Tom in the coffee shop, talked to him for a bit, and then left. When I left I passed through the front hall and saw Barton there talking to Jerome St. George."

"Did you speak to him?"

"Yes, he congratulated me on my bidding ploy and then left."

"Do you remember what time that was?"

I tried to think back. "Well," I said. "The Ryder was number 140 on the list and Barton left about ten minutes or so after it was sold. So it must have been after one o'clock. Joe's auctions usually go at about seventy-five items an hour so the Ryder would have been sold about or a little before one. But yesterday things were slower." I remembered Kevin's antics on the stage, his theatricals wasting precious minutes of daylight driving time. "I'd say it was about 1:15 when Barton left."

"That's helpful," he said.

"Can I ask you a question?" I asked. "Are you going to do all those things like analyze the contents of his stomach? Some pieces of information might make sense to me that would seem irrelevant to you."

"That's very possible. If we bog down we'll be sure to let you know."

"Meanwhile, I should just stay here and polish up my Sherlock Holmes kit. Just in case?"

"Now, I didn't mean it that way, Miss Greene," he said.

"Yes, you did, but it's okay, I don't blame you. Why should you want my help, it'd be pretty dubious from suspect number one."

"I didn't say that you did it."

"It hasn't escaped me that these questions of yours are less than innocent," I said.

The Captain stood up and walked around the room as if seeing it for the first time. I knew they didn't have anything "on me," as they say, but the whole procedure was making me very uneasy. What if, for some crazy reason, they really do think I did it? What other doubts were there? Captain Sheehy stopped his perambulations right in front of me and stared hard down at the floor in front of where I was sitting. His face took on a stern and serious look. "Miss Greene, how come you bought a particular wooden chest? You don't normally buy pieces of furniture. According to Mr. Wickham's records it's the first piece of furniture you've ever bought at his auction."

I was stunned. Christ. "You could make a real case out of that one," I gulped.

"Explain."

"Well, you're right, of course. I don't buy that much furniture at auction, I have all that I need. But . . . oh this is going to sound so lame. That chest . . . I'd sat on it before, during the preview, and, well, you see while I was sitting on it I had felt pretty awful and had been comforted by rubbing my hands over the walnut carvings. When it came up for auction and I was going to walk away having lost both the Ryder and the Inness, although I had the small rug, I wanted something, and, committing the auction-goer's version of suicide, bid simply because I wanted. You can only afford those a few times. Fortunately, this one was cheap."

"You do see our point."

"Of course." Was there a better way to dispose of a body? All I had to do after I'd stuffed it in the chest, was buy the chest, and then dump the body somewhere between Shelton and Boston. The more I thought of it, the more diabolic it became. No one would have ever known Barton had come back to the auction, so he could have been killed there, dumped elsewhere, and I would have had the perfect alibi.

"What did you think when you saw Mr. Morley's body fall out on the stage?" he asked.

"I didn't think. I responded."

"What did you hope to find when you rushed onto the stage?"

"I guess that Barton wasn't really dead, though I knew he was."

"You *knew* he was?"

"I mean anyone with half a brain knew he was. The thud he made was so heavy and solid there was no question." Sheehy picked up his hat and took a step toward the door. "That'll be all for now," he said, "but could you, in the next day or so, think over what happened yesterday and call us if anything occurs to you that might be significant?"

"I'll tell you something that will convince you I didn't do it," I said, feeling candor was the best course.

He put his hat on and took another step toward the door. "What's that?" he asked.

"You're going to find my prints on the African sceptre. I picked it up during the preview."

Captain Sheehy nodded to Sargeant Rizzo who wrote a note on a pad. "Thank you. You've been very helpful." Then they were gone. I stared at the doorway through which Sheehy had just passed and listened as they walked across the gallery and out the front door.

Liam stuck his head around the door. "How'd it go?" he asked.

"Not so great. Turns out I'm prime suspect, number one. At least I would be if I were them."

"But you didn't kill Barton," Liam exclaimed, as if truth were justice.

"We know that, or at least I do. But they don't. I had every reason to kill Barton, apparently."

"Can I do anything?"

"No, I just want to be alone for a bit. I can't think straight."

He nodded, sighed, and disappeared back into the workroom, leaving me to pace my office as if it were a cell. I was dazed and incomprehending.

I think perhaps only three people came into the gallery that morning, which was just as well. I was having a hard time focusing on anything. As soon as I'd stop my wandering and try to concentrate, images from the day before would pour into my head as unerringly as the sun poured in the windows. I'd see Barton on the platform, Kevin and Joe standing there motionless. I'd see Barton smile at me as he stood in the hallway with Jerry. What *was* there about that smile? It had been a little different, I thought, with a touch of the old Barton in it. Or was I merely still searching desperately for new significance from his gestures, something to give him life after death? And all these images were seen in the glaring light that Sheehy had so purposefully flicked on. I was deeply worried and didn't want to know it.

It was not a day filled with promise, and all the surprises were unwelcome.

Liam popped up at twelve-thirty and said he was going out for a bit and would be back at two. When he returned he found me in the kitchen, an uneaten deviled ham sandwich in front of me. He was carrying a big box and a little box that he stuck in the refrigerator. After he'd gone I peered in and found an orchid corsage. For a moment I couldn't imagine what the hell Liam was playing at or going to do with an orchid, but then I remembered. Oh Christ, I thought, I promised him we'd go and it's tonight.

It was the annual Museum of Fine Arts Council party. It was supposed to be a ball-like affair because there was dancing and music, but it was more like a bash because these things were getting more crowded and stuffy, in the can't-breathe sense, every year. Actually, they were getting more stuffy in the other sense as well, as more and more young people with money wanted to be young people with money and social position. Not that I had anything against the Council, I didn't, it brought needed capital and attention to the museum. I'm just not a great lover of Big S society because it usually ends up with more pretenders than princes.

So Liam's big box had been a tuxedo. If I hadn't felt I owed him something I probably would have begged off going but by six I was absurdly grateful for a reason to do something else beside wander around the gallery, drink coffee, stare out of windows, and worry. If nothing else, the Council party would be a diversion from thoughts of Barton and the abysmal sense of loneliness and loss as well as anxiety that had been assailing me all day. One's man's death reminds you of another, one loss of a different pain, and that day I'd relived every single one of them.

I'd also gone over and over my conversation with Sheehy and had liked it less every time. My only comfort, nasty though it was, was that in talking to the others he'd have to learn something that would clear me. He'd have to know by now that I couldn't have done it.

We left at six-thirty. Liam looked radiant in his tuxedo. I had helped him with his tie and as he reached into the refrigerator to hand me his surprise I thought he was really remarkably handsome and well on his way to being a yuppie if he didn't watch out. Somehow,

I thought, his irreverence might save him. At least he'd
never pretend.

As I suspected, the place was jammed. The bash was
held at the museum's new I. M. Pei wing, in the courtyard, and in every available nook and cranny where
you could squeeze a bar or a band and a dance floor.
From the outside the museum looked like a palace with
lights ablaze and banners flying from the turrets. Inside it looked like a freshman orientation party, thou-
sands of faces searching for other faces, everyone
determined to have the time of the year, which it was.

Liam and I squeezed our way in. He wanted to check
out the food first. He claimed that if we didn't get
something in our bellies by eight it would be all gone
and we would be dead hungry for the rest of the night.
I agreed, as I would have to nearly anything. Having
someone else direct my steps made it just possible for
me to function. Taking my hand he threaded our way
through the door to the courtyard where tables laden
with crabmeat and oysters and such like were surrounded
by black tie nibblers. On the way through the crowd I
smiled at the people I recognized. At least two had the
good heart to simply touch me as I passed and remark
that they were so sorry to hear about Barton. If anyone
had asked me for the details I think I would have stuck
my heel into his or her toe. But no one did. I couldn't
tell whether it was manners or incapacity to deal with
something as off-beat as murder, but whatever it was, I
was grateful.

Liam munched crab and I sipped champagne. I wondered if Tom would show. I was pretty sure that Silky
would not. Although he was a member, he said he felt
out of place at these affairs. I had tried to convince him
to come the year before, but he had maintained that
not only was he too shy he was also too short and could
never see anything more than other people's shirt studs.
I looked around the courtyard, nodded at a few heads
I knew, and turned to Liam who had stepped back to
the table. Tom was standing in his place, right by my
elbow. He looked, oddly, perfectly natural in his tuxedo, the black-on-white contrast suiting his angular and
sharp face.

"Hi," I said. "Been a strange day, hasn't it?"

"Yeah, you could call it that. Wasn't normal, that's for sure."

"No, not normal at all. Sheehy been to see you too?"

"Who's Sheehy?"

"The detective in charge of investigating Barton's murder. You mean he didn't come by today?" I didn't like the implications of what I was hearing.

"So they're on to you already. Pity. I thought you were cleverer than that."

"Tom, that's not funny. I'm beginning to get really worried."

"Wasn't in the best of taste. Sorry. You know, I been thinking about yesterday and what stands out in my mind is how normal Barton was."

"What do you mean?"

"Well, he obviously didn't expect to get killed, did he?" Tom asked. "I mean he wasn't sneaking around looking scared or furtive or anything different at all. Whatever happened must have been as much a surprise to him as to everyone else. I would have liked to have seen that."

"Did you hate him that much?" I asked, at the same time thinking that Tom had more insight than I had given him credit for. Barton *had* seemed normal, he *would* have been supremely surprised.

As if he realized he'd said too much, Tom quickly added, "Not enough to kill him, but enough to watch the surprise on his face."

I felt sick. It was as if Tom had seen Barton's surprise, didn't just imagine it. I moved away from him wondering for maybe the hundredth time why I ever had anything to do with him.

Liam saw me coming and quickly packed his mouth with the food he had in his hand.

"You act as if you've never eaten in your life, Liam. It's embarrassing."

"You kidding? You should see some of those people go at that food. Eating's the 'in thing', you know." He put his hand on my back and guided me to a relatively body-free corner of the courtyard.

"Want to dance?" he asked.

"It's been ages, I'm very rusty."

"But I'll bet there's a dance in the old girl yet," he crooned while leading the way to the foyer where couples were swaying to some old-time swing music. The band started playing "It's the Wrong Time, and the Wrong Place" and Liam smoothly moved us over the floor. He was a superb dancer, all of his motion coming from the hips down while his top half followed effortlessly. So, after a few bumbling starts, did I.

We danced a few minutes and I was just getting comfortable with the sense of Liam so close to me and chiding myself for thinking that he was holding me perhaps a little too tightly, when he suddenly pulled away and stopped dancing. I turned my head to see what was wrong and saw Liam's face for a second register annoyance at the same time I felt my own break into a smile. We were both looking at Ritter who had cut in by tapping Liam on the shoulder. Liam quickly regained his elfin look and shook Ritter's hand.

"Mr. De Ruyter, nice to see you. How's the Luks?"

"Reclining nicely, thank you. How're you?" he said to me. "You look beautiful."

I never blush but I did then, and Liam must have noticed. "Helen always looks beautiful. It's her way," he said with a sense of proprietorship.

"So it is," Ritter agreed. "May I?"

Liam backed away, saying he'd be back to collect me while Ritter assumed the dancing position and I fitted myself into his arms. He was much bigger than Liam, not just taller, and it took me a minute to adjust. Clearly, he too was unused to my shape, so for the first few bars or so we fumbled our steps.

"Suppose we are doomed to always step all over each other?" he asked as we finally got the rhythm.

"No, but it might take some effort," I commented, looking around his shoulders at Liam who was standing across the foyer watching us. I'd never seen him quite so ruffled and had a fleeting sense that I'd seen that same half-smile somewhere before. Then he was joined by an elderly man who engaged him in conversation, and he finally turned away.

Ritter interrupted my thoughts. "Yes, but it might be worth it."

I digested that in silence but felt myself begin to relax. I'd known him less than twenty-four hours but he felt more natural to me than Liam had. I wondered about that and decided it didn't bear too much examination, not then at any rate. We danced for awhile in silence. I didn't feel like talking and that felt fine.

"I have to say one thing," Ritter said finally. "Orchids are just not your flower."

"I know, it makes me feel like my grandmother, but Liam was sweet to think of flowers."

"I think Liam's sweet on you. He didn't appreciate my cutting in at all."

"Oh no," I said, very aware that I wasn't being candid, "he thinks of me as just a nice old thing who is his employer."

"Well, how is his employer today? I meant what I said, you look lovely."

"I'm alright, considering your friend Captain Sheehy came for a visit and he thinks I killed Barton."

"Are you serious?"

"Serious is how I feel. I'm not sure they think I did it, but they sure have a lot of evidence stacked up against me." We stopped dancing and stood in the middle of the dance floor while I told him all the bits and pieces that had surfaced during my conversation with Sheehy.

Ritter whistled. "Sounds solid except for one thing. I can testify as to where you were most of the day."

"That's the hooker. Most of the day isn't all the day."

"But anyone there could have killed Barton and not have been gone very long," he said, taking my hand and moving our bodies over the floor again.

"I know that, but you know what they always look for—motive, opportunity, and weapon, and I've got all three."

"Well, as long as they don't throw you in the clink before dinner tomorrow. Are you free?"

"Yes, if you promise to take this more seriously."

"I am, I'm taking it very seriously. I'm just not worried. 7:30 okay? Uh oh, here comes your keeper."

Ritter smiled and departed as Liam touched his shoulder. As he left, pulling a pipe from his pocket, I wondered whether his tuxedo pants had holes in the knees, and bet that they did.

"I didn't think you knew him," Liam said as we started dancing.

"I didn't until yesterday. He was at Wickham's. In fact he sat next to me during the Ryder sale and was the person I told you about who took over the bid."

"He seems to be showing up a lot for someone nobody knows."

"Liam, come off it. He's a customer and you know how we treat customers. Besides you're being petulant."

"You're right. I'll shut up and we'll have a lovely time." As it turned out, the time we had was not bad but we left soon thereafter. I was truly exhausted and couldn't dance another step. On the way out I saw Ritter across the hall. He waved to us as we gathered our coats from the cloak check counter. As we passed through the main hall I noticed someone standing behind the column to the right of the door. I was too tired to make much of it then, but then I'd done a good job of ignoring reality for most of the day. There was no reason to stop just because Sergeant Rizzo was at the museum ball, in plainclothes.

10 The next day began very much as the previous one had, but in the new day's light many things that pain and confusion had obscured the day before became clear. Principal among them was that Sheehy's visit to me had not been just one of many that he was paying that day. He hadn't gone to see Tom; I had been singled out. And it was no accident that Sergeant Rizzo was at the museum ball. What I had so easily not dealt with yesterday had to be faced today.

I was thinking about this in the kitchen when the back door opened and Liam bounded up the stairs. Seeing him also in the new light he looked just like the old Liam to me, and his discomfort of the night before evaporated like dew in the sun. I had to admit to myself, however, that Ritter had spotted something in Liam's attentions to me that I had missed, and that I'd probably better be a little careful. It was easy for me to see him as a boy, when in truth he was a man only nine years younger than myself. Complications of that sort I didn't need.

After greeting Liam, I peered at him over my coffee cup.

"Why don't you take the day off, you've been on one sort of duty or another for nearly thirty-six hours."

"That's awfully kind of you, but haven't you forgotten one very important fact?" he asked, grinning with delight.

"What's that?"

"It's Sunday." He rocked back on his heels and hooted.

I laughed. "Last of the big givers, aren't I?"

"You don't do so badly. But I'll hang around for a bit. I've some work to do on that little Kensett. You never said, you know, what the police were all about yesterday." Liam helped himself to some coffee and hoisted himself up onto the kitchen counter.

I told him all that happened and then that I'd seen Sergeant Rizzo at the ball as we left.

"I don't like the feel of this one bit," I said, putting my cup of coffee down. "It wouldn't be so bad if I thought Sheehy knew what he's doing but he didn't strike me as very imaginative, more a by-the-book sort who takes the easy route, namely me."

"So what are you going to do?"

"For starters I'm getting dressed and going downstairs to do some desk work."

Liam jumped off the counter, saluted, and went back down to the workroom. I cleaned up the kitchen and eventually made my way to my office.

I sat at my desk and tried to make sense of the invoices and statements that lay in neat piles on the top. But I couldn't concentrate. I got up and walked around my office doing a lousy imitation of Sheehy the stalker. "No," I said to the room at large, "I didn't kill Barton." I know that. Might have wanted to on occasion, might have been angry, and hurt, and a few other things. But no, I didn't kill him. But somebody did, and the sooner Sheehy finds out who, the better.

So who did kill Barton? Most of the people I'd seen at the auction might have had a motive to kill him. And most of us were in the main auction room most of the time, but any or all of us at one time or another had undoubtedly left to go to the bathroom, get a cup of coffee, or simply walk around. All I knew was that I'd seen Barton at one-fifteen or so. When was the chest sold? I opened my briefcase and pulled out the auction catalog. The cover was smeared with gooey egg. I smiled at the sight of it then flipped the pages to item number 280. Figuring the seventy-five to an hour rate, plus some, the chest was probably sold around three o'clock or so, to be generous. So what happened between one-fifteen and three o'clock?

I sat back down at my desk. I knew really what I was going to do, I just didn't want to have to do it. I had no desire to point the finger at anyone but even less did I want anyone to point the finger at me. I think if I'd thought Sheehy was terrifically smart and with it, I might have let the whole thing go, but he didn't strike me as a bumbling brilliant Columbo or a savage Kojak, simply a Boston cop, probably underpaid and with my future in his hands. I didn't like that one bit; it was like going under the knife without a second opinion. Art might be my business and detecting his, but in this case I knew more about the potential suspects and the victim than he ever would. Unless the resolution depended on some strange poison in the stomach lining that only a pathology lab could discover, then I was already ahead.

Where to start? I made a mental line-up. There they were, mugs all. Julie, Tom, Al, Silky, Jerry, and last of all, to be fair, Joe. I didn't know him well but he knew Barton, and who knows what Barton had said to him after the Ryder had been sold?

First in line was Julie. She, I knew, had seen Barton at some point before she'd gone out shopping. I saw her as she had been on Friday, laden with bundles. I picked up the phone and called her home number. There was no answer, so I tried her shop. After a few rings she answered, her voice husky. I figured she was hoping it was Jerry. When I spoke she sounded like Julie again. I asked her if she was busy and whether it would be okay for me to drop over for a bit. She didn't sound thrilled, but then Julie would never be thrilled to see me before she had sewn things up with Jerry.

I decided to walk. Julie's gallery was on Charles Street, so I turned right up Newbury and headed toward the Boston Public Garden. Newbury Street was nearly empty. The day was just as bright as it had been the day before. The sun reflecting off the snow made it almost painful. Boston Public Garden, which in summer is neatly planted with every imaginable kind of flower and looks heavily cared for, that day looked like a wasteland. Huge drifts of snow formed artificial mountains and the intrepid out yesterday had created their own footpaths around them. I crossed the garden, coming out at the Charles Street corner and turned into the street of old wooden-front shops and stores, most of them run by antique dealers, although increasingly the supreme Yuppie establishments, gourmet food shops and restaurants, were making inroads. Julie's shop, Atkins Art and Antiques, and in very small letters, *est. 1975*, was halfway down the street on the left.

Julie carried mostly paintings. About seventy-five percent of her capital was tied up in wall art, but she had some furniture too, enough to make her gallery look like a Regency sitting room, which it did. She'd copied a room from a house in Bath down to the correct flutings on the half pillars by the windows. As I've said, Julie doesn't know much herself but she does know whom and what to copy. I pushed the door open and a little row of silver bells over the door tinkled. The shop was empty. An open copy of *Country Life* lay conspicuously on the couch. Either Jerry had been there or Julie was fishing for that kind of customer. What she really wanted, I thought, was not Jerry as partner but Jerry as a prop.

"Oh, Helen, you scared me," Julie said from the door to her office, which was cleverly concealed behind a tall painting of a door, "you're standing so still I didn't think you were real at first."

"I'm real all right. I wanted to thank you again for the dinner the other night. You were very kind to do it."

"You came all the way over here to say that?" Julie did have a way of getting to the heart of things. So I lied, and told her that I was going for a walk anyway and had just wanted to chat, it being such an odd time, and all that. She seemed to relax.

"How's Jerry bearing up?" I asked.

"Just fine. He's wonderful, Jerry is. So kind and considerate. Such a person! I never in all my life dreamed I'd ever meet anyone like him, let alone spend an evening with him sitting in front of the fire."

"How long is he staying, did he say?"

"He can't leave until all this is cleared up, but I think he's beginning to like Boston. You know it occurred to me this morning, now that Barton's gone, Boston's a wide open market for someone like Jerry."

"You have a point," I said, wondering whether Jerry had thought of that and whether he had much chance at a peaceful moment left in his life.

"Where is he?"

"Over at the Fogg doing some research on some prints, he'll be there all day. We were going to have lunch later then go over to Nickerson's preview for the auction tomorrow but quite honestly, the old crowd just doesn't make it, and I'm sick of auctions."

"I'm a bit bored with bodies tumbling out of chests myself," I said.

"I didn't mean disrespect, Helen, it's just too soon to go to another one, I guess." I could feel the moment approaching and my stomach began to tighten.

"Remember Friday, Julie, when you said you saw Barton? Do you remember when it was?"

"Why?"

"Don't tell me you're not curious?" I said.

"You can't get Barton off the brain, can you?" she asked, nearly hissing at me.

"Come on, Julie, that was over years ago. Barton wasn't that important to me."

"I don't believe it. Once you have something like you had with Barton, that doesn't die, just because he does. One look from him all those years and you'd have gone belly up, anyone and everyone knew that." Julie flopped down on the striped Regency couch and puffed pillows as if domesticity were a defense.

"Julie, you're a real treat. Remind me to come talk to you when I really need comfort someday. But, just as you can't believe me, I can't believe you're not curious."

"I don't want to know," she said.

"In other words you're afraid to know." I walked to the couch and stood right in front of her.

"I just don't want to know, that's all."

"What are you afraid of finding out, that Jerry killed Barton?"

"Don't say that!"

"Why, do you think for a moment Jerry killed Barton?" Of all the people in my line-up, Jerry was last before Joe. The amount of passion it would take to kill might make him sweat. "You saw what happened to his hands, didn't you?" Julie asked. "Do you think that has anything to do with killing Barton?" I wasn't sure myself and wanted to see what Julie would say.

"I don't—he does."

"Oh, I see. If people found out that he was cured they'd think there was a connection? Well, I hate to pull rank, Julie, but I'm a much more likely suspect than Jerry. And it would help me if you'd try to remember when you saw Barton last at the auction. You said when I saw you in the ladies' room that you'd been to East Shelton to do some shopping. When did you leave?"

"I don't know exactly when it was, sometime after the big Bierstadt was sold. I remember that because I had bid on it and was still recovering when I left from actually having bought it."

"Where did you see him?"

"In the hall. He brushed by me and pretended he didn't see me. I tried to say something but he was gone before I opened my mouth. That was the last I saw of him."

"Which way he going, in or out?"

"In."

"Did he say anything?"

"No, he was moving fast."

"Can you remember anything else?"

"No, he looked just like he always did, one hand holding a painting, the other holding his nose lest the smell of humanity get to him."

"Where did he go, did you see?"

"By that time I was out the door, I didn't look back." She paused and flipped the cover of *Country Life*. "Do you really think that you're going to figure this all out? I honestly don't understand why you're bothering. Seems a bit perverse if you really want to know."

"I don't think I'm going to figure this out all by myself. But regardless, it's better than sitting around at the gallery waiting for Captain Sheehy to knock on the door."

"Who's Captain Sheehy?"

"You'll have the pleasure, I assure you. I expect he's no better or worse than any other cop detective, it's just that he thinks I killed Barton. That makes him objectionable."

"You're not serious?" she said, almost with glee.

"I'm afraid so—isn't it exciting," I said echoing her tone. I picked up my gloves from the table where I'd dropped them and started moving toward the door. Julie hopped off the couch and skipped along behind me.

"But shouldn't you be in hiding, or on the run, or the lam, or something, instead of being around in broad daylight?" she asked.

"Julie, I said they think I did it. I didn't say I did do it for Christ's sake. I didn't kill Barton." I think she was almost disappointed. If she could get rid of me and Barton in one sweep, what a bonanza. Julie was not simple-minded, just single-minded. She wanted to win. And that was all she needed to know.

11 I walked back up Charles Street wondering about what Julie had said. I couldn't remember exactly when the big Bierstadt had been sold but it had been after the Inness, I was sure of that, and that had been some time after the Ryder. I did remember seeing Julie walk up the aisle and go out which could have been the time she left to go shopping.

When I got back to the gallery, I went to my office and opened the catalog from Joe's auction to the index. Bierstadt was number 204. The Inness was number 152, the Ryder had been number 140. I put down the catalog and leaned against my desk. If I had seen Barton with Jerry in the hall at about one-fifteen, or thereabouts, and Julie had seen him coming back in about an hour later, what had happened in that hour? What had made him come running in like that? All I was sure of was that he'd left, gone home, and come back, for some reason.

I sat down on one of the chairs by the fireplace and stared at the burnt logs and ashes. The gallery was shut and the workroom quiet and still. Liam must have gone out before I got back. It was in fact the first time since Barton's death that I was alone with mental faculties vaguely intact enough to think about what had happened. What had made Barton come back? Maybe, I thought, it had nothing to do with the people at the auction at all. Maybe it had to do with something Barton discovered at home, something that he was involved in that was totally unrelated to all the little fires that had burned so fiercely at Joe's auction. This was the first happy thought that I had had in connection with Barton's death, and if it were true that he was wrapped up in some bigger conflagration than all my little pals could set, perhaps Sheehy would focus his attentions elsewhere. Most of all I was concerned about Silky, but even in my rush of optimism, I didn't want to examine the cause against Silky too closely.

I pushed myself out of my chair and went into the workroom, closing the door to my office behind me. I stood looking around me for a moment. One of these days, I thought, I'll have to clean this place out. After my father died I hadn't bothered to clean out the cabinets of half-completed pieces, the unfinished sketches, the old canvases, frames, and pots of dirty brushes that he and Barton had used. I had left it and it had stayed pretty much the way it had always been until Liam had arrived. Now that Barton was gone, it suddenly became more imperative to clean it out. Where once I could pretend it was sheer laziness, now not doing the job would be too clearly mawkish sentimentality. Barton's death was having the effect of cleaning up my life. I reflected that Jerry's aftershock was far more noticeable than mine.

Jerry. I thought of him sitting over at the Fogg and considered what Julie had said. It amazed me to think that she would entertain thoughts of Jerry as a partner in bed or out while harboring the slightest doubt about the possibility of his murdering Barton. But then Julie's ambition knew no limits. I thought too that if there was a likelihood that Barton was involved in some other transaction that might have flared up at Joe's, Jerry would be the person to know.

When I went to Julie's it was with only half a hope that I'd learn something, think of questions to ask. I wasn't sure whether what I'd found out was important, but anything was better, even facing Jerry's galloping sense of guilt, than standing in the mausoleum, which was what the workroom was beginning to feel like.

I backed the car out of the alleyway, turned up Newbury Street, took a right at Fairfield, crossed over to Marlborough, and backtracked to Berkeley where I could pick up the Storrow Drive to get to Cambridge, Harvard, and the Fogg Museum.

Cambridge is a small town of enormous contrasts. Much of Harvard is beautiful, and the Charles River, as I drove by it that morning, was serene in its serpentine coursing between Cambridge and Boston. In the summer, the Charles is dotted with white sails of small boats and the sculls from the university boat houses. But the Charles, and Harvard, are only a small part of Cambridge. The rest is undistinguished and human, a sadly neglected fitting for the jewel of the east.

I crossed the Charles at Andersen Bridge, which connects the business school and the rest of the university, and drove toward Harvard Square up J.F.K. Street, through the Square, and around the yard to the back of the faculty club where, if you are only going to be a few moments, there are always a few parking spaces. The club, red brick with white columns, is right next to the Carpenter Art Center, which is right next to the Fogg Museum (Harvard's own) on Quincy Street.

Once inside the Fogg, it wasn't hard to find Jerry. The print room is right off the main gallery and Jerry was its sole occupant. His finely combed head was bent over a large portfolio of prints. He was so absorbed he didn't hear me approach and nearly jumped when I spoke his name.

"What a surprise and a pleasure," he said gathering his composure by smoothing his tie and patting one side of his head. "What brings you to these ivied halls?"

"You," I said. "Can we talk for a few moments?"

"As many of them as you'd like," he said, standing up and leading the way out of the room. He seemed in great spirits, his dandy frailty of Friday lifted from him. "How about some coffee?" I asked. "There's a shop just down the street a bit from here." We left the Fogg and turned left down Quincy, crossed Mass. Ave., and finally settled into two small iron seats at the Pamplona coffee shop on Bow Street. After we ordered, Jerry sat back in his seat and put his hands flat upon the table. Then he held one long hand out to me. It was as steady as a surgeon's.

"You're being terrifically gallant about not mentioning it," he said, "but you needn't. I've decided to tell the police all about it and let the chips slide around as they may."

"I'm not being gallant at all," I said. "Jerry, I'm delighted about your hands, thrilled for you and for all the paintings you're going to be able to work on, but doesn't it strike you as an awfully odd and improbable motive for murder? Really! You couldn't have known before you bopped Barton that your hands would stop shaking. It would seem to me that exactly the reverse would happen. So even if you benefit, even if you did kill Barton, it's my bet your hands won't stand witness against you."

"I disagree," he said. "You are being kind. But if my hands stopped trembling because Barton is dead or died, it does mean that there was a strong emotional component to my problem and that it was somehow related to Barton. I'd be suspicious if I were the police."

"Jerry, you sound as if you'd like them to suspect you. I swear you think you ought to pay for this somehow." I pointed to his still quiet hands upon the table. The waiter appeared with our coffees and we sat quietly for a moment sipping them and licking cream from the rims of the cups.

Maybe that was the key to Jerry's calm hands, I thought. He could work with guilt, but as a success, as a free human adult, he'd be a failure. Julie and Jerry could keep each other happily miserable for years.

"What did you want to talk about then, if not . . . ?" Jerry asked, looking at me a shade more hopefully.

"Let's assume just for a moment that neither of us killed Barton. For the sake of this conversation anyway, okay?"

"Fair enough."

"Okay. You and I saw Barton together in the hall, after he bought the Ryder. Remember?"

"Couldn't forget it," he said.

"Do you know what Barton was going home for, or what he was going to do?"

"I think he was going to do some writing on the book. I tried to call him at one point but no one answered, so I don't know if he'd got home by then or not."

"How was the book going? Was he having difficulty or running into imponderables or anything like that?"

"Not at all. It was going magnificently. It's a wonderful book, Helen, the ABCs of restoration. It will be a Bible. And because Barton was such a good style copier it's full of fabulous illustrations on how to attack certain different periods, indexed by problem. Just fabulous."

"So you don't think he'd have come back because of something to do with the book?" I asked.

"In all that snow? If Barton was anything, he wasn't the outdoor type, you know that." I did. Even Barton's car was barely made to be driven in the real world. Jerry continued, "No it wasn't the book. And the Ryder is fine."

"I know, that's why I was hoping he was in some other deal you'd know about."

"I tell you I don't. He was as secretive as ever. I never knew. He had been excited more than usual that day, but given the day that it was, that shouldn't be surprising."

"No, I was a little excited more than usual too." I sat back. What was it? Again I had that sense that something was wrong or different or not resolved just around the corner. It was the feeling I'd had sitting in Barton's study. Nothing had been wrong or out of place. Everything had been absolutely normal.

"Jerry, when we went back to Barton's, did you notice anything odd or out of the ordinary?"

"No, everything seemed in order."

"What about Walter?"

"Appropriately stunned. He'd been gone most of the day. He left in the morning before Barton did, and wasn't due back until that night."

I took a long drink from my coffee cup and sat back in my chair. Jerry looked away and stared at the wall. "This is all very strange to me," I said. "I don't normally go around asking questions like this. I'm sorry I'm making you uncomfortable, but it is important."

"Oh, I know it is and I'm not uncomfortable because of anything you've said. It's funny how things happen isn't it? The other day, I was tied up in knots, fearing Barton's influence, yet needing it, and now he's dead, and I can't for the life of me see why he was so important."

"Jerry, do you know anyone who would have wanted to kill Barton, besides us, of course?"

"What about that Ewart fellow, the one that Barton took the Ryder back from. He was livid with rage the last time we saw him."

"Do you know Tom?" I asked.

"No, I've never met the man, though I've heard enough about him from Barton to make me want to stay miles away." I put my cup down hard on the table and gripped its edges.

"Did it ever occur to you, Jerry, that every one of your acquaintances in Boston has been previously described to you by Barton and that those descriptions might not have been altogether accurate? You're a big boy, judge for yourself." I was mad at Jerry and at Barton too. What I didn't need was Barton directing my investigation into his death from his grave, or wherever he was. For such a neat man he'd left a terrible mess.

"But isn't Tom a little shady?" Jerry asked, finally.

"Seems to me shady depends on the size of the tree," I said, standing up and putting on my coat. "If you think of anything, will you let me know, I'd appreciate it."

We went out into the brilliant light of the day and Jerry put on his Daruma hat and took a deep breath of the clean air. Intrepid Harvard students on bicycles skidded around icy corners. Down the street the Charles shimmered in the sun.

"New York doesn't ever smell this way, clean and fresh, almost country," he said taking another breath. "I think it might be a time for a move, would you like that?" he asked, taking my arm as we walked back up toward Mass. Ave.

"Would my opinion matter?"

"My dear, your opinion is the only one that does." He turned his head and smiled at me broadly from under the fuzzy brim of his hat. I liked Jerry, I really did, but if he was thinking about turning his attentions on me, Julie was going to turn something else on me, and that I wouldn't like. I smiled noncommittally, waved, and turned into the faculty club walkway.

When I got home the gallery and workroom were the same tombs they had been when I left. They say that activity is its own reward, and I believe them. I felt much less at Sheehy's mercy than I had in the morning before seeing Julie and Jerry, but once home the disquiet that Sheehy's visit had caused set in once more. So what, I thought, if I've convinced myself that Julie couldn't have killed Barton or that Jerry didn't have the heart for it, or that it was unlikely that Barton was involved in some other transaction that was connected to his death. All I'd done was narrow the focus toward myself, and I didn't see clearly what the next step should be.

I climbed the backstairs from the workroom to my apartment above and went into the kitchen to make a cup of tea. When it was done I took it with me into the living room and lay down on the couch facing the Newbury Street windows. Most of the furniture was either left-over early American or Victorian, heavy and dark. I was lying on a Duncan Phyfe couch. Across the room on the other side of the fireplace was an upholstered rocker that Abraham Lincoln had sat in, between the windows was a Sheraton bureau, and all around the room was scattered the occasional odd chair covered in a pale green damask. On the floors were a collection of orientals, the density of their color adding to the room's ancient air. Placed at random on the floors were about six Persian saddle bags that had been turned into pillows. I suppose it was these that had led Jerry to think the room a pasha's palace. The only changes that I had made since my father had died were to have the dark red wallpaper removed and the walls painted a light milk lavender with white trim.

As I lay there sipping my tea I wondered what my father would have thought of all this. He'd have been horrified by Barton's death as we all were, but I thought the thing that would have struck him the most was the coincidence of the death with the maelstrom of events that occurred on the same day. Dad was never a believer in accidents. Every event has a long history, he'd say. He often told the story of how his favorite dog had been run over when he was a boy.

Apparently, the dog had been hit by a man who was distracted by his angry and frustrated wife. The wife had just discovered that twenty years ago her mother had hidden letters from another man whom the mother had not wanted her to marry. It was on driving home from his mother-in-law's house, his wife fuming by his side, that the man struck the dog. My father always said the mother-in-law killed the dog, and that if you look hard enough you'd find the real reason for things.

Well, Dad, I thought, if there's reason to all this it's escaping me at the moment. I could see all the people but I couldn't see the reason. Why would anyone want to kill Barton? I must have lain there for quite awhile and even dozed off a bit because the next thing I was aware of was of someone moving around in the kitchen. I rolled off the couch and walked a little groggily down the passage to the kitchen. Liam was squatting in front of the refrigerator shifting its contents around.

"Where have you been?" he asked, "I tried to call a couple of times and no answer. I was beginning to get worried."

"No need. I was out. Saw Julie at her gallery and then St. George at the Fogg. Didn't learn much," I said, leaning against the counter still not sure what Liam was doing in the refrigerator.

"What on earth for? I'd have thought you'd want to avoid all of them, for awhile anyway."

"I just wanted to find out some things."

"What things?" Liam asked.

"After our talk this morning I realized that if I didn't do something to try to find out something, my future was in Sheehy's hands, and that prospect doesn't please me one bit. So I thought I'd just see what others had to say; maybe they know something that will tell us who killed Barton, or at least something to prove I didn't."

"Did you learn anything that will help?" Liam asked, shutting the door to the refrigerator. He started to pick up some paper bags and put them away in the closet underneath the sink.

"Not much," I said, "just that everybody saw everybody somewhere sometime. The whole mess makes me feel grubby. If you'll excuse me, I think I'll take a shower before going out."

"You're going out?" he asked. His glossy hair fell over one side of his forehead as he tilted his head at a slight angle and looked a little quizzically at me.

"Yes, why?"

"Well, I had it in mind you'd be wanting company still, so I got us a bit of a wee dinner, that's all."

"Oh, Liam, I am sorry. I didn't expect for a minute that you'd want to take care of an old lady for another night. I just assumed you'd be going home. I am sorry. Of course, I can stay, but I did have plans."

He shrugged his shoulders and lifted his palms upward as if to say, "What's a man to do but try?"

"Is it so important that you'd pass up some of Rebecca's squab for it?" he asked, his face breaking into a crinkled grin.

"Yes, I'm afraid it is, and that's a low blow, Liam. Squab. How could you?"

"It was easy. Marinated bamboo shoots and strawberry cheesecake do anything for you?"

"Oh, I didn't know you could be so cruel. Fiend, horrible child, get thee hence," I said putting dismay in my voice. But Liam wasn't laughing any more. He looked suddenly very serious and older.

"I'm not a child, Helen."

"Of course, you're not," I said quickly, seeing hurt in his eyes, "I'm just playing. I didn't mean for a minute that you're really a child."

"Just putting on a good imitation right? Just a thespian at heart really," he said, striking a melodramatic pose.

"That was quite a recovery," I said.

"But the patient almost died because the wound went deep," he said.

"Oh, Liam, get off it. I said you weren't a child."

"Yes, you did, but you didn't say I am a man and irresistible."

"Oh, Christ, you are irresistible. Besides, I don't know what I'd do without you. So don't be so dumb."

"One squab and one turkey to go," he said, calling over his shoulder. "You're right, I am dumb. But do me a favor if you need anything, please ring. I will be home. You may think you're an old lady, but to this man's eyes you're a pretty fabulous woman." He said this staring right into my eyes, no glint of mockery filling his.

"Oh," was all I could respond. Liam leaned forward and kissed me, then turned and crossed the kitchen and opened the door to the stairs. Just before closing it behind him he stuck his head back in for a second. "I mean it," he said.

After he was gone, the kitchen seemed duller and strangely still. Almost as handsome as Barton and almost as neat, Liam had been saved by his humor and his Irish sense of the absurd. I wondered if he knew how really irresistible he was, and decided he couldn't. Shaking my head, but still moved, I flicked off the light and went to take a shower.

Ritter chose a small restaurant in Cambridge, The Voyagers, maybe a block away from where Jerry and I had had our cup of coffee that morning. Ritter had picked me up around seven-thirty, admired my Han pot from a distance, as well as the rest of the inventory. He said he'd been torn between the large Luks that he'd finally bought and the Malone. I said there was always tomorrow. He said we'd better eat before his acquiring appetite took over.

Before dinner he told me who he was and what he did. The mathematical doodads I'd watched him draw during the auction were a clue. He had been an engineer, had gone to MIT, and then started his own software business. It had done so well that he was in danger of ruining it if he kept playing with it as if it were a toy, so he turned it over to a professional management team and he retired very early. Now he was in search of something else to sink his money and energies into.

"Do you buy much art?" I asked, after the waiter had removed the soup dishes.

"Not a lot," he answered, "but enough. It's the only

way I can satisfy my fantasy to be an artist. Creative buying."

"Did you ever try?" I asked.

"Once I took a year off from MIT and tried to paint. I was pretty bad. Things kept looking like gray washes. I had a terrible time getting color to look like color, so I quit."

"But you'd been at it just a year."

"Yes, but I had a good enough eye to know what it was supposed to look like and knew I'd never be able to replicate it. So I took the gentleman's way out. Besides I knew I'd look ridiculous in a tweaky little beard and a beret."

"You could have tried a sombrero."

"Thanks, but I think I made the right choice. I'm also not messy enough."

"Messy?" I asked, sitting back so the waiter could put my main course in front of me.

"I know I've all sorts of stereotypical notions of what artists have to be like, and one is messy and liking it. I'm afraid I'm too organized and analytical."

"Without the organization it's all whistling in the wind," I said.

We lapsed into silence then, and I realized I wasn't really hungry. To be polite I started poking at bits of food on my plate.

"You're not eating," Ritter said, leaning across the table. "You're shifting your food into little heaps to make it look less, but you can't fool me. Want to talk about it?"

"Talk about what?" I asked, putting my fork down.

"What else could be on your mind? Murder. Simple uninteresting things like that." Ritter put his fork down too and sat back in his chair. "Let's have the whole thing," he said, "if it'll help."

"Well, you can tell me one thing. What were you talking to Captain Sheehy about on the stage after the auction? You seemed to be talking like old friends."

"We are. We went to grade school together. He still lives on the street where he did then, in the same house with his mother. He's been rising slowly through the ranks all the time I've known him. At school he was the worst first baseman we ever had, but boy he was determined. Never got to be very good, but he was so dedicated that he got on the team anyway. Lost more outs at first base that year than any team in history."

"He's still doing it," I said, "rising above his skill by sheer dedication. He scares me, so I spent the day trying to do his job for him. And that makes me mad."

"A policeman's lot is not a happy one," he said.

"No kidding. Anyway, I figured that I'd know as much if not more about Barton's connections and what was going on with his life than Sheehy, so I tried to talk to some people today to find out what they knew. I was just trying to piece things together."

"How's the puzzle look?" Ritter asked, and began to eat again.

"Full of holes. It seems that Barton must have come back to the auction for some reason. I saw him leave soon after the Ryder was sold and that was about one-fifteen. Jerry St. George and I were both in the hall and saw him go at the same time. Then all I can guess is that Barton went home and something happened to make him come back. Jerry said he called Barton at some point but that no one answered. Then round about two o'clock Julie saw Barton come in on her way out to go shopping. Between that time and the time he tumbled out of my chest is up for grabs. I haven't talked to Tom Ewart, Silky, or Al yet but they were all there except for Julie who went shopping."

"Julie is the little squat version of Lana Turner?"

"That's Julie. She'd love that description. She's madly in love with St. George. He's the one you were bidding against. Tom is the one that I had take over the bid. Al, well, he's an ex-partner of Barton's. He claims Barton owes him. They all had reason to want Barton out of the way, but I can't see any of them really doing it."

"Julie's too small to lift Barton into a chest." Ritter said.

"Yes, but it's not that, I just can't see any of them being mad enough. You know, going around the bend to do it. Because one thing is fairly clear, as Tom said, it must have just happened on the spot. I don't think it was premeditated."

Ritter put down his fork and knife and looked at me across the table as if he were studying a possible purchase.

"Are you really doing this because you think Sheehy is going to try to nail you? Or is there another reason we're not talking about?"

"I think it's because of Sheehy, not to mention Sergeant Rizzo who was at the ball last night."

"So were a lot of people. It's not likely he was tracking you alone. You know, it just seems odd to me that you haven't mentioned Barton himself in all this. Just how well did you know him?"

"Are you asking a personal question or one about my insight into his taste in art?"

"I don't know. I think it started out as an insight question, but let's assume it ended up being a personal one."

"How personal?"

"You really don't want to answer this one at all, do you?" he said, taking a sip of wine. "Look," he said, "I've clearly not made you feel any better. As usual I've followed my foot with my big mouth. I'm sorry."

"You really want to know what I was thinking?" I asked.

"You bet I do," he said.

"Well, I was thinking," I took a deep breath, "that I didn't want you to know about my relationship with Barton because sometimes it's something I'm ashamed of. It's sort of like admitting to someone that at one time in you life you had a wart on your nose or something like that. You know it's stupid, you know it doesn't matter, but who likes warts."

"I don't believe you," he said.

"I'm being as candid as I can be," I said a mite huffily.

"What I don't believe," he said sighing, "is that you would worry what I or anyone else would think about your whatever-it-was with Barton."

"Oh, I care all right, but it occurs to me that you do a super abundant amount of worrying about whether other people are okay. Maybe you wouldn't bump into so many things if you weren't so studiously trying to protect them yourself."

"Boy, that comment came right out of the blue."

"No, it didn't. I just realized you were being so concerned about me, whether you were making me feel better or hurting me in some way, when all you'd done was to ask me how close I was to Barton. At the idea, not the reality mind you, of my fragility, you turn into the hulk."

"And?"

"The reason I was having so much difficulty answering you is not because I was going to fall into some faint at the mention of the dearly departed but . . . but because I didn't want you to think I still, that I . . . because I don't."

"Strangely enough, that's just what I wanted to know." He smiled and sat back in his chair. "You know what I can't figure?" Ritter said finally, lighting his pipe. "What I can't figure out is how whoever killed Barton did it. The chest that Barton got stuck in and the monkey sceptre that he got hit with were both in the preview rooms and people were walking in and out of there. What does Joe have? At least three or four workers plus Kevin and his wife, children, and office help who stroll in and out of the rooms all the time."

"Not to mention the people who aren't supposed to be there." I thought of Silky prowling around the preview room after the Sloan had been sold and replaced on the wall. "That day, though, a lot of the time Joe's men were dealing with the snow and were outside more than usual. Someone could have been in the preview room unseen most of the time."

"Where was the chest?"

"Probably in the little room where the Inness was, where I first saw it, then most likely it got moved at some point to the passageway between the preview room and the gallery."

"What about the sceptre?"

"That was in the main room when I saw it, but it could have been picked up and carried around and put anywhere."

"It hadn't been sold, had it?"

"No, it was going to be one of the last items. Whoever did it made sure that the murder weapon wouldn't be missed for a long time."

"I bet it was pure dumb luck. As you say, whoever killed Barton had to act very quickly, probably right after Barton was seen by Julie in the hall. I don't see how that person would have had the time to decide to kill Barton, and then check the catalog to find a convenient weapon that was listed at the end of the auction."

"There's another reason I'm doing Sheehy's work, besides Barton," I said. "When I went to Barton's with Jerry after the auction, I just felt something was wrong. The Ryder was there on the easel and nothing seemed out of place. But something teased at me, and it's been gnawing away at the back of my mind ever since. I don't know why it's so important, just feels like it is." I described the feeling I'd had sitting in Barton's study while Jerry was out of the room. "It felt like I was missing something. Something so obvious I should have been able to see it, but I couldn't. For awhile I thought it was probably just a question of knowing that Barton was gone. But I've lived with that for a few days now and the feeling is still there about his study. Even if I can't figure it out, I'm curious as to why it should be so important for its own sake."

"Maybe for the simple reason that you described it in terms of missing something. I'm always a hell of a lot more worried by things that aren't there, that I don't know about, than by the things that are there." He leaned back and signaled the waiter, who came over and poured us some coffee.

"I don't want to think about it now," I said, knowing full well that the next day it would be all I thought of. I took a sip of coffee and leaned back in my chair.

"Ok. Let's not think about it. Want to go dancing?"

"Dancing?"

"Sure. Seems like a good thing to do, we didn't get much of a chance yesterday." Ritter said putting down his cup and folding his napkin on the table. He beckoned the waiter, who was slumped against the far wall discreetly picking his teeth.

"I'm not sure I feel like dancing," I said.

"Someone once said to me something I'll never forget. He said 'It takes a lot of work to have fun' and he was right. It doesn't come easy. I know you don't feel like dancing but it might be fun. You might have a good time. I know I would. Are you sure?"

"Sure."

"How about a drive and then dancing. Give you more time to think about it." He smiled at me and I had to smile back.

"You win."

We drove to the Marriott on Long Wharf and danced overlooking the harbor. By the time we left, we had gotten pretty good at it.

12 The next morning was a real improvement over the previous ones. As Liam bounced up the back stairs for his cup of coffee and soggy croissant I was dressed and singing.

"It must have been a nice dinner," he said, leaning back in the kitchen chair and wiping crumbs from his mouth.

"It was," I said. I smiled. "I'm sorry about last night. You were an angel to think of me."

"Takes an angel to make me think," he said. He sat the chair back on its legs and came over to where I was standing by the kitchen sink. He laid his arm along my shoulders and gave me a gentle squeeze.

"You okay this morning about everything else?"

"Not really, but I'll manage."

"You going to do any more snooping?"

"Or in other words, am I going to be responsible and stay in the shop all day and work like some downtrodden people who shall remain nameless?"

"I didn't say that, old dearie, you did." Liam put his head at an angle and grinned at me.

"I'll be gone this morning, but back this afternoon. I promise."

"We have cold squab for lunch. It's the best I could do."

"Oh, Liam."

"I wasn't hungry, really, and besides I had gotten it for you." He put his cheek next to mine and gave me a kiss near the corner of my mouth. He then quickly moved away and poured himself another cup of coffee.

"So," he asked, "who's on top of your suspect list today?"

"Only a few left," I said. I looked at Liam and wondered what would happen the next time he kissed me. What would I do if he didn't move away? I quickly turned my thoughts to Ritter and his uncomplicated and thoroughly desirable solidness.

Liam left to go downstairs to open the gallery and I cleaned up his crumbs from the kitchen table and put away a few days' accumulation of dirty dishes. So where was I, I thought, what holes need plugging? My list was pretty short but the implications of it could be huge. One, I wanted to find out about my chest. Where it had been. Two, where had Tom gone after Barton left, and three, where had Al and Silky been? As soon as I thought of Silky I knew why I had not wanted to continue talking to Ritter about the murder the night before. Maybe the reason I couldn't find the reason my father would have searched for was because it was beyond reason, as Silky had been the other day the last time I'd seen him. Maybe there was no reason at all, just madness.

I went downstairs and told Liam I was off to Nickerson's auction. There was a Kensett and a Swift I wanted to see. I like the drive, and besides I knew I'd find at least a few people I needed to see there, and although the idea of playing Sheehy with my friends didn't thrill me, neither did the depression that would descend as soon as I stopped moving and acting on my own behalf.

Nickerson's auction gallery is just south of Boston off the Southeast expressway in Hull. In the summer and spring there is a dividend in going there. You can sit outside at the clam shack across the street and have fresh clam cakes or little necks while taking a break. During the winter, however, the end of the Hull peninsula, though bleak and grayly beautiful, is a little remote for most fireplace-hugging Bostonians. I love it, though, and will go to Nickerson's for an auction simply for the ride out along the surf wall. That day, for obvious reasons, there was less traffic than on most and though I had some difficulty getting up one ramp on the expressway, for the most part I had no trouble. Once on the expressway, the Mercedes growled along.

When I pulled into Nickerson's driveway it was about eleven-thirty. The auction would be beginning in a few minutes, so I decided to take just a quick look at the items. The official preview had been the day before but like Julie I hadn't been in the mood. I never really expected to find much at the gallery at Nickerson's, as he rarely has fine paintings. Most of his stuff is Victorian, oak chests with marble tops, ugly hall stands, and break-fronts. On occasion, though, you can find a nice primitive or a good example of some of the lesser painters who travelled up and down the coast during the mid-to-late 1800s that he'd pulled out of some old farmhouse on the North Shore. Also, on occasion, you might find a piece of oriental pottery that some sea captain had picked up and that had sat unnoticed and unrecorded as such on someone's dining room mantle for over a hundred years. I had found the Han pot in a Nickerson auction just a few months before, but because these finds are rare, I don't spend too much time examining the items in the preview room and never feel as if I missed a golden chance if I don't.

As I crossed the lot to the front door, the wind whipped hard around the corner of the building. Behind me the surf pounded and, across the street, the snack bar's metal Coke sign clattered and squeaked on its hinges. On the roof, a few gulls perched as if still expecting a diner to drop a clam.

At Nickerson's the preview is held around the edges of the auction room itself. The seats, about three hundred of them, fill the center of the hall. The items to be auctioned that day lined the walls and occupied a considerable space at the back of the hall. As I entered the back of the room I thought that whoever had killed Barton at Joe's couldn't have done it so easily here. The only places out of view in the whole building were Hal Nickerson's office behind the platform and the small kitchen at the back of the hall where hot coffee and soggy tuna-fish sandwiches seemed to be in permanent residence.

Along with the change in scene, the cast of characters

had shifted as well. From the back of the room I could see Al leaning against a wall with his arms folded across his chest and a cigarette stuck out of the corner of his mouth. On the other side of the room Joe was talking to a woman in a blue hat. I guessed he wanted to check the Swift as well—there was no other reason for him to be there. Aside from these two, however, none of the others were present. We all have our different ways of dealing with things.

I decided to leave talking until last, and look first at the items lining the walls. I took a quick turn around the room and as I had expected, saw little of interest. The two paintings I'd come to see weren't in good condition. The Swift's surface was badly chipped and the Kensett's looked as if someone had used it to line a cat box. They were early items in the auction as well, so Hal didn't think they were worth trying to hold the crowds with. I checked the wall again where Al was and saw him moving along it to the back in the direction of the coffee and sandwich counter. I decided to head him off. I approached from behind and poked his shoulders. He jumped perceptibly at my touch. He wheeled around and glowered at me.

"Boy, are you nervous," I said. "I didn't mean to alarm you."

"I'm not nervous," he said. "You didn't alarm me."

"It's a nervy time, though, isn't it?" I reached for a styrofoam cup of coffee and put some dry cream in it. "What happened at Joe's had the effect of making things kind of real didn't it?"

Al didn't waste a minute. "I can't believe Barton's dead. It's sort of like getting up and having nothing to do."

"Have the police been around to see you yet?" I asked.

"Jesus, no, what would they want me for?"

"They've come to see me already. They'll get us all before long. What did you tell them at Joe's?" I asked as innocently as I could.

"What do you want to know for?"

"Because the whole thing bores me obviously." I took a sip of coffee, it was barely warm. While Al registered my comment, I fixed my eyes on the front of the room where Hal was setting up his lectern.

"Okay, okay," Al said finally, "I told them that I saw Barton drive in 'round the back of the building and get out of his car."

"What were you doing out there? It was snowing a blizzard!"

"Checking it, what do you think? Look, regardless of what I might have said to you about Barton, I was the last one to want him dead. He's no fucking good to me dead, how'll I get my share of what he owes me now that he's dead?" Al had a point. It seemed that if he'd been handed the monkey sceptre and Barton's head at the same time, he wouldn't have done it even if he could have.

"What time did you see him?"

"Must'a been about two o'clock or somewhere in there, I don't know. Natch Barton didn't run right over and pump my hand or anything."

"How did he look?"

"Just like Barton always looks, like he was dressed for some fancy ball. But I didn't get that close to him, you ought to ask the person he was with."

I knew that some wells ran deep but I had no idea how long it would take to reach bottom. Trying not to sigh with annoyance and relief, I asked, "Who was with Barton?"

"I don't know, I couldn't see. It was snowing like I said, and I knew it was Barton only because I saw the car come in and he got out and like that. But I couldn't really see him, couldn't tell you whether he was smiling, or spitting wooden nickels. Anyway, after that I went back inside."

"What about the person with him, was it a woman or a man, big, short, or what?"

"You don't get it; it doesn't help anybody because I didn't see the person. The best I can guess is someone pretty short. It was snowing too hard. Could have been one of Joe's guys. They were all over the place. A car pulled in right after Barton's, that person might have been able to see more."

"That's a big help. Thanks."

"What are you really doing this for?" he asked. "I think you're being really dumb."

"That's not funny," I said.

"Maybe, but you're sticking your nose out, or haven't you figured that out yet. I know I'm no killer, never wanted Barton dead, fat cat goes off and gets himself bumped off before I can get my share, but if I were, I wouldn't be sitting here talking to you about all this. I'd be worrying about how much you knew and be looking for another monkey sceptre lying conveniently around. Like that." He snatched at a fly with his bear paw hand and flung it to the ground. I felt a tinge of cold hit the base of my neck.

"I'll be careful," I said.

"Oh, I don't worry about your head being bashed in, more scare tactics I'm thinking of. You have a way of making me feel guilty even when I know I didn't do anything, so when you hit the person that did, it follows you're going to make him really squirm." He hunched his shoulders and saluted slightly with one hand before moving away.

I went outside to the parking lot for a breath of fresh air. How had I ever thought Al was a lummox? He talks like one and acts like one but here he had just presented me with a penetrating insight into what I was doing. It was fairly sobering to realize that up to that point I could have met with the twin of the monkey sceptre and never have known why. There on the parking lot I didn't suddenly turn brave and fearless, but I lost my innocence. Before it had seemed merely an intellectual assumption that someone I knew had killed Barton, now it seemed a hard reality and my well-being became extremely precious to me. I decided to stick close to the crowds; it didn't escape me that Barton met his maker in full daylight in another hall with three hundred people in it. At that moment I felt very vulnerable. I listened hard for sounds, but heard only the distant sound of a motor starting up and a whirr of rubber as the tires took hold and the car moved off.

I was alone out in the silent open, too easily able to imagine my body lying on the ground, a bright red trickle running down the side of my head and spilling onto the snow. A carnation of death would be blooming on my chest. Aside from the fact that I didn't fancy myself ending up looking like some photograph on the cover of a cheap thriller, I didn't want to be scared. Most of all I didn't want to be scared. If death came, and it came quickly, I thought, who would mind? Barton didn't know of his death and was hit so quickly that for him dying was simply not completing a thought and not knowing it; painless and unaware. But I hate being scared. Even as a child if I could do something without thinking, I'd do it fearlessly. And I did things on impulse a lot, jumped off cliffs into quarries, scaled trees, and crept across roofs. But if I had time to think and realize how dangerous it could be then I couldn't move. Unlike Hamlet, consciousness, not conscience, makes me a coward.

My parking lot soliloquy went something like this: To live or not to live, to hell with the nobler mind, what about survival? What good are hoops of steel, grappled or not, if the thing they wrap around is stone cold dead in the market? But then how about care, the fabled raveled sleeves of which seems to be in a perpetual snarly heap? One could, I suppose, leave it up to the Sheehys, but that wouldn't do any good. I'd be merely keeping help from myself and, as the young prince says, there's the rub. And I wouldn't, no matter where I was, be able to turn the brain off, stop worrying, or probably stop myself from talking to the person with the slings and arrows of, oh, I'd probably get mine with a New Guinea poison dart.

My soliloquy was disturbed by the loudest sound in the world, crunching snow in silence. Joe appeared around the corner of the building and stood a ways from me surveying the parking lot.

"We look like a scene out of some Italian movie," I said, finally.

"What are you doing out here?" he asked.

"Antonioni," I said.

"What?"

"Never mind. I'm out here freezing. I was just going to come find you," I said, walking over to where he stood. "What are you doing out here?"

"Getting a breath of air."

"I just lost a few," I said, "Can I ask you about Friday?"

"What about it? It stands etched in my mind. It was awful. But I've already said that so many times in the last couple of days, I can't imagine how many, frankly."

"What if Barton really were killed by one of us, that's the most appalling thought, don't you agree?" I was trying here to sound merely interested and conversational. Al had a point. I thought if I did run into the sceptre-wielder my question-asking might not appear so suspicious if it sounded simply like girlish gossip.

"I haven't even begun to think of it in that way," he said.

"But how can you avoid it? He wasn't killed in his own living room by a thief, or on a dark street somewhere by a mugger, he was killed while at a place of work where someone must have had a strong reason to do it. It's got to be someone *you* know at least."

"I don't know everyone who was there personally, Helen. That would be impossible. No, I frankly think you're on the wrong track there altogether. I don't think anyone we know did it. It was someone from Barton's past."

"Did Barton say anything to you to give a hint that he was worried about something?" I asked.

"No. He seemed completely his usual self."

"You didn't talk about anything special. Say, when he came to your office?"

"Not at all, he brought in Mr. St. George to introduce him to me, which was a nice thing for him to do as I'd heard of St. George and did want to meet him. And we merely talked, had a cup of tea, you know the usual thing before an auction."

"What about after the Ryder. How'd he seem to you then?"

"Oh, Helen, I am so sorry about that. I know how much it meant to you," he said. He started patting his arms with his hands. It was getting cold—the sun was moving behind some thick cover—so we started walking slowly back toward Nickerson's back door.

"That couldn't be helped, Joe. We did everything we could."

"I wasn't sure who that fellow was. The big one sitting next to you. You know if you're going to have someone bidding for you, you ought to at least let the auctioneer know before you switch horses midstream."

"Joe, that's ridiculous and you know it. I could have any number of people in the hall bidding for me, all on the same piece if I wanted to. It'd be stupid, but I could do it."

"It's just not smart," he said reaching down and picking up some snow.

"That sounds ominous."

"It's not ominous, Helen. It's just not done." He threw a snowball at a tree.

"Joe, this doesn't sound like you. Who have you been talking to?" Before he answered I knew. Barton one more time. It seemed Barton's grasp was going to be long-lasting and far-reaching.

"Just what did Barton say to you after the Ryder? You didn't make this up all by yourself."

"He didn't say anything." Joe reached down for some more snow.

"Oh, come on, Joe. He did too," I said, stopping to pick up some snow myself. Two can play at this game, I thought. "He warned you that if you lost control of your auctions the way you lost control of the bidding on the Ryder, people wouldn't consign their more valuable pieces to you and that soon you'd be a second-rate auction house once more. He said that what had happened doesn't happen in the big houses where auctioneers really know what is going on and are in on almost every deal before the bid comes up. Auctioneers are not supposed to be surprised, right? And just as an added fillip he said that if you really wanted to succeed you'd better learn more about your business, or he'd send people elsewhere." I'd got this far, knowing I was right, and suddenly aware that I was moving on dangerous ground. Here was another motive and sure enough, I was involved again.

Joe's face was getting paler at every word, and his wattles were quivering. Don't scare away the golden goose before the eggs, dummy, I said to myself. Back off.

"Joe," I said in a voice I hoped was soft and helpful, "Joe, everything Barton said is wrong. You can't be in control of everything, and people do have a right to have as many fronts as they want. All you're responsible for is making sure you don't miss bidders, and get the highest one."

Joe started walking back and forth in front of me as if on a small moving sidewalk. All the time I'd been talking, he had been pounding his right fist into his left glove with every step of his right foot, like a mechanical soldier gone beserk. But then he stopped. He banged his arms to his sides, as if at rest.

"I don't need you telling me my business either," he said finally, beginning to walk again.

"So he did pump you full of junk."

"It was more subtle than that."

"It always was with Barton. What did he say?"

"You about covered it. But that's not what he was really mad about, you know."

We had reached the back door by this time, so we leaned against the wall. At least we were out of the wind blowing off the ocean.

"No, I don't know. What was he really mad about?"

"He was furious, you know in that controlled efficient way he had, about that man with you."

"What?" I was truly dumbfounded.

"Oh, yes, he was angrier I think about that."

"But about what? The fact that I had someone bid for me or what? It doesn't make sense."

"Helen, stop being so naïve. Of course, it makes sense. You and Barton may not have been close for years in that way, but I don't think you were ever out of his sight, not really. He always knew where you were, who you were with, what was in your gallery, how you were doing."

"Would he appear interested, ask questions, and all that? How do you know this?" I could feel my chest getting tighter and the air in it going colder. I didn't like this trick Barton had of tickling me from the grave until it hurt.

"Nothing direct, just implications made, comments, and things like that. You could tell."

I didn't want to know Barton had cared, I really didn't. It was painful and the breathing was getting more difficult, but I couldn't not know. "What did he say Friday?" I asked, finally.

"He wanted me to find out everything I could about that fellow you were with. He said that if the bidding had stopped, I'd have had to take a large bid from him, and I had no way of knowing who he was, and that was irresponsible of me. He wanted me to find out, and tell him, and, of course, not tell you. Though he didn't say that, it was obvious from everything he did say."

"But why?"

"I think that what had happened really got to Barton. He had the Ryder but suddenly, you know, you were on your own, it was obvious to everyone there. You weren't afraid of him—which, Helen, for years you have been, you must admit. When you went for the Ryder in that innovative manner using first the big fellow and then poor Tom, Barton got the painting but he lost you. You were the only person who could take Barton on in that way, lose, and still win. He was dented all right. But it wasn't that that got him, it was that you wouldn't need him."

"But I haven't needed Barton for years," I protested.

"No, but have you ever distinctly *not* needed him? In any event, he took all that out on me, and on the man you were with. If a man was ever close to tears, frankly, it was Barton. He was that upset."

"I'm sorry you got it in the neck, Joe. Believe me I never imagined Barton . . ." I couldn't continue speaking. Suddenly all the words fell over themselves to get out of the way. My throat was bursting. Poor Barton, so tight, so withdrawn he could never ever have let me know. For the second time in forty-eight hours I wept hard, but this time it was for Barton, not me. The poor mop-headed, brilliant man had never been happy.

Joe stamped his feet while I dried my face and wiped my nose and sniffled myself back into composure.

"Sorry," I said.

"Me too, it's been an awful, awful business. There I

go saying it again." He turned and started to open the door. Just then something occurred to me.

"Just one thing more, please. Do you remember where my chest was during the auction?"

"The chest Barton was found in?"

"That's right. My chest. I bought it."

"My lord, so you did. What a coincidence. How awful. Most of the time it was in the small back room. Practically no one went into that room during the preview. A bad mistake, that. Think I'll take that wall down and open up the space."

"Was the chest very heavy?"

"Couldn't you tell? It's massive."

"Do you think it would have been as easily moved with Barton's body in it as not?"

"Oh, I'd think so. Barton wasn't very big you know and the chest weighed so much. I don't think the boys would have noticed the difference. They certainly didn't remark on it."

"That opens up the horizons instead of narrowing them down but, nonetheless, it's a start. Joe, thanks, you've been great, putting up with my blubbering not to mention all my questions."

"No problem. Take care of yourself." He opened the door and left quickly as if relieved to get away. I had never known Joe very well personally, but now I did. We had suddenly met in Nickerson's parking lot, after all these years.

I decided not to go back inside. I didn't really want the Swift or the Kensett. I didn't really want much but to get this thing over with now that it was started. I wanted to get away from the idea that all those years Barton had been watching from a distance, as some dark-eyed and seething Heathcliff with a strange passion, for that is what it must have been. For the first time I realized that when he had lived with us I had been just a kid and he had been a grown man. What could he realistically have seen in me? All the way along his behavior had been more questionable than mine and I'd always assumed the opposite. It had always been upside down. I knew things would never be the same for me again, but right then I didn't have the luxury to think of what would come in the future, my concentration was on the next few hours.

But what next? Who was the person in the lot that Al had seen with Barton? If Barton had driven back in and met someone in the lot was it a prearranged meeting, and what was it about? Or had that person said something in the lot that had drawn Barton back into the building? I tried to think back to Friday. What had happened? Where had Tom gone after he stormed past us in the hall? He had gone outside but had he stayed there all that time? It didn't make sense that he had but maybe he'd gone somewhere and come back. Maybe he was in the car that came in behind Barton. I tried to remember everything that had happened Friday that connected Tom with Barton, and, suddenly, I realized that Tom knew a hell of a lot about what had happened between Barton's leaving the hall and when he came back. Whether he'd tell me was another question. In any event it was worth finding out, and I wasn't going to learn anything leaning against Nickerson's wall.

I looked at my watch. It was then about two o'clock. I wondered where Tom was and how to find him. I slipped in the back of the hall and called his number, but there was no answer. On the chance he'd come back I decided to drive over. Activity was becoming a drug.

13 The drive back to Boston was a far more sober one than the drive out. Then I'd been upset, and curious, and worried. Now I was upset, curious, worried, and determined. I reflected how Barton had been right about so many things so many times, not least of all Friday: the world is up for grabs, and I was no longer a groupie.

I drove up Commonwealth Avenue, the street of small rug dealers, Boston University, and flat ugly motels catering to the twelve-to-two trade. If Comm. Ave., as it's called, were in Paris it would be a boulevard; in Boston, it's a strip. Tom's basement apartment was off the section of the avenue that became respectable, the part that goes uphill. I turned off at Summit and followed a maze of streets around until I pulled up outside Tom's building, a large brick weight upon the street.

I parked the car in the only available space and shuffled along the barely shoveled side path to a small door in the side of the building. I rang the buzzer and listened. Silence. At the end of the path a few steps descended to what serves as Tom's garage and extra storeroom. He often works down there cleaning items outside. Holding onto the railings I picked my way down the icy steps to the garage. It was quiet and seemingly empty. Walking around the outside of it, I peered into the windows. Tom's car was inside as well as some boxes and packing material, but nothing else. As I was walking around the back side of the building, having neither heard nor seen a thing, a hand fell on my shoulder from behind me.

"Oh God!" I cried, and swung my left arm out.

"Hey watch it, for Christ's sake, you want to blind me or something," Tom yelled ducking as my arm swung again. I halted my arm but not until it had clipped the side of his head.

"What are you doing down here?" Tom asked, coming out of the shadows behind me. His long face was encased in an old flyer's hat, the leather flaps pulled down around his ears making him look like Pluto the dog.

"Great question coming from you," I said wiping nervously at my coat as if there were snow on it, knowing there wasn't. "Why didn't you call my name or something? What are you sneaking around for?"

He ignored my question and asked, "What do you want?"

"Just to talk. So much has happened since Friday, I just wanted to know how you felt, you know . . . talk about it like normal people. We didn't get much of a chance at the museum."

"Oh," he said stamping the snow with his foot, "Yeah, well, to each his own. I'll talk to you if you'll talk to me as honestly. I have a feeling the police are going to be pretty interested in anything I have to say."

"Talking to you is like being in a game of snakes and ladders," I said, "up ten steps fall down twenty. Why do you think what you have to say is so interesting? Didn't you tell them everything Friday? Besides, Tom, for my money, the police think I did it and I don't know anything more than you do, probably less. When was the last time you saw Barton?"

"I never saw him again after the deal fell through. Well, that's not exactly true. I saw him through the coffee shop window after he left." Tom climbed the small flight of stairs and leaned against the railing.

"Was he doing anything?"

"No, just walking along. I assumed toward his car to leave . . ." I imagined Barton walking away as I had seen him last, safe, sure, and unsuspecting.

"Can I trust you?" he said quickly and quietly.

"I guess so, depends on what it is."

"I guess it doesn't matter if I tell you, because I know I didn't do it. I lied just now when I said I'd just seen Barton walking away from Joe's. I also saw him coming back."

"When was that?" I asked trying to sound nonchalant.

"About two o'clock."

"Was he with anyone?" I asked.

"No, alone, looked just like he did when he left. That's why it doesn't mean anything, it could be a film that you ran backward."

"Did you tell anyone, Al, the police?"

"No. I don't want the public distinction of being the last person to see Barton alive. You know what that always means. Cops have got primitive mentalities."

I could see it from Tom's point of view. He did have a great motive for killing Barton, and he thought he was the last person, so far, to have seen him. I'm not sure I would have been eager to admit it either.

"Did he look any different; upset, angry, or anything?"

"No, like I said before, he looked absolutely normal, in control. Determined. You know Barton."

"And you say you saw him coming in the front of the building?"

"Of course, if I was standing in the cafe he had to be coming in the front of the building."

"Calm yourself, Tom, you may not have been the last to see Barton anyway, so you can tell the police, the action TV news if you want to alert the media. Julie saw Barton in the front hall before she went out to do some shopping and as he was already inside the building it must have been after you saw Barton, not before." I thought his face would light up with relief. Instead he stared down at his feet, his mouth twitching in the middle as if very small words were trying to escape.

"Help me with one more thing. Then I promise I won't bother you further. You say you saw Barton leaving Joe's, then you say that actually you'd also seen him coming back but it wouldn't make any difference because it was like a film being run backward? Well, what did you mean? Was it actually the same?"

"Seemed so to me, Barton walking away and Barton walking back just seem reverse images, yeah."

"When he left Barton was carrying the Ryder, right?"

"He never let go of it once he had it, that's for sure," Tom replied.

"And when he returned, Tom, he was also carrying a painting?"

Tom turned his head and looked behind him and then peered over my shoulder as if absorbed by something difficult to make out.

"Not sure about that part," he answered, finally.

"Reverse images, Tom. Your phrase, not mine."

He slowly faced me. "Okay, okay, so he was carrying a painting when he came back, what's the big deal? Barton was always hauling paintings around."

It was a big deal. I pictured Barton leaving, and the image was as Tom said, just like he always was. But we always see what we expect to see and don't comment on what we think of as normal. There was nothing more normal than Barton carrying a painting. But when he came back he couldn't have been carrying the Ryder, it was already back on the easel. What he had been carrying was suddenly as plain as the evasive look on Tom's face. Once you saw it, it was obvious.

"But it was a different painting he was carrying when he came back wasn't it?"

"Right. You got it. It's funny, I was afraid you were that smart. I was hoping you weren't. When we talked at the museum 'do' I figured you hadn't remembered and that maybe you wouldn't."

"What happened, Tom, when Barton came back?"

"Oh, it was a case of a little too much booze, fury, and recklessness. I'd had it with Barton, you knew that. He'd been screwing everything up royally for a couple of months. After the deal with you fell through, I was sitting there in the coffee shop and got just plain mad."

"I remember. You stormed by us in the front hall."

"I went out into the parking lot straight to Barton's car and opened the back door. I'd seen him put the print of 'Washington Crossing the Delaware' in there earlier. He'd just slung it in there as if it weren't important." Tom continued. "Anyway, what I did was simple vandalism. I stuck my foot through the print, right smack dab in the middle of the bloody boat and rendered the effing thing worthless."

"That explains the broken glass the police found on the back floor."

"Yeah. At the time, of course, there was no reason to be neat about it."

"So when you saw Barton coming back carrying a painting, you thought he'd discovered it and was coming after you?"

"Thought, hell! I knew it. I didn't know when he'd find it, but I figured it would be when he got home. He wouldn't have seen it, he'd have just got in and driven away. But if he looked in the back seat once, he'd have seen it. Hell, I was waiting for him and I was looking for a chance to swing my fist into his face by that time."

"So, why didn't you?"

"I couldn't. If you really have to know, I blew it. I simply turned cold, scared stiff when I saw him coming toward the building. He was so cool. If he'd been really angry and fuming it would have been one thing, but he wasn't. He looked so cold, he could have killed me. And he was after me, there was no doubt about it."

"What did you do then?"

A slim smile struck his face like a strobe, and then was gone. He looked up to the sky as if searching for a way out.

"What's funny, or was for a moment?" I asked. I knew Tom well enough to know that if anything was difficult, it was being straight where he wasn't sure how the other person would react.

"I was just thinking," he said, "that if anyone had seen me it must have looked funny what I did, but it wasn't a Jerry Lewis movie, it was the real thing and I was scared. Christ, Helen, I don't think I've ever been so scared in my life. When I saw Barton coming and knew he was after me, I turned five or maybe six. I hid. I knew he'd find me if I went into the gallery itself, so I ran into the preview room and . . ."

"Was there anyone else there when you went in?"

"No, I don't know where everyone was at that moment. I could hear Joe's voice from behind the revolving wall, and I had a sense of someone in one of the small rooms off the main one, but no one saw me. Anyway, I ran through the main room across to the passageway, you know, that goes between the preview room and the gallery, and to the first place I could think of."

"Joe's office?" I asked thinking that there was no better place. With Joe on the podium, Barton would never have thought of looking for Tom in Joe's office.

"Not only Joe's office, and this I tell you now but will deny if I read this story in *Antique Weekly* or something, but under his desk. It's funny how some things you don't forget and one of them is that desks make good hiding places. Anyway, I slid under that thing as if it were home base." Tom made a sled of his hands and whooshed them through the air toward the ground.

"And then what?"

"I don't know. That's what's been killing me. I don't know. I sat under that desk for a while, and nothing happened. Then I snuck out of Joe's office, down the passageway and into the back of the auction hall."

"Do you remember when that was, what was being auctioned?"

"No, Joe was gone and Kevin was back, but aside from that I don't remember. I was still on the lookout for Barton, wondering how the hell I was going to get out of there, and wondering where Barton was. Then of course the next thing I know, there he is on the stage flat out and dead. For a moment I was convinced I'd done it."

"I know what you mean," I said, "and I can understand why you were a little anxious, to say the least."

"Yeah, I knew I had the opportunity, double motive, etc., and if anyone found out about that print, I'd have it."

"The weird thing, Tom, is that whoever did kill Barton must have the damaged 'Washington Crossing the Delaware' or know where it is." I remember Tom creeping around the preview room after Barton died. "Is that what you were looking for in the preview room?"

"Yeah. If Barton was dead, then the print had to be somewhere. I was dying."

"Tom, how big *was* 'Washington crossing the Delaware'?"

"Oh, twenty-six by thirty-four or thereabouts, why?"

"I don't know, I was just wondering whether you could have overlooked it, or someone else could have put it away without thinking about it. But it's doubtful, isn't it?"

"Whoever killed Barton had everything to gain and nothing to lose by leaving that print around. That's what I couldn't understand. I still can't figure it out," he said.

"Are you sure you didn't see anything or anyone in the preview room?" I asked.

"No, I was moving very fast. I think I heard Barton come into the preview room behind me, he may have seen me dash in there from the front door, but then nothing. The door to Joe's office wasn't all the way shut, but enough. I could hear Joe still on the loud-speaker, and that may have blanked out any other sound." He paused. "How much do you really care about this whole thing?" he asked finally, as if he had an unmatchable art acquisition that he knew I'd want.

"Do you mean about Barton dying or about finding the killer?"

"Both, but, ultimately, the latter."

"I care a lot. Mostly I guess because I feel partly responsible for why any number of people might have been mad at Barton, you included. But why does that matter anyway?"

"Because you haven't talked about Silky. You know, you can't always tell who was where by who people saw, sometimes it's important who they didn't see." What he said had a familiar ring to it and seemed important but I couldn't concentrate on why at the moment.

"Who didn't you see, when?" I asked.

"I didn't see Silky anywhere until after Barton's death."

"So what? You probably didn't see a lot of people," I said.

"See? There you go. If I'd said I saw him do it, you wouldn't believe it."

"Well, did you?"

"No, I didn't see him do it, but where was he?"

"I don't know, but who knows where Al was all that time either? He says he was in the parking lot but what does that prove?"

"God, he's an old lady about the snow. But he wasn't in the parking lot all the time. And he couldn't have followed Barton into the building, if that's what you're thinking, because he went blundering in ahead of Barton." That fit with what Al himself had said, and I remembered then scanning the back wall for Al and seeing him, a walking snowman, assume his bidding position at around two o'clock. As far as I could remember he hadn't moved again.

"But that still doesn't prove anything about Silky. He went out about twenty minutes after the Inness was sold, that must have been about one forty-five."

"So where did he go between one forty-five and you know when?"

I tried to think where Silky had been, whether I had seen him after he left the auction. I remembered seeing him go through the small door that led to the passage-way to the preview room, but I also remembered that only twenty minutes before he had been acting oddly.

"Tom, that's pretty flimsy evidence to hang someone on, isn't it? Just because we didn't see Silky doesn't mean that he was off beating up Barton. More likely he was off still licking his wounds."

"I was pissed at Barton but I wasn't half crazy and Silky was. You know as well as I do, we all do who saw him. And with that, I'll leave you," he turned and walked away back down the path then stopped and turned back. "You didn't want to come in, did you?"

"No," I said, aware that if Barton had been scoring, he'd have given the round to Tom.

"Next time then, be sure to," he said. Then, stepping back, he touched the brim of his absurd-looking cap and walked down the alleyway. Sometimes I could see why my father befriended Tom, and sometimes I couldn't fathom it. I think on balance it had to have been because, if nothing else, Tom was a caution. He stood watching, and it was better to have him near you where you could see what he was up to than miles away

where the first you'd hear of it would be long after the
ball game.

On the way home it occurred to me that Silky was
probably the person who Al had seen in the parking lot
talking to Barton. If so, Silky would have a lot of
answers to a lot of questions.

When I got back to the center of town, the lights
were all on along Newbury Street, and it was the time
of evening when people huddle into their coats and
rush along sidewalks, like blown bits of paper. I scurried up the back alleyway and through the workroom
door, hurrying to shut it behind me. I could hear Liam
still in the gallery, turning the locks on the front door.
In a moment he appeared in the workroom, and leaned
against the storage shelves.

"Any luck?" he asked.

"No, the Kensett was gritty and the Swift looked as if
someone had tried sharpening a knife on it. Besides it
was ugly." I took my coat and slung it over the rack.

"How about you," I said, "sell out the inventory?"

"The whole lot, you'll be forced into early retirement."

"Terrific, a vacation is just what I need right now.
Whew, what a day!"

"Driving bad?" he asked.

"No, it's not that," I said walking over to Liam's easel
for a look. Liam had talent but he wasn't in my father's
or Barton's class yet. "It was just a slimy day," I said.

"What were you up to? Sounds like a trip through
primeval ooze."

"Not a bad description of it. I talked to Al, Joe, and
Tom, and everyone, even Joe, was racked with greedy
self-interest. Not that I mind looking out for number
one, they just all seemed so excessively selfish."

"Maybe they had all wanted to kill Barton."

"I think you're probably right. They're all going to
profit from his death, that's for sure."

"Were they all at Nickerson's? Must have been a
gruesome gathering."

"No. I saw Joe and Al there, Tom I hunted down.
And don't ask me why I'm doing this," I said slumping
against the shelves of frames and rolls of canvas.

"Okay, I won't." Liam asked if I wanted him to stay

and I said that I thought not, that I was ready to begin life again, on my own. I left him in the workroom looking a little hurt and went into my office to check my messages and my mail that Liam would have left on my desk. There was only one call that interested me, from Harry Dodge who was my lawyer and had been Barton's lawyer as well.

When I called Harry he was full of proper condolences before he got down to business. First he wanted to check with me about the funeral arrangements he'd made for Wednesday the day after next. Then he wanted to know if I'd be willing to be an appraiser for Barton's estate. I said I would, the arrangements sounded fine and after a real hesitation said I'd have a look at the collection. He asked if I could possibly get over there tomorrow, and I unhappily agreed. I wasn't looking forward to going to Barton's again, I was especially not looking forward to seeing the Ryder, though, I thought, it might be the last chance I'd have to be alone with it. Why had Barton wanted it so badly? He had never even liked it that much, calling it my gloom. But, despite what Joe had said, he'd really gone for it and something about that was wrong, the way something had been wrong in his study, and still I couldn't see it. Maybe I would tomorrow, and in the back of my mind I was sure that I wouldn't like what I saw.

I shut up the office and went into the workroom where Liam was still puttering around, closing cupboards, and putting dropcloths over the two easels that held work in progress. He said he'd be done in a moment, for which I was grateful. I was looking forward to a long hot bath and then bed with a bowl of soup, some crackers, a pot of tea, and a long, perfectly lazy luxurious night in front of the VCR.

After he'd gone I carried out my plan without interruption. The phone rang once but I ignored it. I had enough to think about and didn't want my evening disturbed. I felt something like an athlete getting in shape for the main event the next day. Only for me the main event was going back to Barton's and saying a final goodbye to so much that we had shared, so much that had so firmly connected and held me to the past.

I was watching a tape of *Adam's Rib,* enjoying the banter between Tracy and Hepburn, thinking how the brain truly is the most erogenous zone, when the building was besieged with an eardrum-breaking clanging of bells. What the hell, I thought, jumping from my bed and running to the hall and down the backstairs to the workroom. My first thought was that it was a fire, but I knew as soon as my feet hit the bottom floor that it was no fire that caused the freezing cold wind that whipped at my ankles or that lifted the dropcloths from the easels causing them to move like living shrouds in the semidarkness of the workroom.

The back door was wide open, a pale light coming through from the alleyway outside. Something was on the floor just inside the door. I ran across to my office and reached around the door to turn off the nearly deafening burglar alarm. My heart beat hard and I waited a minute by the office door to catch my breath before crossing the room, batting the dropcloths out of my face.

I shut the back door, which was splintered around the lock. It looked as if someone had gone at it with an ax. And then I turned to look at what was on the floor. I didn't know what I expected but what was there made me hold my mouth while the animal in me that was afraid screamed. It was the picture of the African sceptre ripped from Joe's auction catalog, and it was pinned to the floor by a knife.

14 The next day was as gray and as dark as the day Barton had died. It looked like another storm was headed our way, and given how I'd spent the rest of the night, wide awake jumping at every sound, the outlook was definitely not cheerful. The day reflected my mood perfectly. I grumped at Liam's happy morning greeting, and explained what had happened to the door. After exclaiming that he was going to call the police if I didn't, and that he'd be taking up permanent residence in the loft until this mess was cleared up, Liam went off to see about getting the door fixed. I left him to it and shut myself away in my office. I thought of calling Sheehy and almost did, but every time I picked up the phone to dial, I changed my mind. I just couldn't picture Sheehy believing that I hadn't stuck the picture on the floor with a knife myself.

Maybe a vacation was what I needed. I'd been promising myself a trip to Greece for three years and maybe this was the time for it. I sat at my desk and contemplated seeing Delphi again. The last time had been with my father and Barton years ago. Barton and I had sat on the lip of the ancient world looking down the valley toward the sea and I had felt the presence of all time in one place.

But I knew it could never be that way again and I also knew I didn't want to go back there alone. I didn't want to go anywhere where I'd been with Barton by myself; I wanted to wash all that away with a life full of new and saner memories. Most of all, I thought, as I sat

177

twiddling with a pencil, I didn't want to go to Barton's alone, or anywhere until whomever had killed Barton was out of the picture. I had to take the warning seriously, though in full light I figured that it was probably just a scare tactic. But from whom? Who of all the people I had talked to saw me as coming too close? No, I definitely didn't want to be alone.

I flipped through the bills of sale of the previous week and found the slip Ritter had signed when Liam had sold him the Luks. His phone number was on it and with only a slight hesitation left over from my teens when girls didn't call boys, I picked up the phone and dialed. When Ritter answered, and he heard who it was the delight in his voice removed all disquiet. My days of sitting on mountain sides gripped with indecision were over.

I filled him in on what had happened since I'd seen him last, including finding the picture of the sceptre, then explained what the day held for me and asked if he had the time whether he'd come with me to Barton's for awhile anyway. I described what I'd be doing, namely beginning to put Barton's collection in some kind of order, and said I'd appreciate it if he could be there with me. He said he wouldn't dream of being anywhere else.

In a much happier mood I exited from my office and told Liam that he'd have to do without me for another day.

"Wow," he said, "whatever you took in there it works wonders. Where are you off to?" I told him what Harry Dodge had wanted and that he could get hold of me at Barton's if anything came up. Liam squinted slightly as if trying to see something on a very bright day. "You'll be there all day?" he asked with a slightly querulous tone to his voice.

"Most of it," I said, "but I'll call you so you won't get lonely. I should be back by three o'clock or so. Okay, Mom?"

"OK. But stay clear of the snooping. I'm too young to be put out on the streets without a job. You know my concern is nothing personal." He grinned at me and left to open up.

I realized as I left that I hadn't told Liam that Ritter was going to meet me there and wondered why I hadn't. The answer was only too clear. Liam's attentions were getting to be a little too possessive. Maybe I'd have to think of some other arrangement. If he was going to make life difficult, life was going to have to go on without him. I didn't like the idea of starting over with another neophyte but if that's what it would take for me to be able to go in and out of my own gallery without feeling as if I was leaving my aging father behind, then I'd have to do it.

That thought stopped me dead in my tracks. Perhaps Liam was treating me that way because I'd treated him like something that should keep me at home, the way I'd always treated my father and Barton too. If any-more cobwebs fall from my eyes, I thought, as I got into the car, I'll be blinded by sights unseen before.

As I drove over to Barton's I wondered what I would see. And suddenly felt then that the reason my father would have searched for would be something that I could see, should see, and that if I didn't I didn't really belong in the trade. For the first time I had an inkling that all along it was my vision that had been challenged, that it was my capacity to see that was at stake here, not just finding who had killed Barton.

I found a parking space just up Beacon Street from Barton's, a small miracle in the Back Bay these days, and in a few minutes was outside Barton's. Ritter was leaning against the railing at the top of the stairs.

"I rang," he said coming down to greet me and take my hand, "but there's no one in there."

"Doesn't matter," I said, "there's a key." I looked at him quickly as I reached behind the nameplate for the key I'd replaced there when Jerry and I had left on Friday, what seemed to me then years ago. He gave no hint of thinking there was anything too familiar about my knowing where a key to Barton's was hidden: he was as in the present as he appeared. The more I knew, the more I liked.

We went through the outer door and the large inner door to the hall and hung up our coats on the crook between the newel post and the stair rail. Then in silence we walked down the hall to Barton's study. I was afraid that the mood was going to be funereal, but Ritter fixed that.

"Nice digs," he said.

"If you like living in museums," I said, thinking I was already having a nicer time at Barton's than I'd ever had when he was alive. We set to collecting all the paintings from the study and putting them in some sort of order in stacks against the walls. Then for the next hour we combed the house for every painting in every room and took them all into the study. By the end of it we'd piled up a total of 68 paintings representing practically every major school of art. Until they were all amassed in one place I had had no idea of just how vast Barton's collection had become over the years. Numbers of them I recognized, like a small Watteau that he'd restored while he still lived with us and which had hung over his bed in the studio loft. I sighed with pleasure at seeing it again. These were old friends of mine and for a moment I forgot Ritter, his large self stretched out on one of the couches relaxing with a cup of coffee I'd made, and strolled around the room breathing in the glory that was around me.

"It's funny to think what Barton would have done with 'Washington Crossing the Delaware,' it sure would have looked out of place here. So stupid that. He wouldn't have known what to do with it," I said, sitting down on the edge of the couch. Ritter leaned back and stretched his feet across my lap, forcing me to sit back a bit. It felt comfortable, and I didn't mind the holes in his socks.

"Is that everything?" Ritter asked.

"I guess so," I said, but as soon as I said it, I knew it wasn't. "What was it you said the other night about things that aren't there?" I said, sitting up so suddenly that I almost rolled Ritter right off the couch.

"I said," he said straightening himself, "that I'm usually more worried by things that aren't there than by things that are. What's there you can deal with, what's not there is a mystery."

"You may have just connected the dots," I said. No wonder I didn't, pardon the pun, want to see the picture. I'd feared that it would come to something like this, and that I wouldn't like it. "All along it *was* something that wasn't here that was bothering me," I went on. "The Sloan is missing." Poor Silky, I thought, I was afraid that the Sloan might have been that important.

"Can you explain about 'the Sloan,' what that means? I'm just a dumb country boy," Ritter said, breaking my absorption.

"Silky Constantine is just a beginner, and at the auction he wanted to buy that small canvas that looks like a Sloan, remember? Early in the auction? I don't know, it may be, I told him I thought it might be, but I wasn't going to swear to it without examining it more closely. Anyway, he had set his heart on it and you can guess who bought it. Well, it's not here. The Ryder is but the Sloan isn't."

"Couldn't Morley have put the Sloan away somewhere? Would it have to be in plain sight to be here?" Ritter asked, pulling his legs around so that he was now sitting on the couch.

"Could have, but unlikely. Barton liked to leave new purchases around for a few days to get acquainted with them. If I know Barton, the Ryder would go on the easel first thing and the Sloan should have been propped up on his desk over there leaning against the desk lamp or somewhere in plain view where he could look at it."

"Okay, then, and I'm playing devil's advocate here for no purpose except that I can't stand intuitive leaps, only because I'm not very good at them, where analysis should work. Let's assume that for some reason Barton didn't pick up the Sloan, didn't bring it home with him at all."

"That is a possibility. Sometimes he would leave things with Joe or Mat Peterson or some other auctioneers he trusted. He'd check the piece again after he bought it, sometimes to let them take care of the cleaning for him which, because it was he who asked, they would."

"Wouldn't he clean things himself?"

"Only if it was an important painting, then he would. But with something like the Sloan, what'd he pay for it—something like twenty-five hundred? I can't remember—he might not want to bother. Besides Joe's got a good person who works for him. Or Barton may have decided to leave the Sloan altogether."

"What do you mean?"

"Well, sometimes, and he's not the only one to have done this, I do it too, after you've bought something, and you go to the loading dock or whatever to pick it up, you take one look at it and know it was a mistake. Sometimes the best thing to do is unload it right then and there. Barton may simply have taken one look at the Sloan and told Joe to sell it for him in the next auction."

"Is it possible that Barton got home and saw something wrong with the Sloan, a rip in the canvas, a bad bit of overpainting that he'd missed, and drove back with it? Does that sit?"

"No, won't work. First off, there wasn't much wrong with that canvas. And, remember, it was never sold as a Sloan. So he couldn't have discovered it wasn't and had a beef. No, Barton didn't have any complaints with the painting per se. He wouldn't have gone back because of it. Maybe Silky, impossible to believe, but could he have killed Barton in town and taken his body back to Joe's?"

"Nope," said Ritter, "that won't work either. Unless both Tom and Julie were lying about seeing Barton walk in on his own two feet. Besides, would Silky be that stupid? Wouldn't the police eventually think of the Sloan and think of Silky as the obvious suspect?"

"Maybe, maybe not. I think Tom and I are the only ones who know Silky well enough to know how upset he was by the Sloan. Others may have seen him leave, but people move around in auctions all the time. In any event, I can call Joe and ask him if Barton picked up the Sloan. I just know if Barton picked it up, it would have been here when Jerry and I got here Friday evening. He would have liked that little piece just for what it is, regardless of who painted it or how much he had paid for it."

"What if Joe doesn't have it?" Ritter asked.

"I don't like to think about that possibility. It might explain why Barton came back. When he got home he may have noticed the Sloan was gone from his car. That would have brought him all the way back, the way a wrecked Washington never would have. I'm just hoping Barton left it at Joe's for some reason. If he didn't? Well, enough dawdling. I suppose I'd better get it over with." I crossed the room to Barton's desk and dialed Joe's number. It rang for ages and I was about to hang up when finally someone answered. It was Kevin.

I asked him if Barton picked up everything that he bought at the auction. I could hear sounds of people shifting furniture around in the background and people calling to each other across what was probably the preview room. I could picture the activity as the room was being prepared for another auction.

"Would you hang on for a moment, Helen, if your thumbs won't get tired. I'm in the gallery and I'll have to check the records in the office . . . You know, I'm not sure I should tell you, though, all kidding aside."

"Why not?"

"Isn't that police information?"

"Joe's records aren't confidential you know."

He finally agreed and asked me to hang on while he went into the office. In a few moments he was back on the line. "Just a minute . . . hope your neck's okay . . . here it is, Barton bought and paid for two items Friday, number 72 and number 140 . . . now just a moment . . . yes, here it is. He picked up both, too. He took the Ryder himself and I remember putting the other painting in his car for him when he drove around to the loading dock."

"Are you sure of that?"

"Absolutely, here it is in the inventory book. Why do you want to know anyway?"

"I'm an executor of Barton's estate and we're just trying to make sure that everything's where it ought to be, that's all."

"Okay, I see. It's probably all right to tell you then."

"I'm sure it is, Kevin, and thank you." I put the receiver gently back in its cradle.

"Not good, huh?" Ritter asked.

"No, not good. Barton definitely picked up both paintings."

"So now what?" Ritter asked, standing up and going over to the Ryder and staring at it.

"So now I suppose I have to do what I've not wanted to do all along. I have to go see Silky and find out what happened to the Sloan and what he was doing in the parking lot talking to Barton. I'm convinced the person Al saw had to be Silky."

"Okay, hats on, and let's go." Ritter moved away from the Ryder and put an arm around my shoulder while we walked to the front door. I didn't know how to say what I had to say next but figured the direct approach was the safest.

"I don't think you should come," I said, "Silky must be pretty skittish right now and while he just might talk to me, there's absolutely no chance in hell that he'd tell me what happened with you there."

"Are you kidding me?" Ritter exclaimed stopping and pulling his pipe from his mouth. "You're going to go alone to visit a man who you have every reason to believe killed Barton not to mention playing mumbledy-peg at midnight in your gallery and talk to him nicely and calmly about why he did it and you expect me to let you go by yourself? Lady, you have much to learn about me."

"Glad to hear it," I said, recognizing the sanity of his comments which I might, just a few days ago, have pushed aside as so much macho bravado. No doubt about it, he was bigger than me, and while Silky could do me in quite easily if he wanted to, against Ritter it would be the fly attacking the swatter. Sometimes macho makes sense. "But," I went on, "I just can't believe that Silky killed Barton. I can believe he had something to do with it, maybe knows about it, but not that he actually did it. I'm not afraid of him."

We argued about this for quite a few minutes in Barton's hall. Ritter finally gave in, partly.

"Okay, I'll tell you what I'm going to do. I'm going to call Sheehy and tell him what happened to you last night and what you've remembered, then I'm going to go home and sit there until you call me, and if I don't hear from you in an hour, I'm coming over there. I'll just be a curious customer. Surely Silky can't object to those," he said bending way down so he could look

straight into my eyes while he talked, his mouth working hard on the stem of his pipe.

"You're so cute when you're angry," I said.

"Cute weighs two-twenty and when it's angry it weighs
two hundred and twenty angry pounds." He picked me
up and sat me down on the newel post.

"Still cute?" he asked.

"No, convincing, but I'm still going," I said, jumping
down and rubbing my sore rear end. It was still a little
bruised from where I'd sat down hard on it when
Barton had brushed past me in the hall outside Joe's
office.

"I was always afraid I was a bit of a fraud," he said
smiling. He then did the most amazing thing, he picked
up my hand and gently kissed the back of it. I was
about to say something clever but somehow the gesture
didn't call for slick comments. Ritter had a way of
making sure the moment received its due, and I knew
it was a lesson I would enjoy learning. I left him then.
He was standing on the sidewalk in front of Barton's as
I walked down the street toward my car. I knew he was
watching, maybe with as much wonder in his eyes as I
knew filled mine.

15 I drove down Beacon Street, crossed over the Mass Avenue bridge to Cambridge. Silky had a small shop on Broadway. He'd started out leasing counter space in a shop up the street, but when this small one had become available, had gambled that he'd be able to pay the rent. Along that stretch of Broadway there are a number of small shops run by people trying to consolidate customers as well as lines. Because they flank Hubley's auction house, which does a good business, they pick up some drifter trade that ordinarily wouldn't appear in that section of town. Recognizing their kinship and interdependence, the shop owners support each other by lending each other items to make their displays especially enticing. One of their gimmicks is to hang red flags outside their doors when they are open.

That morning, Silky's red flag was flying. I parked the car by the Longfellow School and walked across the street. I checked his window display. He'd borrowed some nice chairs and had made a little sitting room effect in which he displayed his netsukes and some of his glassware. It looked nice. The Sloan would have looked nice on the wall over the chairs, but it wasn't there.

When I opened the door, Silky, who had been arranging some objects in a display cabinet, looked up. He did the closest thing to a blush that a dark-skinned person can manage.

"Hi," I said, "how's it going?"

"Oh, okay, I guess. You?"

"Okay, considering," I said.

He came out from behind the counter. "I feel really bad that I didn't get a chance to tell you how sorry I was about the Ryder the other day. I guess it's a day we'd all rather forget, huh?" He said all this in a slight whisper as if he were uttering a prayer.

"Don't worry about the Ryder," I said, "you had plenty of things on your mind, too, you know ... like the Sloan."

"Oh that. I'm all over that. I can't imagine why I got so upset, it was very silly of me." He shifted his weight slightly and dusted off the counter top with the sleeve of his shirt.

"Silly, but understandable." I wondered how to proceed. Silky was acting self-consciously, but who wouldn't after the display he'd made.

"Silky," I said finally, "you saw Barton after that, I mean did seeing him make it any better?"

"I didn't see him," he said quickly. "Whatever gave you the idea that I did?"

"I'm not sure it matters who said it, but somebody said that they saw you in the parking lot talking to Barton," I said, taking a shot in the dark.

"Look, Helen," Silky finally said, "I'm so scared I can't sleep. Last night Nina even had to get me some sleeping stuff like I was some dumb husband on a TV ad. It was awful, her caring for me. Barton dying in that way. I feel like such a wreck. And ashamed. Don't you think this means something to me that suddenly I'm a wreck? Everyone sees it. Don't you think I know everyone thinks I could have done it? And now you, my friend, come to me and say someone saw me talking to Barton. What is it you know that I don't, because I didn't kill him." He said this all in a low, sad voice as if he were reciting parts of different speeches that didn't quite hang together but which all came from the same play.

"I'm not trying to hang anything on you, but if you go around acting so sheepdog-like, no one is going to believe you don't know something."

"I did see Barton," he said suddenly.

"Did you tell the police that?"

"What do you think I am—crazy? Everyone thinks I'm off my nut and then I'm going to tell the police I saw Barton drive back into the parking lot and actually had a talk with him."

I was astonished. Silky had a bee up his pant leg, no wonder he was nervous. "What happened?"

"You promise you won't go to the police?"

"Silky, I'm not going to promise that. If you tell me something I think is crucial, I'll have to tell. But it may not be. There's only one way to find out."

"Okay, I'm trusting you. After I saw you, you know after the Inness, I went outside and took a walk. I was still upset, you were right. I don't know what I was doing. Suddenly, I saw years of losing out to Barton, even you, stretch in front of me. I realized I'd never have the cash to compete with you, that I don't have it in my bones the way you and Barton did. You don't know, nor did Barton, how much impact it has on people that you've got all those years behind your name. You're sort of a ruler of a kingdom, and you have responsibilities. None of us—me, Tom, Al—is of royal birth either, you know, and with Barton gone you're it for blue blood."

"That's absurd, but go on with the story," I said, thinking that a lot of people do soliloquizing in parking lots.

"So there I was, wrecked, trying to decide whether to ditch the whole thing, and in comes Barton driving *that* car, wearing *those* clothes."

"How'd he seem?"

"Well, not smiling, you know, but intense, like he had the cat by its whiskers."

"And?"

"So I approached the car, I didn't know what I was going to say or do. Maybe I would have killed him. I felt so close to him, I mean, I had been thinking of nothing else for over an hour and there he was. So I went up to the car window and he took one look at my face, which I don't know, must have looked weird considering how I was feeling, and he says, 'You want the painting, you can have it.' " Silky put his forearms on the counter and hung his head over them.

"He said that?" I couldn't believe my ears.

"He said if I wanted the painting, I could have it."

"What did you say?"

"What could I say, I said 'Sure, how much?' Then he said 'Whatever my last bid was.' " I thought of Tom and how he had seen Barton toss "Washington Crossing the Delaware" in his car in a sort of throwaway gesture. Oh, Barton had had a way with people.

"Oh, Silky," I said again, having difficulty not laughing. I was so relieved. And, in fact, Silky didn't have a bad bargain. It was still a nice painting and even if it turned out not to be a Sloan, he could probably make money on it, a little anyway. I had promised to put it in the gallery and I would, gladly. I was just about to tell Silky that at the first hint of cash flow troubles any spot on my gallery wall was his, when he waved his hand in front of my face to keep me from talking and continued himself. He had a way of keeping his audience hanging that made me think he was in totally the wrong business.

"So there he was leaning out of his car looking so rich and I couldn't stand it. I remember my mother once bought a huge ham in the butcher shop when she couldn't afford hamburger just because she saw Mrs. Costello and Mrs. Sicilianno buying roast beef. She couldn't be outdone by those ladies, it was her pride. She came home and cried and cried over that ham. We never enjoyed one bit of it either, because it had cost her so much, not money, you know, to buy it." He took a quick look at me as if to find out if I understood. I nodded.

"Anyhow," he continued, "there was Barton and there was I, so I reached in my pocket and pulled out the cash and paid him on the spot. He looked a little surprised I guess, that was all . . . where I was feeling as if my bones were on fire."

"I wouldn't hit yourself so hard, Silky. It's a nice painting, and frankly, I'm relieved you have it. It was missing from Barton's and I really got worried . . . Well, I didn't really think it, but knew that others would."

"That's exactly the problem," he said. "Who's going

to believe that I, little old glassware baron me, came up with the extra dough to pay for the Sloan? That I even had it in my pocket? I mean really, who's going to believe I didn't kill Barton? And here I am with the painting as perfect evidence that I did."

"You obviously didn't get a bill of sale or anything like that?" I asked, trying not to wag a finger in front of Silky's nose, although he deserved it.

"No, of course not. Who thought Barton was going to die in the next hour? I didn't, he didn't. I mean I didn't think of a bill of sale at the time; I would have later, I suppose, and got one. Besides, Barton seemed in a hurry and I just took the painting. When he handed it to me, I knew I'd never really enjoy it." He put his head down again and took a long gulp of air before looking up.

"Fact is," he said, "I don't want it around at all. Would you put it in the gallery for me, sell it as fast as you can? I don't care what it is or who painted it." I recognized his distress too well. You hate the things that make a fool of you, over which you find you can be a little crazier than you had thought.

"Whatever you say," I smiled, but I was worried. If Silky didn't have a bill of sale, and the police found out he had the Sloan, it was going to be a little difficult to persuade them that he had come by it honestly. I didn't have any doubts he was telling the truth, however. It seemed completely likely that Barton would hand away, as of no import to himself, what he had bloodied someone with merely hours before.

"You said Barton was in a hurry, did he say why?" I asked.

"No, he just looked determined and busy, you know, like it annoyed him because it was a bother."

"Did he say anything else?"

"No, he handed me the painting and drove off toward the building without a word." He stood straight and touched my arm. "Thanks for coming by. I feel much better, not so scared anyhow. Though I don't know what I'll do about the business."

"What do you mean?"

"I'm not sure I have the temperament for it. I get too

wrapped up, if you know what I mean. I think I'll just piddle along on the lower markup for awhile. I'm feeling kind of in neutral right now, you know. I don't think I have any blood left."

As I watched him I thought that he was the second person to remark that Barton had acted far differently from someone going to meet someone scared enough to kill. Of course, Barton did have an overinflated sense of his own imperviousness to the world, let alone its monkey sceptres, but could he have been so blind to murderous turmoil around him? That, least of all, made sense. The one thing that everyone agreed on about Barton was that he knew what was going on, he was in control.

"Silky," I said, "if I were you I'd call the police myself and tell them exactly what you've told me. They'll find out about the Sloan one way or another, and it's better if you tell them. You didn't kill Barton, so don't worry. Just do it."

"Maybe you're right. I'd sure like to get it off my back. I'll bring it round to the shop later, okay? It's at home."

"Under the bed?" I asked.

"No," he said, "but not far from it. It's in the closet." He laughed, finally, and I could see he was going to be alright.

I left Silky's and drove up Broadway, around Harvard and through Harvard Square down Kennedy Street and over the river.

Driving back to Boston, the veil lifted from my eyes, and I saw then what had probably happened on Friday. Barton had never gone home at all. He never would have gone back in all that snow just to crease Tom over the head about "Washington Crossing the Delaware." Essentially, that print meant nothing to him, and sitting in front of a fire did. He'd have called Joe and complained about Tom, then he would have called the police if he'd wanted to press charges. Regardless, he wouldn't have gone back. Even more convincing, however, was the fact that if he had gone back, the Sloan would have been there in the living room where it should have been. It wouldn't have been in his car, he wouldn't have been able to hand it over to Silky. So Barton never got home at all. He probably stopped at a gas station and noticed the broken glass in his back seat and drove back because he was still in the car, not all the way home. And if he hadn't gone home, someone else had taken the Ryder there.

By the time I reached Newbury Street, I thought I knew who had killed Barton and why. I decided not to go to the shop but straight to Barton's. I had no evidence of any sort, just the fallout of my own perception. I was seeing things quite differently. My father's reason was there after all.

I shielded myself from thinking about who had killed Barton by concentrating on *what* was happening. Soon enough I would know if I was right. If I was wrong and nothing happened, what would I lose? Nothing. Was it still so important to be right? Because I owed something to Barton, to my father? No. No longer. I knew that wasn't it anymore. I owed something to myself. Someone had been challenging me. I had forgotten one of the prime rules in this business. People see what they expect to see, and that included me.

When this whole thing started, I was determined to find out who had killed Barton because I was worried about Sheehy. Now I was determined because someone was threatening my very livelihood, challenging my ability to *see* a painting, not to mention turning the Ryder into a poker chip. And to be frank, I think that blow hurt the most of all; that I hadn't recognized the fake when I had seen it.

16 I parked the car a block away from Barton's on Commonwealth Avenue and walked east another block to Dartmouth, crossed, and walked down Beacon. I didn't want to run the chance of being seen, just in case. Ducking down the alleyway that leads to the buildings' backs, which sit ignoring the Charles River like fat fannies on a fence, I walked behind them until I reached the back door. Standing across the alleyway, I looked up at the second-floor study windows. The curtains were still open, and there was no sign of movement within. Fortunately, the back alley had been plowed and the snow removed from the back doors. Barton *would* have a classier snow removal service, I thought, smiling at him. I rang the buzzer and waited for Walter. When he didn't answer I used the key I still had, hoping it worked on the back door as well as on the front.

The key turned easily in the lock, and the door swung silently open into a small dark hallway, at the end of which was a smoky brown glass-paneled door. A trickle of light showed through the frosted panes. I knew the door led to the basement floor hallway off of the kitchen and laundry, and the small sitting room that Walter used. In the center of the hall were the stairs leading to the ground floor. They came up right outside Barton's study door, underneath the main staircase that went to the upper floors. I assumed the light was the far end of the glow from the lone lamp Ritter and I had left on in Barton's study. As the basement

windows were covered and shut out the bleak afternoon light, most everything was in darkness.

I closed the outside door behind me and crossed the
passageway to the inner one. It opened silently as well.
I listened for a moment before stepping into the main
hallway, but heard nothing. I called for Walter but
there was no answer. As I thought, the light came from
upstairs. I made a quick inspection of the basement
rooms but saw no sign of anything out of place. Barton's dishes, like his life, were neatly stacked in their
places in the cupboards and looked as if no one ever
used them. Back in the hallway I moved toward the
staircase and looked up. I knew what was up there, I
knew what I would see, but I also knew I would find it
hard to believe my eyes. Believing my eyes, of course,
was the name of my game, and more than anything
else it was what I had going for me. If they were
wrong, I might as well go out of business.

I slowly climbed the stairs to the main floor hallway
and Barton's study, and stood in the doorway. There
on the easel was the Ryder. I switched on another light
and went over to it. I don't think I've ever looked at a
painting harder in my life than I looked at the Ryder in
those few minutes. Just a few days before, I had stood
there with Jerry looking at it, and if you'd asked us
then, we'd have both probably said that we were examining the painting. But we weren't. We were merely
admiring it. I took out my magnifier and went over it
inch by inch. It was an odd feeling knowing I was the
authority on that painting, but it was a comfortable
one, and I liked it.

Just as I thought, as I had suddenly seen in the car,
this was the real Ryder. The one I'd bid on at the
auction had been a wonderful fake. Whoever had
painted it had done a magnificent job. It had been
perfect, down to the specks, chips, and cracks that
ought to be in a painting of that age painted in the way
Ryder did. But the real Ryder would have aged more,
would have had more and newer and different cracks
in it that I wouldn't have recognized. The fact that it
had been so perfect was perfect evidence that it was a
forgery. Anyone questioning why it was in such good

shape would probably do so more out of amazement than suspicion, as both Tom and I had. But I was certain now. That canvas had not been the Ryder that had hung on my wall for so many years. The one I was looking at had not been on preview before the auction. The old cracks were right, and there were new ones in new places. This was my Ryder, older and wiser.

Leaving the easel, I walked quickly to Barton's desk and dialed the phone.

"You're back," I said, "thank heaven. Am I under the limit? I'm at Barton's, can you come?" I asked, hoping I wouldn't have to fill in the blanks.

"You figured it out," Ritter stated.

"I'm afraid so. Can you get your friend and come right away? Come to the rear entrance, the door is open." I heard my voice drop into a whisper.

"Right away," he answered, and the phone went dead, increasing the quietness in the room which suddenly seemed thick and tangible.

I checked my watch. It said two forty-five. It should take Ritter only a half hour or so I thought, a spark of anxiety igniting my adrenalin.

It was darkening outside, but it was still light enough. I switched off the light I had been using to examine the painting, leaving only the desk lamp burning. I went to the top of the cellar stairs and sat down. My idea was to sit there, away from the study windows through which someone might see me, and wait for Ritter. There was no reason to believe that the person who had killed Barton would know I'd figured it out, and come there. But he might. I was under no delusions about how clever he was. I leaned back against the hall wall, shut my eyes, and tried to breathe deeply.

In the deep stillness that came from cellar stairs I felt the air move and knew as sure as the prickles of fear that raced up my spine that the door to the outside had been opened. Peeling my back from the wall I leaned around the newel post and peered down the stairs. A rectangle of light expanded in the frosted glass of the separating door and then shrank again.

I pulled my head back and waited. Whoever it was on the other side of it, he stood as silently as I crouched at the top of the stairs. I pressed my back to the wall and slowly rose off my haunches moving leftward until, with one motion, I was around the corner and in Barton's study again. The room didn't offer many places to hide. But then, did I want to hide? If this was the person who killed Barton and exchanged the paintings, was I going to hide, let the person come in, make the switch again, and leave? Hardly. I wasn't letting the Ryder out of my sight. And if anyone was going to stop the person from leaving until Ritter and Sheehy got there, I would have to—a job I had never counted on.

Barton had had an intelligent fear of firearms and wouldn't have one in the house, but he did have a set of duelling pistols, beautiful eighteenth-century French, inlaid with silver. I knew they worked because we had fired them once in the country, but the preparation took so long that they were hardly what one fired in anger. But to someone who didn't know, they would look efficient enough. Barton kept them on a bookcase shelf to the right of the fireplace. They lay in a leather box lined in dark blue satin. As I silently loaded one pistol, I heard the inner door to the hallway downstairs open and shut with a small click of the ball bearing slipping into its groove. Whoever it was stood in the hallway downstairs doing just what I had done, listening: ears straining against the silence, like trying to derive new love from an old letter.

The pistol metal was cold in my hand. I wanted the person in the room, beyond the doorway so that backing out wasn't possible. I moved in front of the windows, behind the easel, and behind the desk where someone entering the room wouldn't see me. I rested my arms on the back of Barton's desk chair and leveled the pistol in the direction of the easel. My hope was that switching the paintings would be the person's first action. I had no plans for what would happen after my confrontation. As long as my hands could hold the pistol I figured I'd be all right. In those silent moments I was sure the person could hear my heartbeat and that my nerves' screaming would surely tell him where I was.

He came up the stairs far more quietly than I could

have imagined, because when I heard the first sound, it came from the middle of the staircase. If I am right, I thought, trying to time my prayers to his footsteps, and if I survive, I'll pledge millions to the Red Cross, never smoke again, and try not to be such a crabby bitch to Ritter ever again. Oh God, if I see him again.

My eyes were so intently focused on the easel that I think at least a few seconds must have gone by before I noticed Liam standing in the doorway. I was right, and then I would have given anything to be wrong. But being right, I was somehow emboldened, as if by figuring it out I somehow had more control of the next few minutes than he did. He was wearing his down parka, and under one arm carried a painting, just the way Barton had done the last time I saw him. He stood silently in the doorway for what seemed far too long. I needed him to be in the room, just a few feet, but in the room ahead of me. Finally, he took a step. I must have moved because his head swung around and there he was, his blue eyes meeting mine.

"Oh, shit," he said.

"I know, it's a pisser," I said. "But that's too bad for both of us. Just put the painting down and then sit down on the couch over there and don't move an inch more than I tell you, or I will pull the trigger on this thing. It makes a very nasty hole," as if that weren't threatening enough, I added, "I've seen it do it."

Liam looked at me blankly, and I had a sense that this was a scene he had rehearsed many times.

"You won't, you know," Liam said. "I'm not sure how this will end, but one thing I'm sure of is that you won't shoot me." He stood absolutely still, his handsome expressive face still and hard.

"What makes you so sure?"

"Because you're a silly-hearted and sentimental woman. You spend half your life living a memorial to your father and Barton, of whom I'm merely the present embodiment. After me there would have been others."

"You might have been right, but you're wrong, Liam. You were oddly and sadly more to me than that. But I don't owe anything to anyone anymore. Not now, not today, and not you."

"I don't believe you."

"That's all right, you don't have to. The bullet will hurt just as much whether you believe me or not. Please put the painting down and go sit on the couch." My voice sounded calm but I wasn't. My arms were beginning to lose sensation from holding the gun out from me for so long. My hands shook as they held the gun and my heart pounded. I didn't doubt that I would shoot. I knew I would, but God, I didn't want to, and most of all I didn't want to look at Liam any more than I had to. I hurt, he had hurt me, and that, more than not being able to shoot, could incapacitate me.

He seemed to sense a resoluteness in my voice that he hadn't heard before. He shifted position slightly, indicating to me that I had had some impact on him. He looked around the room as if to find another way out, then with a shrug of his shoulders went over to the easel and replaced the real one with the fake. Carrying the real Ryder he came back to the desk.

"You present something of a problem," he said.

"I can imagine, now why you don't sit on the couch. We're waiting for the police in case you hadn't noticed."

"We're not waiting for anyone," he said, and with a motion quicker than I'd known him capable of he lunged across the desk and grabbed the wrist of the hand that had the gun in it. He twisted it hard. It was all so quick. The sudden terrible pain in my wrist, my fury at being hurt, and my response happened at the same moment; all I wanted was to stop the breaking sound that was coming from my own bones. I pulled the trigger. The pressure on my wrist stopped immediately. Yelping, he leapt away from the desk clutching his arm and dropping the Ryder on the floor. The recognition that I had shot him seemed to infuriate Liam more than the gun wound itself had hurt him. His yelp turned to a growl and he lunged back across the desk, grabbing at me. He jerked me around the corner of the desk sending the only light in the room crashing down landing on the Ryder. I heard the canvas rip, and my heart tore with it.

Clearly Liam's rehearsed play had gone as awry as mine had. I don't think he knew what to do with me, but killing me was clearly not out of the question, and I had to get away and I knew it. I did the only thing I could: kicked, screamed, and battered away at his wounded arm hoping like hell that I was making it hurt even more. The pain must have gotten to him for a moment because he released his grip on me just enough for me to get away. I ran around behind the couch in front of the windows, determined to keep it between us. If he had a gun, it would be all over before I knew it, but the way he had been acting convinced me he didn't.

Liam stood still where I had left him, then reached behind him for the desk set. He pulled out the scissors, and holding them like a knife, street-style, slowly came toward me. I tried to keep light on my feet, bouncing on my toes so that I could dash from one end of the couch to the other. There was no running out of the room from there. I couldn't get past him to the door. Here we were, both of us bouncing on our toes as if preparing to dance, how different from the last time.

I jerked to one side to test his reflexes. They were still good. Liam moved quickly and easily to cover the corner of the couch. He was standing now almost dead center between the two couches. There was just enough room for me to dart in front of the fireplace. I thought I could reach the poker, but the scissors scared me. Almost before I knew what I was doing, I picked up the fire screen, and using it as a shield, bore down on him. He backed away and tried lunging at me with the scissors but the wire mesh of the screen was too tight and strong. It held, forcing him back against the desk. I could never shove him over, I knew that, he was too big. The best I could hope for was to unbalance him and, being near the door, make a dash for it. With his back to the desk, he swung out with his foot and knocked me off balance. I staggered backward trying not to trip, but I caught my heel on something, maybe the lamp cord, and went flat onto the floor, like a kid doing a back flop into a pool.

My head must have landed hard on the marble hearth because my next sensation, it couldn't have been more than a few seconds later, was of cool stone. From my position on the floor I watched Liam push the screen angrily away from him and come toward me with the scissors. I knew he was coming to kill, but I somehow seemed at a safe distance from myself, as if it wouldn't be me that got hurt. I remember having a small debate over the point as if it were a matter of academic interest. One voice in my head insisting that when the scissors stuck I'd feel it, the other as resolutely pooh-poohing the whole thing. I think what convinced me that more hurt was possible was that my head was in fact already banging. It was clear that Liam was going to do something even worse.

My removing of the screen had exposed the fire poker which had slipped and was lying next to my head on the hearth. I reached across my body and grabbed its brass handle. As Liam came at me I swung at his legs with the fire poker; hacking at him as if he were a tree. He fell sideways on to one of the couches, screaming. I scrabbled to a half-couch. The inside of my head crashed against itself trying to find a way out; little angry fists beat against the backs of my eyes. Liam still holding his left leg, stretched toward the scissors, which he'd dropped when I hit him.

"Don't move an inch or I'll knock you so hard you won't see tomorrow, let alone stars."

"Tough talk," he said, sucking in air as if he were sipping hot soup through a straw.

"You bet," I said. Liam chose, apparently, to believe I meant what I said. I think it's smart that he did. The evidence was all in my favor. I was the one who had shot him.

So we assumed a strange scene. Liam had his head leaning against the fat edge of the couch seat, while I perched, like the bird in Peter and the Wolf, "high in the tree," on the back of the couch, the poker held in my right hand over Liam's head. My left wrist looked badly sprained, maybe broken. It had swelled to a gray and bloated doughnut circling my hand. My head went around in circles like a little outboard with no one at the helm. To keep myself from toppling over, I decided to ask the one question that had been nagging at me ever since I saw Liam enter the room.

"What made you come here now?" I asked. "Don't turn your head. Just talk."

"I knew you were coming here and you'd see the painting again. And I couldn't risk it. I called and no one answered, so I decided to chance it."

"And you killed Barton?"

"I'm afraid so. I didn't mean to, but that's the way things happen."

"You mean you went out to the auction to pick up what you thought was the real Ryder and then what happened?"

"What do you mean 'I thought was the real Ryder?' The one at the auction *was* the real Ryder," Liam said, turning quickly around. I lifted the poker as if to swing and he sat back, facing forward again.

"No it wasn't. The one at the auction was a fake. The one you switched it with and brought back here was the magnificent superb real thing."

"But you bid on it!" he said, practically screaming.

"I know, and it'll take a long time for me to get over that."

"I don't understand," Liam said, practically crying as if he suddenly saw that he'd made a terrible, horrible mistake.

"I know," I said, "but I'm not sure it's important that you do. The ultimate punishment, Liam."

My head was swimming and I grabbed onto the couch to get my balance. I hoped I'd stay conscious until Ritter or Walter or Jerry arrived. Where in hell were they all? Whenever someone showed up it would be just in time.

I was right about that. When Ritter and Sheehy finally came crashing up the stairs and burst into the room, I passed out; no maidenly screams or fancy faints. Ritter told me later that as soon as we had made eye contact, I toppled off the edge of the couch and landed on the floor next to Liam who sat impassively through the next hour or so, saying nothing but that he'd talk to a lawyer before he'd talk to anyone.

All this was discussed the next night when I could talk, walk, and eat without losing my balance, and my wrist had been X-rayed. It was broken and put in a cast. Ritter had arranged a small private room for us at Maison Robert, and while they plied us with hearts of palm and quenelles, Ritter plied me with questions.

"How did you figure it out?" he said. "What tipped you off between the time you left Barton's and when you called?"

"It was the Sloan, Silky, everything at once shifted and I began to see what had happened from a different perspective. First off, we knew from what Tom reported that when Barton had gone back he was carrying "Washington Crossing the Delaware." But I never understood why Barton would go all the way back in that snow to Joe's because of that print. It just wasn't that important to him. But as long as we assumed that Barton had gone home, it seemed that the print was the reason he had returned to Joe's. But once I remembered the Sloan and realized the Sloan should have been at Barton's, then the whole picture changed. Either Silky had stolen the Sloan before Barton had left the auction, or Barton hadn't gone home. He simply wouldn't have gone home, put the Ryder on the easel, and left the Sloan in the car. If the Sloan wasn't in his study, then Barton had never gotten there either. No one who was at the auction could have gotten the Ryder to Boston and got back. It had to be someone who wasn't there, who didn't come back, and who didn't know about the Sloan."

"So how do you suppose Barton discovered what Tom had done and what happened?"

"I bet if we check, ask Sheehy, he'll find that Barton stopped for gas or something. He must have turned his head and seen the print smashed in his back seat. He would have been angry, very angry. So when he went back looking for Tom, Tom saw him coming and hid. So what happened then? Barton came striding in coldly furious carrying a painting, looking for Tom. And the first person Barton saw in the preview room? Liam."

"So," Ritter said, "Liam took the Ryder back to Boston to take attention away from it completely."

"Exactly, but what Liam didn't know anymore than I did was that the Ryder at the auction was a fake. And the one he was going to switch it with was the real one. You see, another thing I couldn't figure out was why Barton wanted the Ryder. He never liked it, always made fun of me for loving it so much, in fact he thought Ryder was grossly overrated. Once I'd figured out after leaving Silky's that whatever happened had to do with the Ryder and not any of the other paintings I knew what Barton had done and why he needed to get that painting back."

"You mean that Barton had faked the Ryder years ago?" Ritter asked, astonished.

"He must have. Liam couldn't have done it, he didn't have the original to go by, and besides Liam simply doesn't have that kind of talent. He might have had some day."

"So Barton wanted the Ryder back because it was a forgery and he thought that if you bought it you'd spot it eventually and he'd be caught," Ritter said tipping back in his chair and stretching his legs out underneath the table.

"Something like that. I'll bet he did it, the original forgery, as a bit of a lark. He even helped me sell the painting and I can just see him making the switch way back then as a joke, and then the joke got the better of him and he didn't know how to make good what he'd done," I said, trying in vain to cut my hearts of palm with my fork edge. Ritter watched for awhile and then removed the plate, cut the salad into bite-size pieces, and handed it back.

"Thanks," I said, "I was getting hungry."

"Try asking, it's better than starving," he said smiling.

"I'm learning, I'm learning. Anyway, what must have happened is that Liam discovered the real Ryder where Barton had hid it in the workroom. I'm sure that Liam's original idea was simply to make the switch once I got what he assumed would be the real Ryder back to the gallery. There he'd have all the time in the world to compare the paintings and make the switch. But then I called him from the auction and told him that Barton was going after the Ryder and Liam on a gamble went out to Joe's with the real painting thinking that if he had a chance he'd swap it there."

"And," Ritter said, filling in the gaps, "Liam was there when Barton came in with 'Washington crossing the Delaware,' saw it was his chance to bop Barton giving him time to switch the paintings, bopped him too hard, and put his body in the chest.

"But, wait a minute," Ritter said, banging his pipe on the edge of the ashtray, "there's one very important thing here that I don't understand. How did Liam know that Barton had left at all? If he, Liam, had just arrived on the scene hoping to do a trade of the paintings, how had he known that Barton had left for awhile and come back? And if he *did* know that, why didn't he assume that the Ryder was already back in Boston, instead of in Barton's car?"

I looked at Ritter and loved him for his lack of suspicion. I had wanted to believe it too, that Liam couldn't have killed Barton face-to-face, that he had committed the murder in some sort of adolescent frenzy. But the facts proved it otherwise. We can't always have things the way we want them; nature's canvas is pretty slimy at times.

"Because Barton told him," I said finally. "It's the only way Liam could have known. Barton must have seen Tom dash into the preview room and looked for him in there rather than in the main auction room, and found Liam instead. Barton must have told Liam why he had come back and Liam, realizing the Ryder was safe in Barton's car, saw that here was the opportunity to get it. I'd wondered why Tom hadn't been able to find 'Washington Crossing the Delaware' in the preview room. If Liam had talked to Barton he would have known that taking the print could implicate Tom. He must have figured that the police would make that connection eventually."

"But he couldn't have known about Sloan, could he?"

"No, by the time he went to Barton's car and picked up the Ryder, Silky had the Sloan. Liam was almost but not quite clever enough. So, then not knowing about the Sloan, Liam took the Ryder from Barton's car and drove back to Boston with it to make it look as if it had been there safely all the time, so that Barton's death would be unconnected to it. I bet he also trashed Washington's remains on the way home. What he didn't know, of course, was that he was trading the real Ryder for the fake. And Liam had counted then on my not ever seeing the painting again. He obviously hadn't counted on my distinguishing the cracks that ought to be in the Ryder from the cracks that Barton provided. Liam's good but he's not Barton. Barton knew that the cracks would have aged differently. That's why he was so desperate to get it back."

"What do you suppose Liam was going to do with the Ryder? It would be difficult for him to unload, wouldn't it?"

"Not too difficult. And, remember, Liam wouldn't expect to get a fair market price for it. He'd have been happy with a third. That would give him close to twenty thousand dollars, a nice little sum to start investing in paintings with, paintings that given the business he was in he could probably get for a good price. I think Liam just wanted a toe in the door. He was tired of being an apprentice and wanted what Barton had without working for it."

I fell quiet for a moment thinking of Barton and how his knowledge of painting and how to restore works of art had caught up with him at the end. At the time he had forged the Ryder, I wouldn't have noticed it or would have been afraid I was wrong. But I had grown up and he knew I'd see it eventually. And he must have known I'd never have seen him in the same way I once had ever again. I would have been lost to him forever. He had said that what he had done had been a necessity, and he was right. Maybe that was why, at the last, he had looked for a moment like his old self; he thought he had put things to right. But he couldn't take back what he'd done. To my father's way of looking at things, Barton had been killed by his own hand. His death was implicit in his forgery.

I thought, too, of Liam and all his interest, and how close he had been to being right about the role he had been playing in my life. The more he knew about Barton, the more he was to me. I shuddered. Ritter leaned over and touched my hand.

"Eat a bit, take a drink, they're gone," he said. I did and felt better.

"I'd like to make a switch myself," Ritter said smiling. "This place for mine, if you're finished. We'll have dessert there, okay?"

"At last," I said. "I thought you'd never ask."

And so we did, and still are, with Walter, who, after he decided Ritter's favorite, lemon meringue pie, was a dish worth perfecting, has turned them out once a week with the meringue burned just right. Jerry, who did move to Boston, fixed the Ryder which now hangs in The New Bedford Whaling Museum, where it should have been all along. We sold the chest, but kept the tureen.